Praise for Heather Cochran's debut novel
Mean Season

"This first novel has considerable emotional heft
that works seamlessly with the comic relief....
Whether describing a passionate first kiss or a
fatal tragedy, Cochran makes this story sing."
—*People*

"A poignant, gently comic story
about growing up and moving on."
—*Publishers Weekly*

"Heather Cochran's page-turner had me
from the first word. The characters are
unpredictable, funny and ultimately touching."
—Pamela Ribon, author of *Why Girls Are Weird*

The Return of Jonah Gray

Heather Cochran

MIRA®

MIRA®

ISBN-13: 978-0-7783-2360-0
ISBN-10:   0-7783-2360-9

THE RETURN OF JONAH GRAY

www.MIRABooks.com

Printed in U.S.A.

10 9 8 7 6 5 4 3 2

To David and our new tax deduction

Thanks are due to everyone who lent support and guidance throughout this effort—my parents for their consistent support and interest; my first-draft readers and thoughtful critics, David Allen, Zoë Cochran and Todd Laugen; all those who assisted with my research, including folks at the IRS and Dr. Bob Laugen; my wonderful and challenging editors, Farrin Jacobs and Selina McLemore, and my steadfast agent, Katherine Faussett.

Chapter One

I MIGHT HAVE BEEN MORE DISAPPOINTED HAD IT NOT been so predictable. Martina and I were at the Escape Room, the dive bar where we'd meet after work, maybe one day in five. Martina would have gone there five in five, but she'd always been drawn to dark places and men of a certain unwashed quality. Me, I found significance in the fact that the bar was equidistant from my work and my house. Not precisely equidistant—wouldn't that have been a fantastic coincidence though?—but within a tenth of a mile, assuming my measurements were correct. Having been an accounting major, I was trained to interpret the world through double-entry ledgers, where a debit on one side balances a credit on the other. At the bottom of the columns, if you add and subtract correctly, the totals match up. So I took symmetry as an encouraging sign, whether in a financial statement or bar location.

I was sipping my beer and leafing through the book I'd brought with me when Martina rushed back from the bathroom and practically leaped onto the bar stool beside mine.

"Sasha, I want you to meet someone," she said.

"Well, I want you to meet someone, too," I told her. "I want us both to meet men who are generous and kind and delight in who we are. I swear, my mother wants me to settle for any guy who will have me. But I'm not going to settle. So I'm thirty-one. That's not old. Who says that's old?"

"My God, would you please stop talking," Martina said. "Sometimes, I don't get the way you're wired. I meant, I want you to meet someone *specific*. His name is Kevin."

"Oh," I said. I looked around. I didn't see whom she was referring to. "And Kevin is?"

"In the bathroom. I just met him in line. He was asking me about you. He'll be out in just a minute."

"He was asking about me? And you're giving me a minute warning?" I asked. She knew I needed more time than that. "You *know* I need more time than that. You know I like to be prepared."

"Prepared for what?" Martina asked. "The most we're talking about is bar chatter."

"Prepared for everything. What to ask. What I want to know. What I'll say. What he'll say back, then how I'll respond to what he says back."

"How are you not exhausted all the time? Just relax. Give the guy a chance. I promise you, he's not the usual Escape Room fare."

"So now there's something wrong with the usual Escape Room fare?" I asked. "What, he's some freak? Some anomaly?"

Martina shook her head. I followed her gaze to the man at the far end of the bar, the one whose cheek rested against a coaster, his hand upending a bowl of popcorn. Martina looked from him, back to me, smiling as if she'd won something. "How long do you figure it would take you to prep for *him*?" As she looked past me, her eyes went wide.

"Okay, there he is. There's Kevin," she whispered, vacating her bar stool. "Make eye contact. Be nice. And what is that book? *Principles of Accounting?* Jeez, Sasha, it's as if you were trying to make things harder for yourself."

I looked up to see the Escape Room anomaly. The first thing I noticed was his smile. He had a nice one. More than that, he had the friendly face of a boy who might mow your lawn or hang a set of shelves for you. In short, the kind of guy who showed up at a dive like the Escape Room maybe one day in a hundred, and usually by mistake. He was a statistical outlier, and a cute one at that.

He looked at me. "Hey," he said.

"Hey," I said back.

He pointed to the stool that Martina had just left. "Mind if I sit?" He held his hand out. "Kevin Carson."

I shook his hand. "Sasha Gardner."

"Does that mean that you garden?"

"No, I'm afraid it doesn't."

He smiled. "I always thought Sasha was a boy's name."

It wasn't the first time I'd heard that. Most people I met didn't understand my name's origin. "In the States it's either," I informed him. "But you're also right, since it's the diminutive of Alexander in most of the former Soviet bloc. Russia, Belarus, Latvia, Moldova. Almost all the Sashas there are male."

"Moldova?" Kevin repeated.

I wondered if I had mumbled. Maybe it was just loud in the bar. "Moldova," I said, louder and hopefully more clearly. "You know, in there between Romania and the Ukraine. The capital is Chisinau?"

"Chisinau?" he asked, stumbling over the pronunciation. "That's a city or something?"

"Well, some people call it Kishinev, but you've got to figure that's just a dialect difference. Besides, I'm not one for splitting hairs." A minute in, and I was already lying to the guy, for I split hairs on a regular basis.

"I was just going to ask what you were drinking or start with the weather or something."

I felt my cheeks flush. Why was I always assuming that people would be as interested as I was in lesser known facts and smaller topics, things that I found fascinating?

I thought quickly. "Maybe I'm Moldovan," I said.

"But you don't have an accent."

"Or maybe Moldovan-American."

Kevin nodded. "I guess I should have thought of that. I forget that everyone's not a mutt like me. So who's from Moldova? Your parents? Your grandparents?"

I didn't want to lie to him again. "The truth is, I'm not the slightest bit Moldovan. That I know of, at least."

He laughed. "Maybe we should start over," he said. "Read any good books lately?"

Martina had shoved my dog-eared copy of *Principles of Accounting* into my purse, but I could still see it peeking out. "I did have a great-grandmother from Romania. Family legend has it that we're all part gypsy." As I said it, I picked up my purse as surreptitiously as I could and stowed it at my feet.

"Now you're just pulling my leg."

"It's true," I said. I could almost feel the words forming, the story of my great-grandmother as told through the generations. How she'd long sworn that we had nomadic blood. But I caught myself just in time. I realized that I wanted Kevin to stay and that a long-winded and unprompted account of my family history was an unlikely aphrodisiac. Besides, my father's Anglo genes had washed out my mother's gypsy swarthiness along with whatever remained of the ancestral wanderlust. I'd lived in California for twenty-six of my thirty-one years at that point, and with light brown hair and blue eyes, I didn't look like any gypsy.

"Can you tell my fortune?" Kevin asked.

"Well, I could, but I'm off the clock," I said. "I do see an intriguing stranger in your future."

"I see one in my present," he said.

Oh, he was good.

We talked for the next ten minutes, throughout which I managed to keep the conversation relatively light and avoid referring to any Eastern Bloc countries. He was funny, relatively new to the East Bay, and worked as a building contractor, renovations mostly. Martina, meanwhile, had taken the bar stool on my other side and struck up a conversation with the man next to her.

"I understand you've already met my meddling friend," I said, elbowing Martina. She looked over and smiled at Kevin.

"In line," he said. "Cheers on your promotion, by the way. Marketing crackers, did you say? Got any samples on you? These pretzels are stale."

"Premium packaged edibles," Martina said, nodding. "It goes way beyond crackers, my dear. And I don't. I'm waiting for my next assignment. Oh, this is Carl. Carl, this is Sasha. That's Kevin."

"Hey," Carl said, with a wan nod. He seemed uninterested in any detour in his conversation with Martina. He fidgeted with his key ring. From where I sat, I could see that it sported a Porsche trademark.

"So your friend pitches food. I build things. What do you do?" Kevin finally asked me.

"Besides hang around with barflies?"

"Those weird facts in your head didn't get there by accident. And it's a pretty head, if you don't mind my saying."

"You know, I got it on special over at the dollar store."

I meant it as a joke, but he frowned a little, as if trying to gauge whether I was serious. "You're a little kooky, aren't you?" he finally asked.

It had taken him all of fourteen minutes to notice. Martina would probably count that as a record.

"I don't mean that as a bad thing," he added quickly. "But seriously, where do you work?"

I felt my heart rate rise a little. I wasn't ready. "You know, the usual. In a building. Inside a cubicle. Behind a desk."

"So where's the desk?"

"Not far. Approximately 2.56 miles from here," I said. "You could walk it, if you needed to. I mean, I didn't. I drove."

"2.56 miles, huh?"

"Give or take. I had my reasons for measuring it," I added, when I saw his frown return. I wanted the smile back.

"And what do you do there, besides sit and look cute?"

"That's about it," I told him. "Looking cute accounts for ninety percent of my billable hours. It's a huge growth industry."

"No, really." He was waiting, and at some point, I would have to answer him.

"Truthfully, I work for the government. I'm a civil servant," I finally said.

Sometimes that would be enough. Some guys would have stopped pressing for details and let me relax. But not Kevin. He was determined. He was focused. In other circumstances, those traits would have been appealing.

"Better than being an uncivil servant," he said.

"Only when cornered," I said. "Then I scratch and hiss."

He laughed. "So who do you civilly serve?" he asked. "We do a lot of government work. Maybe I'll come visit you. Do you have a card?"

Martina must have overheard him. Suddenly, she was at my elbow. "So, Sasha, Carl was just showing me his shoes. Show Sasha your shoes," Martina ordered, pulling us both into their conversation.

Carl held out his leg. The black leather of his loafers was shiny and even, as if he'd taken them from the box that morning.

"They're Prada," Martina said. "This season."

"Wow," I said, though I didn't trust a man who wore triple-digit shoes. I preferred Kevin's dusty work boots.

Carl's shrug belied how much he cared. "You gotta dress the part," he sniffed.

"And your part is?" I asked.

"I work over at Morgan Chase," he said.

I knew the investment bank, so I nodded. "What do you do there?"

He paused, narrowing his eyes ever so slightly. "Well, I'm temping right now."

"Martina, maybe you can tell me where your friend works," Kevin said. "She's being evasive."

"Evasive, huh? Isn't that ironic." Martina laughed.

"How do you mean?" Kevin asked.

"Sasha just likes to control the flow of information. She likes knowing what's going to happen," Martina said. "She's not the most madcap person. She prefers to be prepared."

"What, are you a Boy Scout leader or something?" Kevin asked, quite seriously.

"What? No."

"Isn't that their motto?"

"Be Prepared?" I asked. "Well, sure. It's the motto for both the Boy and Girl Scouts and the scout movement in general, which was founded, as you may know, by Robert Baden-Powell, who was known as B.P., bringing us full circle to Be Prepared. But no, I've never been a Scout. And Martina, I'll have you know that I'm just as madcap as anyone else in this place."

"You're right. That was incredibly madcap." Martina rolled her eyes.

Carl pulled out his wallet with a flourish. "I'll get the next round," he announced, as if to force the conversation back in his direction. He handed his credit card to the bartender.

As he passed it over, I noticed that it was an Elm Street Optimus card. I knew the brand. Not from personal use, but I knew of it. It was one of those secured credit cards, typically given to folks with major blemishes on their credit reports. From that single glance, I knew that Carl was paying upwards of twenty-five percent interest, probably a penalty for previous financial misdeeds.

I smiled, and not because he had bad credit. I smiled because, at that moment, I probably knew more about Carl-the-temp's real life than anyone else at the Escape Room. If they were the right details, all you needed were a few.

"Thanks, man," Kevin said to Carl. "I'll take another beer."

"I meant that I'd buy for the ladies," Carl said.

I watched Kevin's sweet smile fade.

"Temp work not paying like it used to?" I asked Carl.

Martina put a hand on my arm, but I was irked. He could cover his fancy shoes but not a simple happy-hour beer?

"It's not like it's a long-term gig," Carl said.

Martina turned to me. "Play nice," she said.

"Why?" I asked. I looked at Carl. "I wouldn't think a guy in your financial situation would spend like that on shoes."

Carl stopped smiling. "You don't know anything about me."

"No? How's this? You're an over-extender. You're all plans, always with a scheme, but you're not much for actual work. You drive a fancy car, but I bet you're behind on your payments. You seek out women with good incomes, because your own money never comes in fast enough. You want everything before you've earned it. You saw the Prada shoes, so you got them. You saw Martina sit down and you figured for the cost of a few cheap drinks, maybe you'd get lucky. Besides, if you stay over at her place, the repo man won't be able to find your beat-up old Porsche. And you'll give Martina your work number, because you don't expect to finish out the week there. Then you'll start the cycle all over again. Another temp job, another bar, another girl."

Carl had waved to the bartender before I finished speaking. "Give me my card back," he said, his features furrowed all together.

"Is any of that true?" Martina asked. She unfolded a napkin that had been written over. "Is this your work number?"

"It's not fucking true," Carl snapped, right before he got up and stalked out of the bar.

Martina turned back to me. She didn't look upset. In fact, she was sort of smiling. "It's not like I was going to end up with a guy who spends more on shoes than I do," she said.

"That's what I figured. He wasn't your type."

"But sometimes it's better to wait for the whole story. You'll never know everything. You can't."

"I've heard Carl's story more times than I can count," I said. "I know it backwards and forwards."

"You really ripped that guy a new one," Kevin said. "How did you know all that?" Even before I turned to look at him, I knew that his smile was gone and it wasn't coming back. Kooky was bad enough, but now I had scared him.

"Go ahead," Martina said. "Why not?"

I pulled out my business card and handed it to Kevin. He looked at it, then dropped it onto the bar, as if it had burned his fingers.

Sasha Gardner
Senior Auditor
Internal Revenue Service

"I guess you see all types," he finally said.

"All types," I agreed.

Soon after, Kevin excused himself to go feed his parking meter. I wasn't surprised when he didn't return. Then again, I was rarely surprised anymore. It was my job to notice details, see patterns of behavior, and infer attitudes, motives, tendencies and likely actions. Once you've learned to do that, you start to realize how predictable most people are. There's actually a degree of comfort in that.

"Two guys scared off in record time," Martina said. "That was fast, even for you."

"I didn't scare them off," I said.

"Right. It must have been me," Martina said. "Didn't that Kevin have a nice smile?"

"Contractor," I explained. "They get audited an average of three times throughout their careers. A lot of cash expenses. I knew as soon as he told me."

Martina shook her head. She reached into my purse and pulled out my accounting book. She placed it on the bar between us. "Guys skip the brainy girls."

"That's not always true."

"Okay. Guys skip girls who can assess penalties with interest."

I conceded the point.

"And he was cute," she went on. "If you'd just said that you work at the Gap, you'd be on your way to a first date right now."

"I don't work at the Gap," I reminded her. "That's the problem. That's always the problem."

Chapter Two

SO PEOPLE SOMETIMES TRIED TO AVOID ME. SURE, I might have wished it were different, but I was an excellent auditor. Not everyone could do my job. Not everyone could build lives atop quantitative foundations or look beyond numbers to the events and decisions that put them there. The best auditors love to unravel the story that lurks in the data, to see hidden meanings and solve the puzzle. They have an eye for detail and great powers of concentration.

At least, they should, and I always had. Only, sometime earlier that month, I had started to drift. I couldn't trace it to a single event or day. I'd only realized it once inertia had taken hold—like a cold you think you can keep from catching, or maybe it's just allergies, and then one day you wake up clogged and froggy and foggy. Looking back, it felt gradual. I was late for work a few times one week, and again the next. I noticed that the muscles in my thighs were a little sore from bending at the knees to sneak by my colleagues' cubicles. My calves felt stronger from taking the stairs more often to avoid running into my boss in the elevator. And then there was that feeling, more and more frequent, of having barely dodged a pothole or avoided a stray banana peel.

Luckily, I'd been at my job long enough to know the minimum amount of work I could do without raising concern. I hadn't even noticed the extent of my distraction until the day that my friend Ricardo, our office's hiring manager, found me in the supply closet.

"Are you okay?" he asked, after knocking on the door.

"Sure. Why?" I asked back, looking up from a box of pens.

"Uh, because you've been in here for, like, twenty minutes."

"Oh please."

"You have. I saw you go in and thought I'd wait, but you never came out. I thought maybe you were having a tryst." He looked around the closet to see whether anyone else was hiding amid the office supplies. "What *have* you been doing?"

"Thinking, I guess." I hadn't realized it had been twenty minutes.

"Thinking? In here? About what?"

I decided to be honest about where my mind had been. "Legal pads are yellow, right? And the original highlighters were yellow, too."

"Yeah, so?"

"So wouldn't they have been useless on a legal pad? I think maybe that's why highlighters ended up branching out into blue and green and pink, while legal pads remain yellow."

"There are white legal pads," Ricardo said. "I've seen them in all different colors."

"Sure, but when you think 'legal pad,' you think 'yellow,' don't you?"

"Honey, unless I'm bedding a handsome lawyer, I don't think about legal pads."

"And then there are these ledger books, which are always light green. My theory is that they're green because they're reminiscent of the dollar bill, since they're intended to hold financial data. But that begs the question of whether ledger pads are also green in England. Because the British pound isn't green, and that might imply a totally different color origin."

"I don't get it," Ricardo said.

"You asked what I was thinking about."

"I mean, why are you worrying about this? You've been in here for twenty minutes contemplating the history of office supplies? It's August, sweetie. Every other auditor is complaining about the workload. I assume you're snowed under, too. Is everything okay? You're not in trouble, are you?"

"You think I'm not getting my work done?" I asked, careful to sound indignant.

"I'm just pointing out that maybe your investigative energy could be put to better use than in here."

I made a show of taking a box of pens before returning to my cubicle. What he didn't say—maybe he didn't know—was that I *wasn't* getting my work done. I hadn't been for weeks.

Before that August, I'd taken pride in my ability to plow through, audit after audit, without a drop in focus. But the morning after Kevin's unceremonious leave-taking from the Escape Room, I'd begun to review a return, only to find myself eavesdropping on Cliff, the auditor who sat on the far side of my cubicle wall. Later that afternoon, I had spent twenty minutes trying to deduce which grocery chain would be carrying the best peaches—based on proximity of the largest stores to local trucking routes. Moments after, I'd found myself wondering why horses and cats and dogs have hair but rabbits have fur. Ricardo was right; I was in trouble.

In my double-wide cubicle at our Oakland district office, I stood up, jogged in place, did a few jumping jacks, then sat back down. I stared hard at the paperwork on my desk, hoping that the brief burp of exercise had forced blood into my brain. Ricardo had a point: the auditing season was in full swing. Stacks of folders had massed on my worktable, each file representing a return awaiting my analysis. I had to buckle down. I had to find some momentum or fake as much. I was a senior auditor, not a veterinarian, nor a fruit whole-saler, nor an office-supply historian. I was supposed to be setting an example.

Then the phone rang, and I imagined that it might be Kevin, feeling guilt over his graceless getaway from the aptly named Escape Room. Maybe he had memorized my phone number and was calling to apologize. Maybe he'd called the IRS switchboard and asked for an auditor named Sasha. It wasn't outside the realm of possibility. Near the edge, maybe, but not beyond it.

"Sasha Gardner," I answered, glad for the excuse to close the file in front of me.

"So *S* is for *Sasha* then," a man said. It wasn't Kevin.

"In my case, yes." I wasn't sure what he meant by the comment. "May I help you?"

"You're not even a man," he said. It sounded like an insult.

"That's true," I agreed. "Though, as you probably know, Sasha is a male name in parts of Eastern Europe. How can I help you, sir?" I always tried to be polite at work. During any audit, and in the nec-essary correspondence before and after, I strove to remain detached but formal. I called people *sir* and *ma'am* and addressed them by their salutation and last name, assuming I knew it. There were strict codes of behavior to be followed when interacting with the public, and I took a certain pride in adhering to them. People will grasp at any excuse to hate the IRS, and one of my jobs was to keep them empty-handed.

"My name's Gordon, and I'm calling to tell you to stop what you're doing. Just stop it! Cease and desist!"

I glanced at the pad of paper on my desk. Earlier, I'd been doodling. Pictures of sailboats and rough waters. Pictures of trees, uprooted, leaves piling and swirling around them. "What I'm doing?" I repeated.

"Pestering an honest, upstanding, hardworking man," the man named Gordon said.

"Do I know you?" I asked. "Was I pestering you?"

Gordon harrumphed into the phone. "You'd like that, wouldn't you? You'd like to get your mitts on all of us. Well, you won't. Not if I can help it," he said.

"But—" I tried to cut in.

"You make trouble for the people who don't deserve it and can least afford it. You dig and you pry, but for what?

"Sir—" I tried again.

"All you need to know is that I pay my taxes so I have as much right to say this as anyone." Then he hung up.

I stared at the phone as if it could explain what had just happened. The IRS receives a slew of complaints every tax season, but they're shunted to the consumer-affairs department, not to individual auditors. Had there been a complaint about my work? Had I audited Gordon in the past? It seemed to me that he would have said as much had it been true. And I thought I would have recognized his voice. I traced back through the current tax season. What had I done that was so awful? The truth was, I'd hardly managed to do much of anything.

"That is not a happy face."

At the entrance to my cubicle stood Ricardo and Susan, an auditor a few years my junior.

"I just got the strangest phone call," I said, trying to shake Gordon's voice from my head. "What are you two up to?"

"We have a question," Susan said.

"Susan didn't believe that some people eat dirt when they're pregnant," Ricardo said.

"Dirt?" Susan asked me. "Come on."

"Not just while pregnant," I said, "but apparently it's more common then. *Pica disorder* is what it's called. If I'm remembering right, the official diagnosis requires eating non-nutritive substances for more than a month. You know, dirt, chalk, paper—"

"Paper?" Susan asked.

"Legal pads?" Ricardo added, with a smirk.

"And we're talking about adults?" Susan went on.

I ignored Ricardo and answered Susan. "*Pica* is from the Latin for *magpie,*" I said. "I guess those birds will eat anything."

Ricardo turned to Susan, a broad smile across his face. He held out his hand, palm up.

"Fine. You win," she said.

"Win what?" I asked.

"I bet Susan that she could pick any topic and you would know some weird fact about it," Ricardo said. "And I was right. You are our resident warehouse of useless information."

"Pica's not useless information," I said. I had audited someone with the disorder a few years before. There'd been a question about whether the psychological treatment was deductible. There had also been a few chewed-up pages in the file. "No information is," I said. "It just depends what you need it for."

"I should have asked the one about code-breaking," Susan muttered.

"Like the Enigma?" I asked, before I could stop myself.

Ricardo started to laugh.

I was irked. "I have to get back to work," I said. I made a show of standing up, walking to my table and pulling a folder from my stack of upcoming audits.

"Sweetie, I meant it as a compliment," Ricardo said. "We both did. Didn't we, Susan?"

"Sure," Susan said, only less believably.

I thought of Martina's comment, about guys avoiding smart girls. Maybe she'd been wrong. Ricardo claimed to appreciate my magpie mind. Of course, I hadn't realized that he'd been using it to earn money. And besides, Ricardo didn't swing that way.

I made a show of glancing inside the file I'd taken from the table.

"I suppose we've all got work to do," Susan said. I saw her glance at my stack of folders. "Some of us more than others." They left me alone then.

"Resident warehouse," I muttered.

"You say something, Sasha?" Cliff called through our mutual wall.

"Nothing," I called back. I looked again at the file I'd pulled off the table, then closed it and dropped it back atop the pile. Every folder represented someone who had already been notified of his or her upcoming audit. They weren't going to wait until my inertia was gone.

But then my phone rang again. Maybe it was Kevin.

"Sasha Gardner," I answered.

"Sasha Gardner," a woman repeated back. Her voice was wavery, watery, but her words were determined. "I'm calling to say that I think you have some nerve."

"Do you?" I'd never considered myself particularly brave.

She didn't answer. She just kept barreling on. "You're harassing one of the best people I've ever known. If you'd only take the time to know him, to talk to him, you'd see."

"Who are you talking about?" I asked, understanding at once the sort of nerve she'd meant. My cheeks started burning. "Who is this?"

"But no, you have to drop your poison into his life. Now, I don't know what sort of a family you were raised in, Ms. Gardner, but I hope you take a good look at how you're spending your time on God's green earth and move on to better things. He's had a hard enough year. Look at all he gave up. And for what? To have you bothering him? How about planting some happiness for a change and letting go that misery you sow?"

"Who are you?" I asked again. "How did you get my name? Do you know Gordon?"

"I'm a concerned citizen who felt an obligation to tell you that you work for the worst branch of our government."

"The IRS isn't its own branch," I said. "We're a part of the Treasury which is a part of..." She had hung up. "Never mind."

I replaced the handset. In my previous six years at the service, I hadn't received even one complaint. Now two in one afternoon? I looked around my office for clues. I listened for Cliff's voice, wondering whether he was receiving the same phone-line vitriol. How could I defend myself when I didn't know what I'd done, or to whom I'd done it? Who was this "he" that both callers had referred to?

I was so flustered that when my phone rang again, I barked into it. "I know—I'm awful. There, I beat you to it, didn't I? Surprised?"

"Uh, this is Jody in reception. Your three o'clock appointment is here."

"Oh. Sure, Jody. I'll be right there."

I had to get it together. I took a deep breath and glanced at my watch. That made me smile and, at least briefly, forget the phone calls. It was three o'clock exactly. They were right on time.

I had predicted by the way they prepaid their bills that the Ritters would be punctual. I had a clear-cut image of them in my mind: Donald Ritter, the avuncular former radio-station manager, his stomach straining against the spongy weave of a golf shirt, his all-purpose, slip-on sneakers, and Miriam, who'd only started to work that year, half time at a children's clothing store. She would get her hair set every week, was a crossword fanatic and probably carried her knitting in a public-radio tote.

I didn't know if the image I had built would be accurate, of course. I was never sure before I got an auditee into my cubicle. But I enjoyed the puzzle immensely, as well as the interim between the moment I wasn't sure and seconds later, when I was. Imagine a life. Have you got it? I mean, have you really got it? Well then, let's raise the curtain and bring out Donald and Miriam.

I walked into our no-frills reception area and looked around. Three sets of folks were waiting. One guy, off the bat I knew he was way too slick. He wore a perfectly tailored suit and crocodile loafers. My folks, the Ritters, they were savers. They weren't wealthy, but I reckoned they'd been saving ten percent of Don's take-home for the past twenty years. The guy in the suit—he'd dropped some serious cash (or more likely, credit) on his threads.

And anyhow, the crocodile man had an oily, better-than-you-are air. Donald and Miriam were softer than that, more hamburgers and horseshoes. The year before, they had donated an old car to a children's hospital and hadn't even claimed full value.

The folks by the door were too young. I knew that the Ritters had recently moved into a senior-living community, and both members of a couple usually had to have passed fifty-five to buy into such a development. Call me a warehouse, but that was the obscure sort of rule I got paid to keep track of.

"Ritter," I called out, looking directly at the couple I had pegged as Donald and Miriam.

They stood. Tote bag and slip-on sneakers. I loved being right.

"I'm Sasha Gardner," I told them. "Would you follow me, please?"

They looked unhappy to see me. I got no joy from ruining their day, but you can't complete an audit without a face-to-face interview. It gives people a chance to explain themselves. Auditing might sound formulaic, but even I'd been surprised a few times. Sometimes, I would think I had someone pegged as an evader, and she'd arrive with a God's honest explanation about the terrible year she'd had (and that's why her numbers had gone all to hell). Other times, a taxpayer I thought I would surely let off would sit down and start lying through his teeth, even about the legit stuff. It didn't happen often, but it happened.

"Here we are, Mr. Ritter, Mrs. Ritter," I said when we arrived at my cubicle.

"Call me Mitzi." As she folded up the newspaper she'd been holding, I could have sworn I caught sight of a crossword.

"Mitzi, then," I agreed. "Have a seat."

I noticed her staring hard at me. "You're so young," Mitzi Ritter finally said. She turned to her husband. "This girl can't be older than Molly." She turned back to me. "You're not, are you?"

"Molly?" I asked.

"Our daughter," Mitzi said. "You don't know that? They said you'd know everything about us."

"They?"

"Our new neighbors got audited once," Don Ritter said. "Everybody has an opinion."

"I don't know everything," I said. "But we don't mind the rumor if it keeps people honest." I smiled at Don Ritter to try to put him at ease.

He didn't smile back.

I had assumed that the Ritters had kids by the size of their former house. "I take it Molly's not a dependent anymore," I said.

"Oh no. She's been out of the house since, gosh how long has it been, Don?"

"Ten years," Don said.

"Has it been that long?"

"She'll be twenty-eight come December."

"Time sure flies," Mitzi clucked, then turned to look at me. "How old are you?"

I saw Don Ritter roll his eyes.

"Is that rude?" Mitzi asked. "It's only because you look so young."

"You think everyone looks young," Don said.

"I'm thirty-one," I told them.

"So young," Mitzi said.

"So listen, Mr. and Mrs. Ritter. I mean, Mitzi. I imagine you weren't exactly thrilled to receive my notice of your audit."

Mitzi looked at her husband, who frowned, sitting a little higher in his chair and pulling his golf shirt down over his belly. Mitzi tried a smile. "There was a bit of language. I won't repeat it here."

"I know how you feel," I said.

"Have you been audited, too?" she asked, eyes wide. "They do that?"

"Actually, no. Yes, they do audit auditors. I haven't been tagged yet though."

"Then you don't know what it's like," Don said.

"Well, my father's a certified public accountant, and my mother is a busybody. I kind of view my childhood as a series of unwelcome investigations."

"I suppose it could have been worse," Don Ritter said. "At least we've still got our health."

"That's a blessing," Mitzi agreed. "Can't take that for granted."

"No, you can't," I said. Indeed, it was a subject I could have spoken about at length. Deep down, I knew it was the reason behind my current distraction. But other audits were waiting, piled high upon my table. I smiled at the Ritters. "Let's get started, shall we?"

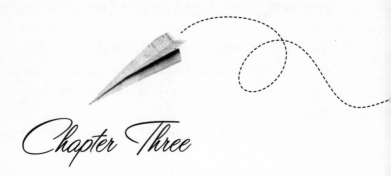

Chapter Three

THROUGH THE FRONT DOOR, I COULD HEAR MY phone ringing. I was just getting home, jacket and book in one hand and mail tucked under my arm, digging through my purse to find my keys. I hated that. A ringing phone and my response was practically Pavlovian. My heartbeat would quicken, and I'd bolt into overdrive, rushing, trying to shove my key in the lock, tripping over my purse, skittering across the room, and what were the chances it would actually be someone I wanted to talk to? Nine times out of ten, my desperate lunge got me to the phone in time for a sales call. Or, as on that day, my mother. And I'd been in such a fine mood leaving work.

"You sound like you're out of breath," she said. "You're not getting enough exercise, are you?"

"I just got home," I told her, picking up my purse, my mail, my jacket, my accounting book. Disappointed for some reason. Who did I expect that elusive tenth caller to be? Who would be worth the lunge and the scattered mail and the bent book jacket? No one sprang to mind.

"You work too hard," my mother said.

"It's not even six yet."

"Long and hard aren't the same thing." My mother had held a part-time job for about six months, twenty-six years earlier. Apparently, it had given her a lifetime of insight.

"Were you calling about something in particular?"

She sighed. "I was just thinking about you and Gene."

I looked at my mail and frowned. "What about Gene?"

"I want you to be happy, sweetheart. Are you happy?"

I *had* been before I'd answered the phone, I thought. There had been no more blistering phone calls, and the Ritters' audit had gone well. In my analysis, I'd discovered that they hadn't taken the full deduction on the appreciation of their former house (at issue was an upgraded bathroom), so I had sent them away with a refund. They were so surprised and relieved that they had invited me to a barbecue at their house that coming Labor Day. Of course, I wouldn't go. Auditors never got involved with current or past auditees, not outside the office. It was important to remain impartial.

Still, it was nice to be asked and even nicer to feel as though I'd performed a public good rather than a necessary evil. Don't get me wrong—auditing is about fairness. I mean, I pay my taxes. And people living in this country and driving on its roads and breathing its air, well, why should some folks foot the bill while others sneak off? But this audit had been different. I had actually made the Ritters' lives *easier*. I liked the feeling that left me with—a sense of pride and satisfaction that drained dry as I spoke to my mother.

"Sure I'm happy," I told my mom. "As much as anybody else." That I'd been off at work of late wasn't something I would ever admit to her. She would have leaped at an opening to tell me that I was in the wrong profession.

"I don't believe you," she said. "What's up with you and Gene? I want to know, but you don't have to tell me."

I was long since sorry that my key hadn't slipped away from my fingers in the bottom of my bag, at least for a few more seconds. Couldn't I have hit another red light on the way home? My mother was an expert at the "I'm not overstepping, I'm just interested" armtwist.

"Nothing's up with me and Gene."

"What's that supposed to mean?" she asked.

"It means we're not dating anymore. Like I told you."

"It was your job, wasn't it? That job is always interfering with your love life."

"You're the one who's always interfering with my love life," I reminded her. "Gene had no problem with my job."

"And I don't have to tell you how unusual *that* is. You don't toss a guy like that out with your dirty dishwater." An image of my exboyfriend, shrunken down and bathing in my sink flashed into my mind. It was not appealing. "And you two have so much in common," my mother went on.

"We do?" That got my attention. She may have been the first person to say that about me and Gene. Most of my friends had chalked us up to a case of opposites attracting. Martina's standing line was "He's milk toast to me, but whatever makes you happy."

"You both work for the government," my mother pointed out.

"And? I have as much in common with the first lady."

"You're not saying—"

I cut her off. "No, not a lesbian, Mom."

"Because that would be fine," she went on.

"Gene and I broke up last month," I reminded her.

"You never said *why*."

"It wasn't because I'm not into guys. I just wasn't into him. He just—he never noticed anything. He only saw what was right in front of him. He never saw *me*."

My mother sighed. She sounded as if she was settling in. "Marriages are work," she said after a time. "But they're worth it."

Mom often used her marriage to my father as the example on which all unions should be based. She tended to gloss over her threats to leave, their trial separation years before, and the difficult times before my brother Blake was born.

"Gene and I only dated for six months. We weren't married." I don't know why I felt obligated to point that out. In some recess of her mind, she must have known it.

"I'm just saying that no one's perfect," she said. "You're not perfect. Your father certainly isn't perfect. Even *I'm* not perfect." She didn't sound convinced about that last part.

"Thanks for the pep talk. Big help."

"Are you sure it wasn't because of your job?"

Neither of my parents was happy that I worked for the IRS, and they'd never made any effort to conceal their feelings. Indeed, I had wondered a few times before whether my longevity at the Service stemmed from the fact that I liked the job and was good at it, or because I was determined to prove my parents wrong. I had expected the negative reaction from my father who, as an accountant, took an adversarial view of the institution. But I had always expected my mother to be more supportive—if only because of the social promise held out by the auditing group's lopsided male-to-female ratio.

Plus, she'd always been a numbers person. Even before I was learning the same concepts in school, she would tutor me in math, using examples from real life.

"Suppose you wanted to buy a hundred pairs of shoes," I remembered her saying, "but the first store only has six in your size. What percent would you still need?"

"Why would I need a hundred pairs of shoes?" I had wondered. The absurdity of the idea was probably why I remembered the example years later.

"Oh princess, every girl eventually does."

"I don't," I had said.

I remember her sighing. "Let's just say that the price was right."

The most meaningful numbers in my mother's life had long been those on price tags. When I was growing up, my mother would discuss returns nearly as frequently as my CPA father, but to her a return meant that something hadn't fit right when she got it home.

"How can you be so sure that it wasn't your job that drove him away?" she now asked.

"Because I was the one who broke up with him. Because nothing was easy with Gene," I said.

"And you think your father was always a peach? Remember when he brought home that crazy boat?"

"The sailboat? The Catalina? Of course I do."

"And none of us knew how to sail."

"I learned," I reminded her.

"You were the only one. I couldn't wait to be rid of that thing. You remember that boat?"

"I loved that boat."

It was called a Catalina 22 because it was twenty-two feet long.

I could still hear my father explaining that. It was a little sailboat, not suited for much more than day-tripping around the Bay. My father had bought it during the summer I was fourteen, coming home and announcing the purchase to my mother, my brother Kurt and me. My mother hadn't received the news well. She preferred to be the one who made our family's splashy, spontaneous purchases. She reminded us that she was prone to seasickness. Why, she could barely stomach lying on a float in the pool.

Only once had the four of us ventured out on the boat together, and after that, it was just my dad and me. I was always up for a sail. I liked the bluster of the wind, even when it was too biting for comfort. I liked the spray that kicked up as the boat galloped over wakes. I liked the nuanced adjustments we'd make as soon as the wind shifted direction.

But that following winter had been a rough one at home. That was the winter my mother took a breather from the rest of us, holing up for a week in the family condo in Tahoe. Maybe the Catalina was one of the things she took issue with. Maybe my father simply knew what it would take to bring her back home. I don't know when he sold it, only that the Catalina was gone by the time the following spring turned to summer. And when Blake was born, not long after, the subject of a replacement sailboat was effectively tabled.

I had always planned to buy one of my own. It was the reason I had saved my babysitting profits throughout high school and on into college. I imagined myself living out of the little cabin as I sailed up and down the west coast, stopping off at small, natural harbors to camp along the shoreline. I would rent a small apartment near the marina in San Rafael—or in the town of Tiburon if I was really lucky.

And while other people spent their weekends pressed up against city crowds, I'd shove off and sail away.

Don't get me wrong. I know I wasn't the first person to land far afield of a childhood dream. Most people probably do. And the fact that I had never followed through on my plan wasn't a daily hang-up. I had a nice house in an appreciating neighborhood in Oakland, a secure government job, friends and family nearby. It was a fine life to be leading—even if it wasn't the one I'd imagined, back when I was saving for my own Catalina. Of course I wondered whether things would have turned out differently if I'd bought one, but how can you know that? How can you know where a few random turns might take you? A few random turns might have changed everything. But I hadn't taken a turn off my straightaway for a while by then.

"I should go," I told my mother. Thinking of the Catalina always made me moody.

"We'll see you Saturday then?"

"Saturday?" I asked. "Oh, yeah. Of course."

"You forgot Saturday?"

"No, I remember."

"It's only our thirty-fifth anniversary. It would be nice to have our children present."

"I said I remembered. I'll be there."

"Come early if you want. You should spend more time with your father," she said.

"He could spend more time with me," I pointed out.

"Don't be like that. Not after what he's been through."

I sank a little. She was right. My father had spent the first part of the year battling an aggressive form of lymphoma. Now, in August, he was officially in remission. I had a hunch that my father's illness had a lot to do with my own malaise. The timing didn't feel like a coincidence, but I hadn't wanted to think too hard about it. I just wanted my focus back.

"What about your brother?" my mother asked. "Do you know if he's coming? I haven't been able to reach him."

"Kurt?"

"Well, I can track down Blake easily enough. By the way, don't forget to congratulate him when you see him next. He's over the moon about making drum major. I don't know if Kurt even knows about that yet."

"I think he's been focused on the move and the new job."

"So focused he couldn't manage an RSVP to his parents' party? Martina managed an RSVP. What sort of children have I raised?"

"Speaking of Martina, I really have to go. I'm meeting her in an hour." It was true, but it was also a good excuse.

"How is that lovely girl?" Predictably, my mother softened. Martina wore skirts and dresses. Martina got manicures and waxed her brows. Martina followed fashion trends and kept old copies of *Vogue* and *Glamour* around for reference. Depending on her mood, my mother referred to my look as "messy," "tomboy," or "oblivious." She was always happy to hear that Martina and I were still friends.

"Martina knows that you catch more flies with honey than with vinegar," my mother was always reminding me. Maybe that was true, but who wanted to spend her life with a collection of flies?

Chapter Four

ON FRIDAY MORNING, I MET WITH MY SUPERVISOR, Fred Collins, to discuss the phone calls I'd continued to receive. By then, there had been six. Three livid, two indignant and one whiny. All referring to the poor man I'd wronged. All refusing to provide additional details—except to note that he was a much better person than I was.

"So you're looking for your better half," Fred said, smiling.

"It's not funny," I protested.

Fred seemed as flummoxed as I, though he took pains to assure me that the calls wouldn't be recorded as complaints in my employee file. "And none of them have made reference to a name or a town? Maybe an address?" he asked.

"None. Believe me, I've tried to ask. They always end up hanging up on me."

"So how can you be sure they're calling about the same taxpayer?"

I thought about that. Auditing was based on facts, probabilities and calculations. This was just something I felt, something I was nearly sure of, but without the proof.

"I'm not," I ventured, "but it sounds like it. It's always the same tone. How he's so generous and that he's had such a hard year. They say that he'd never do this to me. Only, I don't know what I've done."

"Put it aside if you can. How's everything else?" Fred asked. "In your work? In your life?"

I didn't want to get into it, especially not with my boss. "Fine," I said.

"You've been here what, ten, twelve years now?"

"Six, actually."

"Only six?" Fred sounded surprised. "Doesn't it seem like longer?"

When I first joined the IRS, I hadn't planned to travel the career track. It's funny what you can wind up doing if you show an aptitude. If I'd been able to choose my talents, I'd probably have chosen something physical. I'd have been a gold medalist on the uneven bars. I'd have sailed solo down the Pacific coast at age twelve. But kids tend to develop talents noticed and nurtured by their parents. Given that my father was an accountant, it was my knack for numbers that was coddled, and it was just as well—I was too tall for a serious career in gymnastics and the Catalina was long gone. Now, at thirty-one, that knack for numbers had elevated me into the position of senior auditor. Plunk into the middle lane of the career track.

Still, I found myself irked that Fred thought I'd been there for so much longer. Did I have the callous look of a lifer?

"Are you saying that I've been here too long, or that I mesh well with our corporate culture?" I asked.

He laughed. "What do you think?"

Suddenly, I wondered if he had spotted my ungainly stack of un-finished audits. But Fred was the one who seemed distracted just then. He was gazing at the framed photograph of his wife that he kept atop his desk.

"I should probably be getting back to my cubicle," I said. A show of work ethic couldn't hurt, especially if he'd sensed my ennui.

"Did I ever tell you how I met Marcy?" he asked, half to me, half to the photograph. Fred Collins was a gentle man and well-meaning, but his stories tended to drone. So I lied and told him that he already had.

"Anyway, I shouldn't take up any more of your time," I said, excusing myself.

I was headed back to my cubicle when I turned a corner and almost barreled into Ricardo.

"Just the lady I wanted to see," Ricardo said.

Beside him stood a tall man I didn't recognize. He appeared even taller in contrast to Ricardo, who was a slight Filipino, no more than five-two.

"Remember how I told you I made an offer for the archives position?" Ricardo asked.

"Not really," I admitted.

"Of course you do. Well, this is the guy. Jeff Hill, meet Sasha Gardner. Sasha is one of our senior auditors. That means that she rules this roost."

"It's nice to meet you," Jeff Hill said. I looked up and found myself staring into a pair of doleful brown eyes. Indeed, I would have thought him disappointed to be meeting me, had he not extended his hand.

"Nice to meet you, too," I said. He was so tall and thin, he reminded me of a normally proportioned person who'd been stretched out. The same mass over an elongated frame. As we shook hands, I felt the tendons and ligaments running beneath his skin.

"Sasha's a lovely name," Jeff Hill said, keeping hold of my hand for a moment longer than was comfortable. "You must be very skilled at your job to be a senior auditor at such a young age."

"I like him, Ricardo," I said. "He's clearly brilliant." I smiled at Jeff Hill.

"Sasha's one of my favorite people here," Ricardo said. "She knows everything about everything. If you ever have a question, just head for her cube."

"He's exaggerating," I told Jeff.

"She's also about the prettiest auditor you're going to find. You should see some of the people we've hired in the past," Ricardo went on. "Men and women. And their fashion sense, heaven help us all. It's got to be the least stylish profession on record. No offense."

"I'm not an auditor," Jeff said, shrugging.

I watched Ricardo give Jeff a quick once-over, his eyes pulling to a stop on the new hire's outdated loafers. The expression on Ricardo's face was a mix of sour disgust and pity. "Right," he said. "Archivist. Totally different."

I didn't think Jeff deserved quite so much sarcasm, at least not on his first day of work. Maybe fashion wasn't high on his list of priorities, but it would have been hypocritical of me to take issue with that.

"It was nice to meet you," I said. "I guess I'll see you around."

"You will," Jeff replied.

Indeed, he stopped by my cubicle not two hours later.

"Don't tell me Ricardo sent you in here with a question," I said. "I'm so tired of him placing bets on me."

"Ricardo didn't send me. I came up here on my own," Jeff said, then he took an audible sniff. "Your cubicle smells cleaner than the other ones on this floor." He looked around. "It *is* cleaner."

"I try to keep things neat," I said.

Jeff shook his head. "I don't mean neat. That's the tallest pile of file folders I've seen today," he said, pointing to the stack of unfinished returns. "But cleaner. It smells lemony in here. Like a polish."

I tried to act nonchalant. The fact was, maybe two days earlier, in a fit of procrastination, I had decided to reorder my shelf of tax statute books. In doing so, I realized how dusty they had become—and my filing cabinets and the tops of my bookshelves, too. Then I had made the mistake of taking a close look at the walls of my cubicle and found a host of strange stains—there and on the carpet—and ultimately, I had cornered a guy from the night cleaning crew and convinced him to lend me some carpet cleaner and an industrial wet-vac. The lemony furniture polish was my own, from home.

It had taken two days of working surreptitiously, but the fact was my cubicle *was* cleaner than the others on my floor. While I appreciated that Jeff had noticed—and right away—the history of the cleanliness was not something I wanted to explain. It would have been hard to explain it to anyone without sounding, well, obsessive.

"I think the lemon smell might be wafting over from that cubicle," I said, my voice low. I pointed to the wall I shared with Cliff.

Jeff Hill nodded. "Listen, Ricardo and I are going to lunch today, over to a place he suggested. Mexicali's? And I thought, if you had no other plans, you might join us."

"I do love their enchiladas," I said, although I'd heard that Mexicali's had once been closed by the health department, and I said a little prayer each time I ate there. "What time are you going?"

"What time do you want to go?" he asked.

"I don't know. What time did Ricardo say?"

"Uh, one?"

"One works. I've got an errand I need to run first. I'll meet you there?"

"But you're coming, right? I can put you down as an affirmative?"

"I'll be there."

"Is that a definite affirmative?"

"A definite affirmative?" I asked.

"Some people say they'll show up and then don't. This is California. People can be flaky."

"You're asking whether I would knowingly misrepresent myself?"

"Some people do."

"Of course they do. My career is based on that assumption. But I said I'd be there, so I'll be there."

I thought I saw him smile a little, just a glimmer, before he went all serious again. "Then I'll see you at one." He nodded and turned on his heel. He was so tall, I could see his head bobbing above the cubicles as he made his way back down the hallway.

"Odd," I found myself muttering, but I was also wondering what might get him to smile more.

I had a hard time finding parking, so it was five past one by the time I rushed into Mexicali's. I looked around for Jeff and listened for Ricardo's laugh (he had a whoop that could cut through a football game). But I didn't see either of them.

I turned to the hostess. "I'm looking for a party of two that came in maybe five minutes ago?" I told her.

"Sasha?"

I spun around to see Jeff.

"See, I told you I'd be here. Am I early?" I asked. Even as I checked my watch, I knew that I wasn't. I know that some people set their watches five or ten minutes ahead, in order to think that they're late and then supposedly arrive on time. The only time I ever tried to fool myself like that, I remembered that I'd set my watch ahead, automatically did the math and still arrived when I was going to arrive. All I had done was add extra equations to my day, and I got more than enough subtraction practice on the job. I didn't like to be late, but I always knew when I was and when I wasn't.

"Five minutes falls just inside my margin of error for punctuality," Jeff said. "I hope you're hungry."

"Should we wait for Ricardo?" I asked.

"No need. He had to cancel at the last minute."

"So no definite affirmative from him." I'd never known Ricardo to be too busy for lunch.

"Shall we sit?" Jeff asked.

I nodded. So it would be just the two of us, me and a somber near-stranger. "So, tell me something," I said as we sat. I figured I might as well find out about the guy.

"Like what?"

"How you ended up at the IRS. Where are you from?"

With that, Jeff told me that he was originally from Fresno and that the rest of his family still lived there. He said that if he hadn't become an archivist, he would have gone into entomology.

"Insects are fascinating. So highly detailed. Such precise movements," he said.

He explained that he had moved to the Bay area four years before and that he lived in a big apartment complex down in Fremont. As he spoke, he adjusted the placement of his water glass, arranging it in the precise center of his napkin. He did the same with a second napkin and a bottle of picante sauce. Then he picked up the saltshaker.

He caught me watching. "You're wondering what I'm doing," he said.

"Sort of," I admitted. Actually, I had been wondering whether he'd been aware of his actions. Apparently, he had been.

"I've got a touch of OCD," he said. "Obsessive-compulsive—"

"Disorder," I said, nodding. "I see."

"It's not anything dangerous," he said.

"I didn't think it was."

"It's better than being a slob," he said. "It doesn't intrude on my life."

"I'm not bothered by it. Really."

"I like to keep track of where things are. And I like precision," he continued, "in almost everything."

"I imagine that's a useful trait in your line of work."

"Where is precision not useful? You need it in your job, too," he said. "But yes, in archiving, it's absolutely essential."

Jeff's entire body seemed to lift up when he spoke of archiving. He was a big fan of the database system the IRS used. It was the same one he'd worked on in his prior position, in the archives of the Oakland Police Department. He spoke of an archival conference he made a point of attending each January.

"A lot of archivists have real wild sides to them. Every January, a lot of us attend this conference and those guys, they go a little crazy."

"And you?"

"Do I go a little crazy?"

"Do you have a wild side?"

He paused for a moment. "Not really, no," he said. "I used to want one, but now, well, I think I get more sleep this way. Do you?"

I thought about it. I thought about the big plans I'd once had and the house and job that kept me company these days. "Not lately," I had to admit.

"No loss," Jeff said. "Impulse control is an underappreciated trait these days. And I like to plan ahead. I like to know what the future might hold. There's a real comfort in that."

I noticed, as our meal went on, that Jeff began to look uneasy. I wondered if something was troubling him about the imprecise way I was eating my enchiladas. Or perhaps his burrito was causing heartburn. I didn't ask. I barely knew the guy.

Finally, Jeff Hill took a deep breath. "I found something I think you'll want to see," he said.

"Oh God, where—in your burrito?" I looked into what remained of my enchiladas.

"My burrito is fine," he said. Very deliberately, he slid his plate aside and wiped his place setting. Then he pulled a few sheets of paper from his back pocket and unfolded them, smoothing them against the table. He tilted them so that I could see.

The pages had been printed off a Web site called "Gray's Garden," a site about horticulture—plants and flowers and such.

"Oh, I get it—my last name is Gardner, so you were thinking gardening. Actually, I'm not really into plants. All that dirt." I slid the papers back in his direction. "My mother is. I don't know— maybe it skips a generation. Thanks for the thought though." I wanted to head off any gardening pitch he might have been approaching with. I knew my mother could get pretty obsessed with her seed-lings. What would this guy be like?

Jeff frowned. "This section isn't about gardening. Read what the guy says, right there." He pointed.

I leaned in. Indeed, the pages Jeff had printed out weren't about gardening at all; they were about being audited. Probably someone's sob story, I figured. I'd seen a few of those in my time. First-person angst-filled narratives about the hellish experience of meeting someone just like me.

But as I continued reading, I realized that this one was different. This was a first-person narrative by a man who was about to be audited, not by someone like me—but *by* me.

Most of you know about my past year, he wrote. *It's been one thing after another. I've been waiting for a cyclone to touch down in my yard, or maybe a swarm of locusts. Well, the wait is finally over. Turns out that I'm getting audited. In yesterday's mail, a letter arrived from our friends at the IRS. Imagine my excitement when they informed me of my upcoming appointment with "S. Gardner, Senior Auditor."*

He included, word for word, the letter he'd received—the one coldly notifying him of the upcoming audit—then went on to describe the dread he felt at the prospect of meeting me.

Does S. Gardner know the upheaval he or she has just dumped upon me? Does this person—and I must assume that S. Gardner is indeed a living, breathing human, and push aside the ghoulish images in my mind—have any idea of the wake he or she creates? I wonder how many people have met S. and emerged smiling, he wrote.

"So *S* is for *Sasha,*" I heard myself saying, just as Gordon, the first of my angry callers had, upon hearing my name.

"It's from a Web site out of Stockton," Jeff explained. "Someone must have told the guy your name. In the following section—I didn't print it out, so you'll just have to believe me—he's figured it out."

"Stockton?" I repeated.

"The man's name is Jonah Gray. Do you know him?"

"Jonah Gray?" I shook my head. "Where did you find this?"

Jeff Hill sat up straight and started to fiddle with the salt and pepper shakers, arranging and rearranging them. He cleared his throat. "Online," he finally said.

"Do you garden? You said you lived in an apartment." I didn't know which was stranger, the Web site or the fact that Jeff Hill, a man I had met not four hours before, was the one showing it to me.

"I used to garden a little. Back when I had a lawn. Too much dirt. And I really don't like earthworms." He shuddered.

"I thought you said you liked insects," I said.

He looked very serious. "Yes, insects. Not worms. Segmented worms are a hermaphroditic mess."

"But how did you find this?" I pressed, holding up the pages.

Jeff Hill took a deep breath and looked straight at me. "I looked you up," he said. "And when I found that site, I thought you'd be interested."

"You looked me up? Like a search? Like a police search?"

"I didn't go to the police," he said.

"I thought you said you'd worked for them."

"Sure, I could have gone to them. But I prefer to do my own research."

"On me?"

"On anyone."

"What I mean is, you were doing research on me? Why? Why would you do that?"

"Because I liked your looks and Ricardo said that you weren't dating anyone."

I sat back in my seat, not sure where to go next. Was it the truth? It was certainly flattering. And I didn't doubt that Ricardo would volunteer information about my dating status to anyone. It was the proactive research that had my head spinning. What sort of person did that? A stalker sort of person or just someone who was careful and detail-oriented? Was I just behind the times? Maybe everyone did that sort of research these days. I wondered what else he'd found. Hell, I wondered what else there was to find.

"So you did some quick research and then asked me to lunch? Or was it the other way around?"

"Does it matter?"

That wasn't what I was expecting to hear. "I hardly know you," I said.

"I realize that."

"This Jonah Gray person, I don't know him at all."

"So I'm ahead on that score," Jeff said. He smiled for the first time since I'd met him. It was a nice smile, actually. It lit up his face and helped to balance out those solemn eyes.

I held up the printout. "Can I keep this?" I asked.

"Be my guest."

"About the other stuff," I said. "I'm flattered. I am."

"You don't have to say anything. I'm not asking you out."

"You're not?" I found myself vaguely disappointed. I wasn't sure whether it was because I found Jeff Hill oddly appealing or because I had expected him to ask for something more. I mean, you don't usually tell someone that you like them and then just go about your business, la-di-dah.

"You want me to?" he asked.

"I don't know," I said.

"I'll take that as a maybe," he said, smiling again.

Chapter Five

GRAY'S GARDEN—THE WEB SITE—FOCUSED ON PLANT cultivation in California's various flora zones. There were fertilizer reviews, discussions about the weather and complaints about garden pests, both common and unusual. People wrote in for advice, something the owner of the site, Jonah Gray, dispensed generously, when he wasn't musing about various garden topics. In a cursory review of the site, I gathered that Jonah Gray resented nonnative species that required heavy watering, lamented the loss of indigenous oaks throughout California, and felt that Stockton's insistence on pruning trees between April and October was actually helping the dreaded "eucalyptus borer" decimate entire groves. Otherwise, he tended to keep things upbeat.

As I had admitted to Jeff, I wasn't much of a gardener, so I wasn't particularly interested in the plight of oaks or eucalypti. I was bent on finding the references to the IRS, the audit and, in particular, me. I found what I was looking for in the discussion area. That's where Jonah Gray had pasted the audit notification letter that had been generated by an IRS database around the same time I'd been assigned to his case. Had I been more focused that August—or rather, focused on my job instead of cubicle cleaning and legal-pad history—I would already have begun my initial analysis of Jonah Gray's return, and his name would have rung familiar when Jeff had mentioned it.

A number of people had replied to his first post about the audit, adding details from their own experiences with the IRS and whipping up the man's anxiety with (mostly) unfounded rumors.

JasperDad wrote: *I have heard tales. You be strong, Mr. Gray, sir. Don't let them take an extra red cent.*

Skua87 wrote: *This is exactly why I hide my money in my mattress.*

MaxiMoss wrote: *I never understood how good people could become auditors.*

JasperDad replied: *Good people don't.*

Two days into the discussion, Hydrangeas01 had informed everybody that *S* stood for *Sasha* and that I was female. I wondered whether Hydrangeas01 was Gordon, my first caller.

I felt as if I were eavesdropping. Here they were, talking about me, wondering about me, with no idea that I was watching. I felt like a celebrity might, albeit one of those celebrities that people find a perverse pleasure in hating.

"You didn't call me back." It was Ricardo, poking his head into my cubicle.

I glanced at my phone and only then noticed that the voice mail light was blinking. "You're right," I said, turning back to my computer screen.

"Does this mean that you've found your focus?" Ricardo asked. "Sorry I missed lunch."

I looked up at him. "When are you going to stop trying to set me up?"

"As soon as I find the right guy for you. Or your mother does. But I'm determined to win this one."

"And when are you going to stop betting on me? I'm not a horse," I pointed out. "You really think Jeff Hill might be the right guy for me?" He was certainly bright and seemed refreshingly straightforward. I had found that I liked how he'd wasted no time in asking me to lunch. Gene had been so indecisive.

"How'd it go?" Ricardo asked. "Any sparks? He said he was going to ask you to lunch as soon as I mentioned it. He's got great follow-through. And he's very detail-oriented."

"He's also obsessive-compulsive," I said.

"Even better."

"He ran a background check on me."

"He's thorough," Ricardo said. He sniffed. "Do you smell lemon?"

I shrugged and pointed at my computer screen. "His research pulled up the site of some guy I've been assigned to audit. The man's been writing about how he dreads meeting me, and imagining what I'm going to be like. In this part here, he pictures me at my desk, counting beans. And then he goes on this tangent about beans and other legumes and how they're often maligned in speech but incredibly nutritious and easy to grow."

Ricardo frowned. "Is that supposed to be an insult?"

"I don't know," I said. "But all these people on his site are up in arms on his behalf. They're telling him that I'm awful. That I'm a monster. That I'm wicked and bound to bleed him dry. This guy Jonah, he never actually says anything bad about me, not that I've found, at least. He wonders and he worries, but he's mostly just self-deprecating. I don't know what to think."

"Give the guy a break. He's being audited. He can't know how charming you are, my little bean counter."

"You're just trying to get back on my good side."

"How am I doing?"

"What should I do about Jeff Hill?" I asked him.

"Did he ask you to do anything?"

"No," I admitted.

"Then there's no decision to be made, is there?"

When Ricardo left, I turned to my worktable, to the tall stack of audits ahead of me. Somewhere in that pile, I would find him. Somewhere in there, Jonah Gray was waiting.

"Gray, Gray, Gray," I muttered as I rifled through the stack, and then, "gotcha!"

"You okay over there?"

"I'm fine, Cliff," I called back. I took the file folder labeled Jonah Gray back to my desk. "So, Mr. Gray," I murmured. "What do you have to say for yourself?"

I already knew that Jonah Gray lived in Stockton, and I wasn't surprised. Many of my audits that year had been from Stockton, the same city my older brother Kurt had recently moved to, about an hour east of Oakland. Since we were a district office, I was often assigned returns from places I'd never been, and Stockton was one such place.

I took note of Jonah Gray's street address: 530 Horsehair Road. Sometimes you could tell something about a person by the street address—whether it was a small or large apartment building or something that sounded like a town-house development or even a post office box. But 530 Horsehair Road was an address that didn't give much away. I made a mental note to ask Kurt whether he knew the street.

I glanced at Mr. Gray's personal information. *Jonah F. Gray. Social Security number: 229—*

I stopped. Now *that* was a number that told me something. Told me quite a bit, actually, and got my pulse going a little faster.

They say that most Americans live within fifty miles of the place where they were born. My experience with tax returns bore that out. Most California taxpayers offered up Social Security numbers showing allegiance to California, whether they were born there or were naturalized there. And if Jonah Gray had been from California originally, his Social would have begun with a number between 545 and 573, or else between 602 and 626.

But Jonah Gray was not from California, not originally at least— 229 came from the East Coast, from Virginia. And specifically, it came from the southwestern corner of the state, from the rolling green hills at the cusp of the Blue Ridge Mountains, almost to Tennessee but not quite. The number 229 was from Roanoke, an old Virginia city along the salty banks of the river that gave it its name. I knew this because 229 began my Social Security number, too. So, 229 meant that Jonah Gray and I were from the same place, probably the same town, perhaps even the same zip code. That wasn't just rare—it was something I had never before seen.

So he was a Virginian originally, but like me, he didn't live there now. How long had he lived around Roanoke? I wondered. Had we crossed paths before? When had he left, and why? Had he been brought west by his parents, as I had been, years before? Or had he moved later, on his own volition? And how on earth did he end up in Stockton, in the agricultural belly of the San Joaquin Valley? Kurt had moved himself, his sons and his wife there to assume a tenure-track geology professorship, which he'd been torn about accepting *because* of its location. Stockton wasn't commonly considered a hub of culture and industry. Indeed, it was known as a place to drive past without stopping. Then again, I realized, a lot of people might say the same about southwestern Virginia.

My phone rang.

"Are you busy?" Martina asked.

"I know why I've been getting those calls," I said. I told her about Gray's Garden. "I'm only telling you his name because he's already discussed the audit on a public Web site."

"Yeah, yeah. Your protocols." On the far end of the phone, I could hear her typing. "Ah," she said. "Huh."

"Huh, what?"

"I like him. Is he single?"

"Are you kidding?" I asked.

"No. Is he?"

"I don't know."

"You didn't check?"

"I didn't get to that field yet. You like him?"

"He's got a good sense of color, for one. It's an attractive site."

"So you mean you like his Web site."

"It's inviting. Attractive site, attractive guy," she said, as if I should have made the same connection.

"That's not a given," I pointed out.

"Well, he sounds appealing. If he grows plants, you've got to figure that he likes working with his hands. And I do like a guy with good hands. Did you check yet?"

"He's from Virginia," I said.

"So what? Oh, I forgot. You lived there, didn't you?"

"I'm *from* there," I corrected her.

"But you've been in California practically forever."

"But I'm *from* Virginia. And the same part that he's from." I couldn't explain, but I felt that this was important, even though it was true that I'd spent more than three-quarters of my life elsewhere. I looked back at the first page of his return and felt a sudden flutter. I realized that I didn't want to share the news with Martina, but I had to. She wasn't going to forget she'd asked.

"He's single," I said.

"He is? Perfect," she said. "Where does he live? Or maybe I should just write to him through his Web site. I'm totally going to write to him."

"He lives in Stockton," I said.

There was a pause. "Oh." She sounded disappointed.

"I've been assigned a lot of Stockton audits this year. It's random. I don't know why."

"Never mind then."

"What, just because he's in Stockton?"

"Geographically undesirable, my dear."

I felt myself smile a little.

"So what does Mr. Stockton do anyway? No way this site is a full-time gig."

In his file folder, I flipped to the back of his return, to the field just below his signature. "He's a journalist," I told her.

Journalists weren't often targeted by the Service, but like a number of my assignments that August, Jonah Gray was a randomly chosen compliance audit. Every year, a sample set of taxpayers gets tagged by pure chance. I appreciated compliance audits for the challenge of not knowing what to look for, but I did sympathize with folks on the receiving end. Out of the blue, they were ordered to gather their records and justify their claims and often had to bring in a certified public accountant to weed through the process. And still, maybe half the time, the IRS wouldn't find anything amiss. My father, an accountant for going on forty years at that point, liked to say that compliance audits were like revving a car engine once a month. You needed to do it, if only to keep things running. Then again, as a CPA, he got paid no matter how things turned out.

"He's a journalist?" Martina said. "That's like you, only cooler."

"What's that supposed to mean?"

"You've got to figure that auditors and journalists are opposite sides of the same coin. With auditors being the quantitative, nerdy side. No offense."

"How am I the flip side of a journalist? That doesn't make any sense."

"You're both ferreters. You're more interested in finding the truth than pulling down a high salary. Journalists are always sniffing around for a story, looking for the why and who and how. Same as you. I bet he's actually perfect for you. Too bad he's in Stockton."

"And that I'm auditing him."

"I know, I know. You've got all those rules."

Martina had to get off the line to take a call from her boss. After I'd hung up, I sat there, wondering if what she'd said was true. I supposed that I was a ferreter, though I'd never thought of myself in rodent terms. But she had a point. I sorted through bills and bank statements, interest income and mortgage expense and capital gains, in order to find my own version of a story. I was about to do the same with Jonah Gray's life.

I stared at the first page of his return, studying the way he'd printed his address, 530 Horsehair Road, all caps, in black ink. He was obedient, at least in those first few lines. The IRS requests black or blue ink, but I'd seen purple and green, too. And once, pink. You've got to figure a guy who fills out his tax form in pink is daring you to do something about it. In his case, actually, we did. I don't advise people to assume that the IRS has a hearty sense of humor.

Because Jonah Gray had handwritten his address information, I figured he'd moved to Horsehair Road within the past year, and that he'd prepared his own return. Taxpayers who'd stayed at the same address year after year are sent forms with preprinted labels. And an accountant would have printed the return straight from a computer.

I respected a self-prepared return. It took more effort, but it meant that Jonah was someone who wanted to know where his money went. I'd seen plenty of people get into trouble by signing everything over to CPAs, though I'd have caught hell if I ever told my father that.

So Mr. Gray was a journalist, I thought. I glanced at his W2 (stapled, as requested, to the front of his return). His employer was the *Stockton Star,* which a quick bit of research confirmed was Stockton's local newspaper. But the salary he'd been paid was too low for a reporter, even at a small city rag. That meant he was part-time or that he had taken the job midway through the previous year.

Then I noticed a second W2 stapled beneath the first. Now I was getting somewhere. Before he began working for the *Stockton Star,* Jonah Gray had been earning fully three times as much as a writer for the *Wall Street Journal.* What's more, he'd lived in Tiburon. Tiburon—the same marina hamlet in Marin County where I was going to dock my Catalina. But why would anyone leave Tiburon and the *Wall Street Journal* to write for the *Stockton Star?*

"What the hell is all this?" Ricardo was back, standing before my desk, his arms crossed. "I can hear it all the way over in my office. You can't be getting any work done." He looked toward the ceiling and shook his fist.

Only then did I notice the construction noise that drifted and clanged down from the fifth floor. When had that begun? I worked on four, and it was rare that sound would seep up or down from the surrounding levels. Usually, my floor's sounds were white collar—the papery flutter of returns being slipped in and out of folders; the soft metallic click of a file cabinet closing; the clitter-tick of a calculator. But now, hammering, sawing, the clamor of pipes being hit and the whir of machinery clattered around my cubicle.

I hadn't heard them until Ricardo came in. Had my concentration returned?

Without waiting for an invitation, Ricardo pulled up a chair and sat down. "I thought I would hide out over here for a few minutes, but this is chaos," he said.

I watched a flake of ceiling tile drift like snow onto my desk.

"That can't be healthy," Ricardo said.

"Don't you have work to do?" I asked. I liked Ricardo and his visits were usually a welcome break, but I was eager to find out more about Jonah Gray.

"I don't actually. My archivist is hired and the next sexual harassment seminar isn't for a month. What are you doing?"

"An audit."

"The bean guy? It's the bean guy, isn't it? Ol' Beanie Beanerson."

"He's a journalist," I said. "He used to work at the *Wall Street Journal,* I'll have you know."

"Oh Lord, really?" Ricardo sounded put out.

"You don't approve?"

"Journalists are so self-righteous," Ricardo said. "It's always, let me tell you what to think, let me tell you what to know. And financial types are the worst. Present company excluded, I mean."

"Maybe the journalists you've met, but on his Web site, he actually invites debate. About plants, at least. And fertilizer." Before I could say anything more, Ricardo held out his hand.

"What?" I asked.

"Give it. Give me the return."

"I'm not really supposed to—"

"Oh, please child. Hand it over."

I handed him the first page of Jonah Gray's return, and Ricardo pretended to skim it.

"Yes, yes, yes, yes, yes," he clucked.

I could tell that he wasn't actually reading it. "What do you think being a journalist says about his personality?"

"Since when do you care about personality?" Ricardo asked, as a particularly loud crack from above sent a piece of ceiling onto his lap. He brushed it off in disgust. Ricardo had a point. I usually focused on what an occupation said about a taxpayer's propensity for fraud. Some, like Kevin the contractor, had greater opportunities than others. With that, I realized that I hadn't thought about Kevin all day. Gene, either. What a relief that was.

"He's probably one of those earnest droners utterly devoid of humor," Ricardo added.

"I know for a fact that's not true," I said.

"You're defending the guy?"

I felt my cheeks redden. "What I mean is, on his Web site, someone was asking about a plant called 'hen and chicks.'"

"Hen and chicks?"

"Apparently, it's a succulent."

"Succulent," Ricardo said lasciviously.

I ignored him. "So he writes, did you hear about the city guy who went to the country and bought fifty chicks? The next week he buys a hundred, and the week after that, two hundred. Finally, the clerk at the country store says, 'You must be doing really well with your chicks,' and the city guy says, 'No. I guess I'm either planting them too deep or too far apart.'" I laughed a little. It was a silly joke.

Ricardo didn't crack a smile. "That's disgusting."

"Oh, come on. It didn't actually happen."

"Dead smothered chickens?"

"I was just trying to make the point that he's not humorless. I was thinking that, being a journalist, he's probably curious, too."

Ricardo perked up. "Curious like bi?"

"No."

"Like weird?"

"No, curious like…curious."

"Like a monkey," Ricardo said, nodding.

"If that helps you."

I didn't know what beat Jonah Gray covered for the *Stockton Star,* or what he'd focused on at the *Journal,* but on Gray's Garden, the man seemed game for anything. One reader had recently returned from a trip to the Cook Islands and wrote of seeing a rare palm, related to the sago, only larger.

I've never even heard of such a beast! Jonah Gray had replied. *You must tell us more. Do you have pictures? Can we see? Do you want me to post them?* Then he admitted to having spent all afternoon researching sago palms and their closer relatives.

Someone like that was an explorer of sorts, I thought, interested in things beyond his own experience. I don't mean that I'd deduced from a Web site on plant maintenance that the man sought to explore faraway countries or vast oceans. But I was willing to bet that he'd be game enough to try out the new Thai place in town.

Not everyone will. By the end of my six months with Gene, I'd noticed that he rarely agreed to try anything new. Gene worked as a mailman and loved that he could wear the same uniform and walk the same route every day. The guy knew what he knew, liked what he liked, and was content—even happy—to exist inside of such fences. He didn't look beyond them, and he didn't want to. Motivating him to go out was always a chore. He'd see movies, but preferred those with actors whose work he knew, and he would study the reviews and synopses beforehand, and even download the trailers. By the time we got to the theater, I felt as if I'd already seen the damn thing. Gene knew this about himself, and he explained that he found the rhythm of his methods comforting. I appreciated the guy's self-awareness and I respected his consistency. He'd never lie and he'd never judge out of turn. All the same, in our time together, I'd grown to find his habits a little stifling.

Ricardo yawned. "Those journalist types are always getting their panties in a lather about freedom."

"I think you just created a hostile work environment."

"You know, freedom of information. Freedom of the press. Blah blah blah," Ricardo said, waving the first page of Jonah Gray's return around.

A loud bang sounded then, and Ricardo and I looked up in tandem. I could hear muffled swearing at the same moment that a drizzle of water began to seep through the ceiling at one end of my cubicle.

"Jesus on a bike!" Ricardo shrieked. He jumped from his seat and ran into the hallway. "Grab a bucket and call security if that gets worse. I'm going to see what gives. You want to bet this is an OSHA violation?" He ran off.

I pulled my trash can under the leak as the swearing from above grew louder. Then I hurried back to my desk. I wasn't afraid of getting wet. The fact was, for the first time all month, I wanted to keep working. I wanted to know more about this Jonah Gray character.

But when I turned back to his file, I realized that Ricardo had been holding the first page of the return when he'd run upstairs. Immediately, I called Ricardo's extension and left a message on his voice mail. Then I called his assistant and asked that Ricardo come see me as soon as he returned.

"He took something of mine and it's crucial that I get it back immediately," I told him.

"I'll leave him the message," Ricardo's assistant said.

"Crucial," I repeated.

"I promise I'll tell him."

Luckily, six years on the job had taught me plenty of ways to move ahead without page one. As the racket continued, some creaking now and continued shouts, I turned to Jonah Gray's deductions.

I hated the standard deduction. I know—it takes less time and it's a lot simpler to use. But to an auditor, it's a black box. Standard deductions kept me at a distance. Itemized deductions were where the story of someone's year would emerge. Itemized deductions could speak volumes about character and passion and luck and changes in circumstance. They humanized the numbers and offered a clearer glimpse into the life beyond.

Sometimes, I'd skim down the page and come away with a vivid sense, almost visceral actually, of someone who was at the top of their game. Luck had shone on them—maybe through gambling earnings or investment income or inheritance—and now it was time to give back. I'd see gifts to a variety of charities, amounts that had been capped at a hundred dollars in earlier years suddenly rising higher. Old cars donated away. Houses bought for relatives. It was heady to experience such generosity, even through the filter of a tax form.

Other times, I'd run across clear markers of financial distress. A home that burned, an insurance report, attempts to value cherished possessions, now ash. A family living at the edge of their means, getting by on advances from relatives and subsidies they never before had to accept. And me, realizing that my audit would be the nadir of what had already been a terrible year.

Jonah Gray's deductions were a mixed bag, but my overwhelming impression was one of renunciation. He had unloaded a great deal in the year before. Old clothing to Goodwill, computer equipment to a teaching nonprofit, a bed and a couch to the local Veterans of Foreign Wars branch. Though any one of those deductions could have been prompted by a deep spring cleaning, taken as a whole they felt like someone saying goodbye to an entire life.

What had caused that? Had it coincided with the move to Stockton? Had he been ill? I noticed that he'd carried some significant out-of-pocket medical expenses. And why on earth had he paid for a membership in the AARP? The man was thirty-three years old.

Whatever it was, it had happened in July. That much I knew. It was July when he'd stopped working at the *Journal,* moved from Tiburon and given away so many of his belongings. It was in July that he'd filled out a loss report, detailing the destruction of a California black oak at 530 Horsehair Road. But were those things related? What had happened?

Knowing how much he cared for flora, I looked closely at the details of the tree loss. The black oak, estimated to have been sixty-five years old, had been plowed into by a truck and mortally wounded. You can't replace a tree like that—even with my minuscule knowledge of greenery, that seemed obvious. But had he valued a tree more highly than his life in Tiburon? Did he move to Stockton as penance?

I turned back to his deductions and that's when I saw it—the donation of a boat to charity. Not just any boat. He had given away a twenty-two-foot Catalina. Of all the boats on all the bays and oceans and lakes and estuaries, Jonah Gray had been sailing around in the one I'd wanted. He'd donated it to something called the American Aphasia Association. I didn't know much about aphasia, only that it was a disorder that affected someone's ability to use or understand words. If that was so important to him, he could have given the Catalina to me, I thought. I had no words for the coincidence.

My phone rang.

"Sasha Gardner."

"He's a good man," a woman said.

"Jonah Gray?" I asked.

She didn't seem surprised that I knew his name. "If you met him, you'd see that this is a wild-goose chase," she said.

"Listen, it's not personal. I'm just doing my job. It's a compliance audit."

"You think you're so special?"

"I didn't say that."

"That young man, he gives. He gives to anyone who asks, and what does he want in return? Nothing. And after all he's been through."

"What has he been through? Why did he give up the boat and move to Stockton? Did it have to do with the oak tree?" I cringed a little, hearing what sounded like desperation in my voice. But it suddenly felt very important that I figure it out. I felt like I had to know the answers. This wasn't my usual, measured approach. More often I made assumptions based on details in returns, then tested them against the evidence I collected. But I could not yet piece together the story of his past year. I found myself at a loss. And yet I wanted to know.

My caller was not inclined to help me. "Like you care," she grunted.

"I do," I said. "We're both from Virginia. And we both sail. Well, I mean, I used to. And, I guess, he used to. Too."

"Then try showing him a little heart. He wouldn't do this to you."

"How could he? He's not an auditor," I said. "And he did publicly post the notification."

"You started it by sending that letter."

"But that was computer generated."

"A real personal touch. That's the kind of thing he wouldn't do. He's a good person, which is more than I can say about you. You're not even good enough to be rummaging through his financial records." She hung up.

Not good enough? I thought. How the hell could she know that? Who the hell was she to judge? Not good enough? At least I didn't prank call strangers. At least I didn't harass honest government workers. I was plenty good enough, I told myself. And besides, shouldn't that be Jonah Gray's choice?

As soon as the question popped into my mind, I sat up with a start. What was I doing? How had I become so riled from an anonymous phone call? That woman didn't know me. None of them knew me. And it wasn't for any of them to judge whether or not I was good enough to audit Mr. Jonah Gray. Ultimately, it wasn't even his choice. It was the IRS that had chosen. And apparently the Service, or its randomization algorithm, had chosen me.

I realized that I had stopped reviewing Jonah Gray's return in my standard way. Instead of following my long-held protocols, I was wandering around this guy's life like a lost soul, skimming forward and backward without any plan at all. Gone was my customary patience—I was acting as if I wanted to know everything all at once, which is exactly how I felt.

But that's not how an auditor was supposed to approach a return. It was not the way I'd been trained to work. I was supposed to review all returns in the same manner, to give them equal, undifferentiated consideration.

I steeled myself and closed his file. Yes, this guy was unexpected, and I didn't know what I would find next, and I wanted to know. But I wasn't going to abandon my professionalism for the sake of some stranger. I would unravel Jonah Gray's story in due time. But I would start over from the beginning, the standard way. That is, once I got the first page back from Ricardo.

When Ricardo finally reappeared, he was dripping from head to toe. The man couldn't have weighed more than one hundred and twenty pounds soaking wet, which he was when he walked back into my cubicle.

"You left with my return. I need it," I said.

"Look at me!" Ricardo shrieked, as the carpet below his feet grew sodden and dark. "They're replacing old water pipes up on five," he said. He flipped his hair back and liquid spattered across my desk. "One of them burst before they got the water turned off. I walked in and got hosed."

"And my return?" I asked again.

"I could have been hurt!"

"But you're not."

"I should have gone to Susan for sympathy," he said. He held out a matted, dripping clot of paper. IRS forms are essentially newsprint, and they don't hold up under liquid.

"My God, Ricardo!" I said, grabbing the paper. It ripped as I took it from him. It began to come apart in my hands.

"I was holding it and then, well, couldn't you hear? I had to protect myself."

"With a piece of paper?" I spread the remains out on my desk. Half of the page had either been pulled off or had disintegrated. It was hard to tell which.

"Everyone knows that newsprint is just a weak mix of waste-paper pulps. You can't expect it to maintain any tensile strength when wet. The fibers are way too short."

Ricardo blinked at me, water still dripping off of him. "Not everyone knows that. Just geeks like you. Believe it or not, that isn't what went through my mind when the pipe exploded."

"Where's the rest of it?" I asked.

"I'm not going back up there," Ricardo said.

The soggy remains on my desk looked like the beginnings of an unpromising papier-mâché effort. And I had a sinking feeling that I was in possession of the healthiest remnant. "That was the original. I'm going to have to request a replacement."

"So call Mr. Bean Man. Mr. Funny Dead Chickens."

"And tell him what?"

Ricardo shrugged. "I don't know. Mention the tensile strength of newsprint. What man wouldn't swoon?"

Chapter Six

WHEN I WAS FIVE AND KURT WAS EIGHT, OUR FAMILY
moved from the outskirts of Roanoke, Virginia, to Piedmont, California. That was back before Blake, back when "family" meant just
four of us—Mom, Dad, Kurt and me. Leaving Virginia was a huge
deal. My father's family had been there for six generations, and Dad
had planned to follow suit and put down roots, his and ours, in the
Old Dominion after finishing his accounting degree at the university in Charlottesville.

My mother, on the other hand, was from California. She'd gone
east on scholarship to Sweet Briar, which she left after three years
in order to be by my father's side at the outset of his career. In the
earliest years of their marriage, my mother had agreed to adopt
Virginia as her own. But during the winter I turned five, the plan
changed. I have this vivid memory of Kurt walking me home from
kindergarten, the door to our house swinging open, the hallway
inside stacked with boxes—giant cardboard containers, some taller
than I was, kraft brown and sturdy. They were the sort of boxes you
might lose yourself inside, the perfect makings for a clubhouse or

tunneled fort. But as soon as my mother came around the corner, I saw something in the crimp of her mouth, and I knew without a word spoken that those boxes weren't for play. Two weeks later, we lived in California.

My mother had insisted on the move, explaining to us that kids in California were nicer than kids in Virginia. I was five. How would I know? Soon enough, though, I would realize that our cross-country move had more to do with turbulence in my parents' marriage. My father had been given a choice: Virginia or his wife and kids.

Sometimes I wondered what would have happened had he stayed behind, but I guess I'm glad he chose us, packing things up and shuttering his fledgling accountancy. He even found a house in Piedmont, a town my mother had long loved, though it was a stretch for them financially. And instead of growing up in Virginia, I became a girl from California, which brings with it a different set of expectations.

A part of me had always sensed that I'd missed out on something to have left Virginia so early. My scattered memories of the place were consistently tinged with the green of its thick, hot summers, its dense forests and its slow, fishy river. My recollections of the move itself are hazy, a pastiche of unrelated images, like puzzle pieces from opposite corners. The purple flower and the blue bird may be part of the same puzzle, but they don't fit easily together. A long plane ride. Kurt crying. Untouched trays of food left outside a hotel-room door. Neighbors that smelled of cigarettes. My old sheets on a new bed.

Three years older, Kurt probably remembered that stretch of time better than I did, but he didn't like to talk about it, except to say how scared he'd been to restart third grade in a new school of strangers, even if Mom had promised that they'd be nicer. I didn't notice that they were any nicer than the kids back in Roanoke.

My parents lived in that first Piedmont house for a few years, then moved to a bigger one, and eventually landed in the four-bedroom traditional on Banner Hill, where I spent my middle and high-school years. Each time we moved, my father would grouse for months about costs and bills and how the hell was he expected to afford it, what with pottery lessons and soccer uniforms and college tuitions for two and then three kids. But my mother had grown up knowing want (her family was from Hayward, down the east bay between nothing and nowhere). As a child, she had dreamed of living in a house with a three-car garage and a pool in Piedmont, a tony little town totally surrounded by the much larger city of Oakland. The Banner Hill house had both the garage and the pool. It was where she felt she had been meant to live, where she deserved to live. And it was where my parents would celebrate their thirty-fifth anniversary.

I arrived at the house at the same time as the Maselins, long-time neighbors from down the block. Mrs. Maselin I barely knew. She was painfully shy and seemed rarely to speak. Their son, Brian, was nice enough and had been friends with Kurt since both boys had been in their teens. And then there was Mr. Maselin.

My own father wasn't easy to get along with, often coming across as aloof and angry at the same time. But at least he didn't hit on every woman in a thirty-foot radius. That was Mr. Maselin's calling card, as was his reference, usually within the first minute of conversation, to whatever he'd most recently acquired—the biggest car on the block, the loudest stereo, the longest wet bar. He was a man of unwelcome superlatives.

I didn't know whether he had ever actually been unfaithful to his wife, Ellen, but he acted as though he wanted to be and as though he would be, should the opportunity present itself. I didn't like feeling that he was constantly seeking an opportunity. And I'd always hated the way his eyes combed over my mother.

The Maselins had pulled up to my parents' house just before I did. They lived four houses down, but they had driven to the party. If I followed them through the front door, I knew I would have to smile politely and hear what new gadget Ian had just bought. Instead, I wound past the side of the garage, back toward the pool. Maybe I couldn't avoid an exchange of pleasantries with Ian Maselin, but I could down a drink first.

My mother had spent months planning the anniversary party, meaning that she paid a party planner and remained available to make hard choices like, yes Stilton, no Muenster. From the looks of the place, the planner had earned her money. In the light of tiki torches, the back patio was washed a golden magical. Someone had trimmed the hedges and scrubbed down the deck. Fresh flowers floated across the pool. There were two bars and three bartenders and a good-looking wait-staff circulated with trays of buttery treats in puffs and crusts.

I grabbed a beer and gazed around the patio, trying to spot Kurt or Blake or Uncle Ed, my mother's older brother. Instead my eyes landed on my ex-boyfriend Gene. Before he could see me, I ducked inside the house and tracked my mother's voice to the kitchen.

"Gene's here," I said.

She looked up from where she stood, hovering over a caterer as he tried to arrange a tray of fruit and cheese. "Sasha! You made it. And don't you look, well, androgynously festive!" She held out her hand and gave me a squeeze.

My mother was wearing the diamond necklace my father had given her for their thirtieth anniversary and the diamond bracelet she had bought for herself "just because." I'd never before seen the outfit she wore, but no doubt it was the finest of several she had acquired for the occasion.

I chose to ignore her comment. "Gene's here," I said again.

"How lovely. I'll have to come out and say hello. Why don't you put some more cheddar on that one," she told the caterer. "Orange is such a nice summery color."

I knew a fake smile when I saw one, and the caterer's smile to my mother was just that.

"You didn't tell me he was going to be here," I said, trying to get her to focus on something other than cheese. I wasn't sure whether I was more frustrated that she had invited Gene or that I hadn't foreseen as much. I should have known; "I didn't realize you'd mind" was one of her set pieces.

"I wasn't sure he'd be able to make it."

"That's not the point," I told her. "I told you that we broke up."

My mother put on her sad face. "So I'm not allowed to see my friend Gene anymore?"

"He's not your friend—he's your mailman. And it's not that you can't see him. Just, a little warning would have been nice."

"He's *your* mailman now," my mother reminded me.

It was true, but that was not the point either. Gene had originally worked my parents' route, which is how my mother had met him. She had found him appealing, in a reliable, rain-sleet-snow sort of way, and over a series of brief conversations, she had ascertained that he was both single and straight. Based solely on these two traits, she had deemed him a perfect life partner for her only daughter.

Gene had transferred to Oakland just before we'd started dating, to a route that included my house. I didn't consider my neighborhood anything special, but Gene had grown up around there, and he'd been angling to get back to familiar sidewalks from the moment he'd joined the postal service.

I'll give him credit—for all the ways he'd irked me while we'd dated, I'd never enjoyed such consistent and timely mail delivery. And I knew that it wouldn't change, even now that we were no longer together. Gene wasn't vindictive in the least, and he took pride in the quality of his work. In a way, he *was* perfect. As a mailman.

"Is he going to make you uncomfortable, sweetheart? Do you want me to go out there and ask him to leave?" my mother asked. "I wouldn't have invited him if I'd known."

I doubted this, but the fact was it wasn't my evening to whine.

"I'm sure it'll be fine," I said.

"That's exactly what I thought!" My mother smiled brightly before turning back to the caterer. "What about grapes? People like grapes."

"We could do grapes if you want," he said. He looked tired.

"Here, Mom," I said, taking her by the elbow. "Why don't you let the professionals do that."

"I'm just trying to help. Scott," she said, turning to the caterer. "I'm not bothering you, am I?"

"I'm sure Scott agrees that you should be out enjoying your party," I said. "Did you see that the Maselins were here?"

My mother must have already been on her way to another thought. When she answered, her voice sounded far off. "Oh, really," she said. "I should say hello."

"Thanks for that," Scott said after she left. He gave me a smile that I liked to think looked less forced.

"She means well." I picked a grape off the platter and popped it into my mouth. "At least, that's what I keep telling myself."

I returned to the patio and found Gene by the pool.

"Hey there, stranger," I said. I'd avoided saying *hi* to him ever since he'd told me that had been a joke in intermediate school. All the kids coming up, saying "Hi Gene," thinking they were so clever.

"Why, hello Sasha." He was always so polite, an otherwise inoffensive trait that had grown to annoy me. It was as if I'd become allergic to everything about him. You break up with someone, and then, maybe to prove to yourself that it was the right thing to do, you find all the ways that the person was wrong for you, wrong for your life or just plain wrong.

"You look as lovely as ever," Gene said.

"My mother just used the word *androgynous*."

"She must have been making a joke."

"She says sometimes she forgets that she doesn't have three sons," I added.

"That Lola is a funny one," Gene said. He gazed at me with that way of his, the one that made me want to run screaming. He was so gentle. So sweet. So nothing.

"So how've you been?" I asked. I hadn't seen Gene since we'd called it quits. To be precise, I'd called it quits. To be totally precise— Jeff-Hill precise—I *had* seen him a couple times as he'd delivered my mail, but I'd stayed hidden behind a window shade.

It's not as if he would have ripped up my catalogs had he seen me, but it seemed easier to avoid eye contact. Maybe I hadn't quite filed away my feelings for him, even though I didn't have any use for them anymore.

"I've been just fine," he said. "Work always slows a little in August."

I nodded. Most things slowed in August. Only the IRS revved up.

"Are you here with anybody?" I asked him.

"No!" he croaked, clearly appalled.

It was a silly question. Bringing a date to my parents' party was the sort of provocation Gene would never have undertaken.

"You seeing anyone?" I asked. I didn't want him back, but I still wanted to know.

"No," he said, with a sad sort of half smile. "One of the other carriers has been trying to set me up with his sister."

"Are you going to do it?"

"I don't know. It seems like so much trouble to go to."

"Have you met her?"

He shook his head, then he shrugged. "I'm not comfortable having this conversation with you," he said.

I nodded. Why did I still need to know every little detail? I had been the breaker-upper—I didn't get to know everything anymore. But even now, he made it easy for me.

"So how's your father?" he asked.

"Fine, I think. His doctor said it looks like a full remission."

"I saw him when I came in. He's gained some weight back," Gene said. "He looks good."

In my job, I heard a lot of people lie. There's a tone to it, an airiness, a carefully constructed casualness. I heard the same in Gene's voice.

"But?"

"What?" Gene asked.

"It sounded like you were going to say something else."

He paused. "No," he finally said. "You know, I never got to know him very well."

"You got off easy," I said. "But speaking of the guest of honor, I see him over there. I haven't said hello yet."

"You should go," Gene said, nodding.

I was suddenly grateful that he'd made it so easy, as if he really did want the best for me. I felt my stomach sour a little. Why couldn't I just be nice to the guy?

"Hey, Dad," I said.

My father looked up and lumbered a step closer. "So you made it," he said.

"Are you kidding? I wouldn't have missed this." I was surprised that he thought I might not have come.

He leaned in for a quick hug and then pushed away, throwing me off balance. My father had always hugged abruptly, as if physical proximity were a reflex which, on second thought, he wasn't comfortable with. I don't know why I still wasn't ready for it.

Though I lived only five miles away, it had been about a month since I'd seen him last. That wasn't an accident. My father and I had hit a rough patch right around the time I took the IRS job, and we'd been skidding for about six years. Back when I was twenty-five and had passed my CPA exam, he'd wanted me to join his accountancy. At least, that's what my mother had said. He'd never actually offered me a job, except to mention that if I ever worked with him, I couldn't expect a handout, and I would need to generate my own clientele and find office space. It hadn't been a terribly compelling pitch, and instead, I'd accepted the IRS's offer.

Ever since, he'd seemed a little angry with me. I could tell by the way he asked about my work, on those very rare times he deigned to broach the subject, that he didn't respect it, and so I'd stopped offering. I figured that he didn't talk to me about his clientele because he thought I might audit them, and frankly, I couldn't have promised not to. You get a lead and you're obligated to follow it. Either way, as the years passed, we seemed to have less and less to talk about. He found the energy to talk to Kurt about geology and to Blake about various school subjects—things he knew precious little about. But with me, the child who worked in the same field as him, my father drew a blank.

Maybe I wasn't the daughter he'd wanted. Or maybe that's just the natural order of things. It's an old song: children grow up, become adults, develop their own friends, buy their own houses, and in so doing, spend less time with their parents. It's not as if my parents were suffering. My mother kept my father busy with shopping trips and golf outings and visits to the wine country and to the condo in Tahoe. It just meant that I didn't see him very often. At least, I told myself that's all it was.

"You're looking well," I told my father.

"Your mother and I were golfing. I got a little sunburned." It was true—he glowed pink under the tiki lights. "You look tired. Audits getting to you?"

"They're fine," I said.

"Don't let the bear get you yet," he said. It was the same admonishment he pulled out whenever he thought I was getting lazy. My father's solution to most any problem was overtime.

"What about you? Everything okay?" I asked.

"Did I say it wasn't?"

"No, I just thought I'd—"

"You always think I'm hiding something."

"I'm not accusing you of hiding anything." I turned to the table of food we stood beside. "So Mom made deviled eggs," I said, hoping that my father's favorite snack might settle his mood.

"Don't you think they look a little weird?" he asked.

The sunny centers of yolk and mayonnaise and mustard looked as golden as I remembered from my childhood. "Do they taste weird?" I asked.

"They taste fine," my father said. "They don't look different? Maybe she used a new mustard. Go get yourself a beer. You want a beer?"

"I already had one. I'm okay."

"There's wine, if you prefer wine."

"I'm going to stick with beer."

"Go get yourself another," he said.

"In a minute."

Ever since my dad's illness, I'd tried to visit more regularly. But once his lymphoma went into remission, back in May, the backsliding began. Sure, I'd tell myself to spend more time with him. Time was precious, we'd been spared, seize the day, etc. The fact is, sometimes those lessons stick and sometimes they don't. Sometimes you realize new truths and sometimes you fall back into the same habits, the same annoyances, the same shilly-shally as before.

My father had nearly died, that much we all knew. But the experience hadn't magically fixed everything. He was the same person as before, if a few pounds lighter, and even that difference was fading fast. We were the same family as before, if a few months older, and my attempts to reach out felt as listless as ever. Not that he ever made it easy. Whenever I called home, he'd talk to me for thirty seconds, maybe a minute, before passing me off to my mother. It didn't matter if I said, "Dad, I want to know what Dr. Fisher said." It didn't matter if I tried to tell him about an audit I was working on. It seemed that he found talking to me as awkward as I found talking to him, as though he was always searching for a reason to end the conversation.

"Oh great, Ed just got here," my father said, and before I could say anything else, he was gone.

Soon enough, Kurt arrived. I had expected him to bring Lori and the boys, but two out of the three of them were suffering from pink eye, and Kurt had insisted they all stay behind. He would have berated himself for years had his kids spread conjunctivitis around the party.

My older brother looked almost relaxed, far from his usual state. I watched him as he said his hellos and made his way through the buffet line. Eventually, with a plate of food and a drink in his hands, Kurt settled beside me into one of the poolside lounge chairs.

"Get enough to eat?" I asked.

"What are you saying? I mean, I know I've put on a few pounds." From childhood through college, Kurt had been your classic meso-morph—average height with an average build. In his twenties though, he'd begun to round out, and now at thirty-four, his sil-houette revealed the growing potbelly of a life distinctly sedentary.

"It was just a comment. Jesus, you're as paranoid as Dad."

"Sorry. I'm stressed out. You don't know what a relief it is to get out of that house and away from everything," he said. "It's chaos out there."

"Actually, I was hoping to see Lori and the boys tonight," I said.

"Well, sure. Of course." He sighed and ran his hand through his thinning hair. He'd been born with my father's fine, dishwater-blond hair, but had lost most of it in the preceding few years. "You seen Blake?" he asked.

"He's spending the night at Barney's."

"He got to skip this? I guess it's good he's not sick. I thought maybe he was sick since I hadn't seen him all night."

Kurt had always been fretful. In elementary school, he worried about me. He worried about missing the school bus, getting lost in the woods and that the apple in his lunch bag would mash his peanut-butter-and-jelly sandwich. When he was a Boy Scout, he worried about squirrels skittering out of trash cans when he went to throw something out. When he was in middle school, he worried that someone would hit him as he drank from a water fountain, mashing his teeth into the metal spigot.

In his teens, Kurt's worry centered on Blake, our "whoops" brother, who was born when I was fifteen and Kurt was eighteen. What if Blake stopped breathing? What if he choked on mashed banana? What if his bathwater ran too hot? What if it ran too cold? In hindsight, I could view it as caring, but at the time, it was really annoying, like having an extra parent watching your every move.

But now, with two boys and a wife at home, plus a new job in Stockton, my older brother was saddled with a new set of anxieties. Still, leave it to Kurt to come up with something no one else would have worried about.

"I hope no one gets too drunk tonight," Kurt said. "Those tiki torches are a lawsuit waiting to happen." I watched his eyes move from the torches to the legs of a waitress who was passing out mini-quiches. They stayed there for some time.

"Been a while since you've been out on your own?" I asked.

He snapped out of his stare and looked embarrassed. "I guess."

"How are things in Stockton?"

"The same. The whole city smells like fertilizer."

"Are you all settled in? Got your cable hooked up? Electricity?"

"Oh, we got it all," Kurt said.

"How about a newspaper subscription?"

"Even that," he said. "We're officially plugged into the local scene."

"What's the newspaper up there called?"

"I think the biggest local one is the *Star*," he said.

"So that's the *Stockton Star*?" I asked. For some reason, I felt that I had to be covert.

"Yep," Kurt said. He took a sip of his beer.

"Is it any good?"

My brother looked over at me and frowned. "I don't know," he said. "We just started getting it. It's a local newspaper."

I rocked a little in my seat before I spoke again. For some reason I was nervous. "You remember reading anything by a guy named Gray?"

"Gray? Gray what?" Kurt asked.

"Jonah Gray."

He shook his head. "No. Why? Do you know him?"

"Just that he works at the *Star*."

"If you already knew the paper, why did you ask me?"

"I don't know."

"What, do you have a crush on him or something?"

"No."

"You do, don't you?"

"Maybe." Only when I said it did I realize that it was true. Much as I hated to agree with my angry callers, there was something about Jonah Gray. Maybe it was the fact that he'd accomplished what I'd only planned to do—live in Tiburon and sail his Catalina 22. Or because he had come from the same corner of the world as I had. But those weren't the sorts of things I would have been able to explain to Kurt.

He turned toward me, interested now. "Really? Some guy in Stockton? What did you say his name was?"

"Never mind. Forget I said anything."

"How'd you meet him?"

"I haven't yet. Not, you know, actually."

"Is this an online thing? One of those dating sites?"

"No. It doesn't matter." I had realized how weird the conversation was going to make me sound, even to my brother, who'd long ago labeled me an oddball.

"Seriously, who is this guy?"

"I'm auditing him," I finally admitted, just to get it over with.

Kurt started to laugh.

"It's not funny," I said.

"Yes it is," he said. "This Gray guy is one of your audits? Jesus, Sasha! First, your mailman and now an audit? You really can't do anything like a normal person, can you?"

"Like study gravel?"

"Geology isn't gravel," he said.

"He seems interesting, is all," I explained. "He's from Roanoke, for one. And he used to sail. And he's a journalist."

"And a total fucking stranger."

"Only sort of."

"That doesn't worry you? I'd think that you, of all people, would want to find out more about him before turning all googly."

"I'm not all googly. I'm not even half-googly. I just think he's interesting. Besides, nothing's going to happen. I don't get involved with people I audit. And even if I did, he thinks I'm some scary bean counter."

"You are," Kurt said.

"I'm sorry I ever brought it up."

"I kind of am, too," Kurt said. He sipped his drink and watched the waitress again. Then he turned back to me. "How does Dad seem to you?"

"Back to his same prickly self as far as I can tell."

"I thought I saw him walking funny."

"Funny how?" I hadn't noticed anything.

"I don't know. Off balance."

"He's probably been drinking since five," I pointed out. Our father often started early.

Kurt nodded, but he looked dissatisfied. Then again, it was his default expression.

At that moment, there was a clinking of glasses, and I could see my mother and father standing together at the top of the small set of stairs that led from the house down to the patio. They were smiling, my father's arm around my mother's waist.

"To my lovely bride," my father said. My mother beamed.

"Should we be up there?" Kurt asked me.

I shrugged. "I think they're fine."

"By now, we've covered most all our vows. She's been with me in sickness and in health. Richer and poorer, and with some of these trips she's got planned for us, poorer still!"

My parents' friends laughed. My mother laughed.

My father was finishing. "To my lovely wife of thirty-five years. Here's to another thirty-five." He gave her a kiss, and their friends cooed and applauded. It was sweet. It really was.

* * *

At any gathering, you couldn't miss my uncle Ed. All you had to do was find the center of the largest and loudest group of people. As an oncologist (though not my father's), Ed had traveled around the world, setting up clinics and medical trials where there had been none before. He had a wallet full of stories about being chased by bulls in Argentina, sailing through the mouth of Gibraltar, trying to outrun a mob in New Delhi.

He loved good stories, too, and as I glanced over at him—later, after the glasses had all been lowered again and the guests had retreated to smaller circles of conversation—he seemed to be taking great pleasure listening to someone's anecdote. I heard him snort and saw his eyes light up. He put down his drink and wiped his broad brow with a cocktail napkin.

"Let me catch my breath!" he said. "A moose? You couldn't make that up!"

The crowd around him was laughing, too. Meanwhile, I stood beside my mother, listening as she described in minute detail the golf trip she and Dad planned to take in November. Even if I had any interest in golf, which I didn't, it would have been a tedious story.

Maybe Ed sensed my envy. "Sasha, you've got to hear this," he said, calling me over.

I took a step toward him as he went on.

"Camille here was down at Yosemite and ran into Marcus—"

I froze in my tracks—my smile, my feet, the air, nothing moved. I heard my mother stop her own story mid-sentence. I saw my father, maybe six feet off, his eyes darting from my mother to Ed and back again.

Uncle Ed's sentence hung there, stalled in his throat. He stiffened, then a second later shook himself free and went on. "Marcus Hunt," Uncle Ed said. "He's a radiology resident. I forgot—you don't know him."

I doubted that the people in Ed's orbit had noticed the stutter in his speech, but you can bet that everyone in my immediate family had. I glanced back at my mother, who continued to watch her brother, as if unsure whether or not to believe him.

"Go on, Mom," Kurt prompted. "You were saying?"

"It sounds like Ed has quite a story," she said.

I tried to see my father's expression, but he was inching away from all of us, slowly, like a cat trying to avoid a fight. He crept off so slowly that at any one second, he looked to be standing still, yet the space between us kept growing.

I was soon back in my chair beside the pool, chatting up Scott and the other caterers as they sneaked cigarette breaks. I liked listening to their banter. It was such a different world from the one I inhabited. Sure, we both interacted with strangers and passed judgment on them. But while I researched, they eavesdropped. While I worried about maintaining confidentiality, they gossiped openly. They also laughed, carried trays, refilled drinks and ate well. And they all intended to do something else with their lives, something larger. Maybe we did share that last trait.

"Has anyone seen Emily?" one of them asked, looking around the party.

"She left already," Scott said.

"She left?"

"Which one was Emily?" I asked, as if I might possibly have had something to add.

"Short blond hair. Great legs."

"With the mini-quiches. I think my brother was admiring her earlier."

"I expect a lot of the guys here were," Scott said. "Maybe one of them took home a party favor."

That's when Uncle Ed wandered over. "May I?" he asked.

I motioned for Ed to sit down. At once, the caterers began to fade back toward the kitchen, as though Ed seemed like more of an adult than me and thus someone who might cause trouble for them. How little they knew. Caterers were frequently audited. All those unde-clared tips.

"Are you enjoying yourself?" I asked Ed.

"I'm having a grand time." He sat heavily beside me. "But I guess I said the wrong name back there."

"It's a sore spot. Always has been. Always will be."

"You think?" Ed asked.

"I know," I said.

Ed shrugged and took a pull on his drink. He looked out over the pool. "I talk to him," he said. "I bet you didn't know that."

I turned to look, to make sure that he wasn't joking. Of course he wasn't joking, I thought. Of course he wasn't.

"You talk to Marcus? Johnston?"

"I talk to Marcus."

"But, you're not even related."

"Sasha—"

"Well, you're not."

"What does that matter? He's a person. I'm a person. We certainly have people in common."

"I'm just pointing out…" I wasn't sure what I was trying to point out. "How? I mean, how often? When?"

He shrugged again. "A few times a month maybe? Sometimes less."

"Does Mom know?"

"Oh heavens, no."

"And Dad?"

"He does."

I turned back to the pool. "Where is he?" I asked quietly. I wasn't sure whether I was supposed to want to know.

"Sacramento."

"California? He's in California? Doing what?"

"Working."

"Construction?" I asked.

Ed looked at me and sighed. "That was five years ago."

The way he said it made clear that changes had occurred that I ought to have known about. I was embarrassed. I searched my mind for any newer information about Marcus, but I had none. I couldn't even remember the last time I had thought of him.

"Does Dad talk to him?"

"Sometimes. When Jacob got sick, it seemed a good time to start something. But you understand, the way your mother is... He's coming down next week. We're having dinner on Thursday. You should come."

"To dinner? Why?"

"Call my office on Monday and my secretary will give you the details. You want to come?"

"I don't know. Maybe."

"Put it in your calendar. I'll drop you a line to remind you."

I nodded. Marcus. Now there was a name from the past.

Genetically speaking, Marcus Johnston was my half brother, though on the day of the anniversary party, I wasn't sure I could have picked him out of a crowd. Marcus was the child of my father and Eloise Johnston, "that woman," my mother called her. "That woman" had been my father's secretary in his first accountancy office, back in Roanoke. I'd never known much more about the affair—not how serious it was or how it had begun or how long it had lasted. Long enough for Eloise to get pregnant, that much was clear. And it must have ended quickly. We were already months into our first Piedmont home by the time Marcus was born.

It seemed a strange subject to be thinking about on that day in particular. The affair had been a stress fracture, straining my parents' marriage to the point of breaking without actually snapping it in half. My mother had stayed, or rather, she had allowed my father to stay. And over the years, especially after Blake came along, the breach had healed into something secure.

All I knew about Eloise Johnston was that she'd moved to Florida soon after Marcus was born, where she could live near her mother. I didn't know whether she had married, bore any other children or anything else about her. Marcus wasn't officially a secret, but nor was he ever discussed, which was the functional equivalent. I read once about the New Guinean word *mokita*, which means the truth that everyone knows about but no one speaks of. Marcus was my family's version of that.

He had come to visit just once that I could remember—when he was eleven. He'd been acting out at home, and apparently Eloise felt that it might help him to know who his father was, or else she'd simply needed a break. She'd put him on a westward plane with little warning. He'd stayed just three days before my father sent him back again, but in that time, he managed to break Kurt's favorite model plane.

I remembered being a little nervous around him, though I was almost six years older than he was. I wasn't scared of him, but he seemed like such a brooding kid and unpredictable. Kurt had gone off to college by then, and as soon as my mother heard that the boy was on his way, she bundled up Blake and took him to her parents' place for the duration. So for those three days, it was just me and Dad and Marcus.

I hadn't heard much of him in the years since. Somehow, I knew that he'd dropped out of high school, although I also recalled that he'd gotten his GED. There had been a run-in at a convenience store—either he'd started a fight or botched a mugging or something—for which he'd spent a few months in a sort of halfway jail. He'd gone into construction after that, and that was the last rooted fact I could recall about him. I had assumed he was still in that line of work, traveling to jobs around northern Florida or southern Georgia.

"When did he move to Sacramento?" I asked. I felt certain I would have remembered if I'd been told he lived in-state.

"Maybe a year ago. After he finished his degree."

"He got a degree?"

My uncle rolled his eyes. "You should get to know him. He's your brother, for God's sake."

"Not really," I said. "I know he is, but I don't know him."

"And why is that?"

"Oh, you know, I…" I faltered. "He just…we never. He's always lived across the country."

Ed looked as if he'd tasted something spoiled. It was an expression I'd never seen on his face before.

"What?" I asked. "He has."

"He was just a kid. You don't punish a kid," he said. "I always figured that you would be the one who got that."

I'd never before received a harsh word from Uncle Ed, and I hated the way his comment made me feel. As if I'd done something wrong, when I hadn't done anything.

"Meaning what?" I asked.

"You're his sister," Ed said, but he didn't get a chance to continue. My mother ran out of the house and called for him, not in a casual way, but in something closer to a panic. People parted to let her through.

"Over here. Calm down," Ed said as she ran up to us.

"You need to come inside."

"What is it?" I asked.

"Your father fell—"

"Is he okay? Should I—" I began.

"You stay there. You stay right there. Ed, come with me."

"But Mom—"

"You stay with the guests. I want Ed to take a look." With that, they hurried through the crowd, now buzzing a bit about things overheard.

Apparently, my father had been in the kitchen when he took an abrupt tumble. The caterers who'd witnessed his fall were unclear what he might have tripped over, but whatever it was, he'd gone down hard. Ed quickly pronounced it a simple sprained ankle, but my father's demeanor proved more troubling. He had accused one of the catering assistants—a girl who had quickly come to his aid— first of causing the fall and later, of trying to steal his watch. The girl had burst into tears.

I figured that my father had simply been drunk. It wouldn't have been the first time. But Ed insisted on a trip to the hospital, to do an X-ray and look for signs of a concussion.

"I'm going with them," my mother told me. "You stay here," she said.

"Why me? What about Kurt?"

"Kurt left already. Something about an early appointment. And with Blake over at Barney's, someone's got to pay the caterers and make sure they get moved out."

What could I say? It was their anniversary. I told myself that I'd count the inconvenience as part of their present.

It was nearly eleven when my mother left for the hospital, and there were still seven or so couples lingering in the torchlight. I stood by the sliding doors between the den and the patio, watching them. I was wondering when everyone would leave when a hot hand settled onto my shoulder.

"Is the old man gonna survive?" I turned to face Ian Maselin. "I can tell you're worried. It's always a shame to see a pretty girl worried."

"I think he'll be fine," I said, trying to inch off gracefully.

"You're probably right. And here I am, left," he said.

"Excuse me?"

"Oh, you know that song, don't you?" He swayed a little bit to get the rhythm down. *"Well, you're right, I'm left, and she's gone,"* he sang. Mr. Maselin was always singing or humming something. Serenades were a large part of his flirtation routine.

"I don't think I know that song," I said, backing farther away.

"No? Oh, honey, it's Tom Jones. You've got to know Tom Jones. *Well, you're right, I'm left, she's gone. You're right, and I'm left all alone.* I've got a whole collection of original records in my media room. You should come by some time and take a listen."

"Yeah," I said, meaning never. "I'd better go pay the caterers."

"I suppose I should scare up that wife of mine," he said. He went away humming. Much as I disliked him, I had to admit, the man could carry a tune.

Chapter Seven

IT HAD BEEN NEARLY ONE IN THE MORNING BEFORE the caterers finished clearing out. Scott had invited me to join a gaggle of them at a bar up in Berkeley, but I didn't want to leave before my parents returned.

"Okay, then. I guess I'll see you around," he'd said.

I'd nodded, though I knew that the statistical likelihood of our crossing paths a second time was slight. I was okay with that. You reach a certain age and the previously spontaneous "why not?" spirit mellows into a more rational "why bother?" Scott was cute and nice, but the fact was I was more interested in a good night's sleep.

Besides, my to-do list the next day was long. Once back in Oakland, I planned to straighten my closet. I was going to get my car washed. I was going to do laundry. I was going to vacuum. I was going to crack open my new book, *New Approaches in Forensic Auditing.*

Those were my plans at least. In the end, the same tasks remained on my list, no checkmarks or lines bisecting them. Instead, I spent the day at my computer, combing through the online archive of the *Stockton Star* and reading everything Jonah Gray had written since taking the job a year before. So much for my determination to follow my standard protocols.

The first mention of him was my favorite.

The Stockton Star *extends a warm welcome to its newest newsroom staffer, Jonah Gray!* it read. I wondered if all new employees went through this public getting-to-know-you hazing.

So how old are you, Jonah?

I'm thirty-two.

And how long have you lived in Stockton?

Only about a month at this point.

What brought you to our fair city?

A lot of things. Family, you could say.

What do you do when you're not hard at work at the best newspaper in town, the *Stockton Star?*

Well, I garden a lot. I used to sail.

And have you ever eaten at Greasy Gus?

Not yet, but I've promised to stop by next week.

As always, the *Stockton Star*'s welcome page is sponsored by Greasy Gus Barbecue on White Oak Way. Don't forget—we cater!

There had originally been a picture attached to the article—an awkward, taken-on-the-newsroom-floor headshot, I imagined—but it wasn't included in the text-only archive.

Jonah Gray had gone from microeconomic trend analysis for the *Wall Street Journal* to covering the police beat at the *Stockton Star.* Though I didn't know much about journalism, it seemed like quite a dive. Soon enough, however, his beat had expanded to cover crime in general—chasing down teenagers accused of theft or vandalism, unruly crowds at local football rallies, stolen farm equipment and at one point, pilfered fat.

Hold on to your fryers, he had written, about four months into his tenure.

The lard rustlers are back. Last week, a manager at the Otis Waffle Hut reported the broad-daylight theft of four fifty-five-gallon drums of used pork grease. Faithful readers of this paper may recall that earlier in the summer, Greasy Gus in Stockton suffered a similar theft. Police assume that the used cooking oil was likely sold to rendering plants where it can be turned into useful products like soap, cosmetics and livestock feed. It can bring in as much as $0.15 per pound. Talk about your greased palms!

If the criminal nature of Jonah's assignments ever depressed him, it didn't show. His style was clear, often lighthearted and revealed a dogged optimism. He ended one article by saying that the police chief "felt certain that the element responsible would be brought to justice." He ended another by pointing out that one hijacked truckload of grade-B lettuce had been found and donated to a local shelter, rather than remind his readers of the second truckload still at large.

More recently, he had been working the local government beat, a shift I inferred to be yet another promotion. For someone who hadn't been in Stockton long, he certainly followed the city's comings and goings.

I was startled from my reading by the ringing of my telephone.

I looked at the clock and saw that it was almost five. I had been reading the *Stockton Star* for nearly three hours.

"Hello?"

"My name is Mel, and I'm a taxpayer," a man's voice said. "I'm calling to lodge a complaint."

"How did you get this phone number?"

"You shouldn't go around auditing people pell-mell like that. You're upsetting the balance of things. It's wrong, I tell you. It's fundamentally wrong. That's all I have to say on that matter."

"So you're a gardener," I said. "You're one of Jonah Gray's lackeys."

"I ain't no man's lackey, lady," Mel said. "I say what I want to say."

"It was just random chance, you know. Chance that he's being audited. Chance that I was assigned to his case," I said.

"Yeah, well, what matters is what you do with the chance," Mel snarled.

"Like calling to harass someone at home?" I asked. "Like that? Right? Mel?"

But there was only a dial tone.

"Dammit," I muttered. The last thing I needed were random gardeners calling me at home. It wasn't appropriate and it wasn't fair, and what I ought to do, I told myself, was report Mel to the phone company or the police (though I had to admit that he hadn't threatened me). But I hesitated. Such a report might get Jonah Gray in trouble, and I didn't want that either. I realized that I felt strangely protective of the guy. My God, I wondered. Was I turning into one of them?

Chapter Eight

I'D NEVER HAD TO REQUEST A REPLACEMENT RETURN before, but I'd heard stories of other auditors who'd had to. Typically, that was a sign of someone on the way out. It wasn't a terminal offense, but when you start to misplace returns, well, you're hitting the bottom of your game. Of course, Jonah Gray's return hadn't been misplaced; it had been destroyed. Thank goodness I'd only handed Ricardo the first page.

It was easy enough to locate the number for the *Stockton Star,* but as I stared at it, I found myself torn. While I was eager to get Jonah on the phone, I dreaded the thought of asking for a replacement. What if he was angry? What if he switched into ferreter mode and began to investigate how his return had gone missing? There would be nothing to stop him from posting the story of its disintegration on his Web site. What if he wasn't the man I'd begun to hope he was, to believe he was? That possibility was perhaps the most troubling.

My heart was beating too fast to call, so I chose to delay a while, to give my approach more consideration. In past years, I'd have begun the next audit awaiting my review. On that day, I killed time in the kitchenette.

Ricardo wandered in after a while and asked after my weekend, and in particular, how my parents' anniversary party had gone.

"Did you know that there's a market for used fat?" I asked him.

"Why? Did something kinky happen at your parents' party?"

"No. I'm just thinking about it. You know, lard, cooking oil. Only used."

"Are you trying to give Susan grist for the mill? She already thinks you're a kook. You don't really have to work to convince anyone."

"I was reading, this weekend, how people actually steal used fat. From fast-food restaurants mostly. You should be glad to know this. It could make you some money. You know, by asking me about it."

"That is true," he agreed. "Where do you get this shit?" He walked over to where I was sitting. "Lordy, what is that you're reading?"

I had spread a newspaper across the table. Now I curled it up.

"Are you—is that—are you reading the *Stockton Star?*" Ricardo asked.

"So?"

"Where did you get that? Where can you buy the *Stockton Star* around here?"

I had to think fast. I couldn't admit that I'd found it at the newsstand near my house. I couldn't possibly explain how elated I'd been to see it carried there, or that I'd struck up a conversation with the newsstand manager about it.

"It's, uh, it was my brother's copy. I told you he lives up there now," I said.

Ricardo seemed relieved. He sat down across from me and shook his head as if to clear it of contempt. "We got that paper when I was growing up. Gives me the heebie-jeebies just seeing its crappy old layout. Oh, hey, Jeff."

I looked up to see Jeff Hill at the coffee machine. I gave him a quick nod, then turned back to Ricardo.

"You always say that you're from Sacramento," I said.

"Of course I do. Who wants to be from Stockton?"

"Oh, come on. Kurt didn't say—"

"Precious," Ricardo said, taking my hand. "It's cows and farms and railroads and more cows and more farms as far as the eye can see. Total snoresville. You couldn't pick a less appealing place to grow up."

"Maybe for you. You know, growing up—" I dropped down to a whisper "—gay."

"Oh honey," Ricardo said, glancing back toward Jeff. "I appreciate your attempt at discretion, but if that young man doesn't know my stripes already, we never should have hired him. Archivists are supposed to be detail-oriented." Ricardo turned around. "Jeff?"

Jeff looked over.

"You know I'm gay, right?"

"In the first minute I met you," Jeff said, without hesitation.

Ricardo patted my hand. "Get yourself a real newspaper. The only use for that one is lining a birdcage."

"Now you're just being harsh."

"Okay, wrapping fish."

"They've got some interesting issues out there," I said. "See, here, I was reading this article about a recent school-board meeting."

Ricardo's expression fell somewhere along the spectrum between horror and pity. "Honey, that's it," he said. "I am getting you out more if it means setting you up with one of my joyriding cousins. A school-board meeting? Those articles aren't even meant to be read."

"He made it seem interesting," I argued. "It was even sort of funny."

"Let me guess, they were debating stolen fat."

"That was a different article."

Ricardo looked at the piece I'd been reading. I tried to pulled the paper away from him, nervous he'd recognize the name of the author. But while Ricardo might recognize detail orientation in others, in his own life, he skimmed over most things. He had held Jonah Gray's return in his hand, but it was just a prop. He hadn't seen anything. He certainly hadn't seen what I saw.

"Imagine the poor soul whose job it is to sit through school-board meetings and then go back and barf them into articles—" He squinted at the byline. "Poor Jonah Gray—whoever he is, he's a better man than I am."

I had come to that conclusion myself. Still, I wished there were a way to know more before I had to call him for the replacement return. Then, as I glanced up at Jeff, it struck me that I had ways of finding out more without ever leaving the building.

"Jeff, are you headed back to the archive room?" I asked.

"You have a return to look up?" He said it as if he already knew. "I'll go now."

"Lucky for you," Ricardo said with a smile.

The big events in people's lives—births, marriages, separations, death—they all show up in tax returns. It's almost as if, every year you pay Uncle Sam, you're adding a chapter to an autobiography you didn't realize you were writing. What you did that year, whom you worked for, what you bought and gave away, whom you lost or added to your life—it's all in there.

I had begun to learn who Jonah Gray was—a sailor, a writer, a gardener, a ferreter like myself—but studying his past would tell me where he had come from. And I wanted to know.

I followed Jeff into the archives department.

"Yeah, so maybe the last seven years."

Jeff frowned. "Seven? That's a long way back. Let me guess, this is for that gardener you're auditing?"

"So you remember."

"Jonah Gray. Of course. It's not a hard name to remember. Have you got his Social?"

"Not with me. I can go get it for you though. I know it starts with 229," I said.

"Do you find that Southerners are more evasive than other people? Professionally, I mean. Do they get audited more?"

I would have taken issue with the question, had I not been so startled by it.

"How do you know he's a Southerner?"

"That Social is from Virginia. In my last job, I made it a point to memorize which state or territory each three-number combination refers to." He looked proud of himself, as if it were a fact he might trot out at parties. In that instant, I understood what Susan and Ricardo and Kevin all saw when they looked at me. It was a little jarring.

"Will 229 be enough?" I asked. "I think last year he had a Tiburon address."

"I'll find him. So, seven years?"

"Unless you've got more," I said. I was joking.

"Oh, I could get ten, but it'll take a few minutes."

"You can get ten? I thought we only keep seven."

"Officially, sure. It's all about who to ask and where to look. You want ten, don't you?"

"Sort of."

"What did this guy do anyway? Must have been pretty bad."

"He ran away," I said.

"He's a runner? From what?"

"That's the part I'm still trying to figure out."

Back at my cubicle, I straightened my desk. I sorted through some office announcements. I wondered how long I would have to wait. I stared at my phone.

I picked up the receiver, then put it down. I wasn't ready yet. I still didn't know enough. I looked around my cubicle, wondering what else to do. I sniffed the air to try to detect whether the scent of lemon still lingered. I looked at my stacks of audit folders, then looked away. I picked up the receiver, then again put it down. I wondered what he would sound like. I wondered what he would think of me. I reminded myself that I could always hang up if he answered. I picked up the receiver and called the *Stockton Star*.

"Jonah Gray, please," I asked the operator.

I was on hold for a moment before his voice mail picked up.

"This is Jonah Gray at the Stockton Star," he said.

So this was Jonah Gray's voice, I thought. It was lovely, like autumn leaves in the sun. Somewhere between tenor and baritone, somewhere between Virginia and California, the sort of voice that would wrap around you when the lights were off, that was Jonah Gray's voice.

"Thanks for your call. I'm away from the phone right now, but please leave a message and I'll call you back as soon as I can." He advised callers that, if it was an emergency, they ought to press zero to be connected to the operator.

I smiled, wondering what sort of emergency calls he might receive. A fire at a zoning meeting? A top-secret source on the school board? A fertilizer spill? A lead on more stolen fat?

I hung up without leaving a message, then called right back. I wanted to hear that voice again.

"This is Jonah Gray at the Stockton Star," he said again, exactly as before.

I closed my eyes to listen. There was barely any trace of a twang in his intonation. Maybe he had left Virginia while still young. My father still had a deep Southern drawl, but his kids had all been raised with California bland.

"Here you go," Jeff Hill said.

I jumped in my seat. I hadn't heard him approach, and now there he was, standing before my desk. I scrambled to hang up the phone before Jonah Gray's voice mail began to record my fumbling. Jeff handed me ten files, all neatly labeled.

"That was quick," I said.

"He didn't give me too much trouble," Jeff said. "Will there be anything else?"

Now that I knew just how detail-oriented he was, I wondered what else Jeff was noticing as he looked around my cubicle. My tax code books, newly dusted and arranged in numerical order. The picture of Kurt and my nephews. The stain on the carpet from the fifth-floor leak. My dog-eared *Principles of Accounting* book. What did he think of the lopsided pile of audits still waiting on my table? And why did I care?

"No, that's all. Thanks," I said.

"Let me know if you need anything else."

"I sure will. Thanks."

"All right then. I guess I'll be going." I had the distinct impression that he wanted to stay, but now was not the time.

"Okay. Thanks again," I said.

As soon as Jeff left, I turned my attention to Jonah Gray's life in the previous decade. I began with the oldest return Jeff had provided me, back when Jonah was just twenty-three and lived in an apartment in South San Francisco, hardly a glamorous address. He was a year out of college—I found the details in his student loan information—and was scraping by as a waiter and occasional freelance writer, selling mostly to local magazines.

By the following year, I saw the inroads he had made at several San Francisco newspapers. Online, I found a restaurant review he'd written of a place I'd always thought sounded great. Jonah had loved it. I found another piece he'd written about a club everyone had said was fantastic. I'd gone once and found it pretentious and overpriced. He'd said nearly the same thing in his review.

Around the time he was twenty-six, Jonah had gotten what I took to be a big break. He'd landed the job at the *Wall Street Journal* and his income rose significantly. I read on, watching as he began to invest in stocks and add to his retirement account. I wondered whether he'd been influenced by his colleagues or simply had more disposable income.

His freelance work petered off from that point, though I did find a review of an art show that I'd actually read before. In fact, I'd gone to see the show because of what he'd said about it. I remembered liking the way he'd described the paintings as "a view into a world I found myself wishing I lived in." I knew that sense of not-quite-regret. I felt that I was peering into the life he'd built for himself in much the same way.

It was when he joined the *Journal* that he left the apartment for a condo in the city, and two years later, he bought a small house in Tiburon, across the Golden Gate Bridge from San Francisco. I figured that was also when he bought the boat, though it wasn't deductible and there were no receipts for it.

As his salary and tenure at the *Journal* rose, his life seemed to grow busy. There were trade journals and conventions, entertainment expenses, expensive dinners out and trips abroad. I found a mention of him in *San Francisco Magazine,* described as "eligible." I cursed text-only archives—again, there was no picture. The writer had grilled him about Bay area dating.

My father has been asking me why I haven't settled down. I mean, I'm thirty, Jonah was been quoted as saying. *Of course, by the time my dad was thirty, he'd done a lot that I'd consider unadvisable.*

So what type of women do you date? the writer asked him. I got the feeling that she was personally interested.

Oh, I don't know. I like them smart and curious. I like someone who might be up for going sailing. I love to sail. I like women who are out in the world.

Is it hard, the writer asked, *to find women who are as successful as you are?*

You think I'm successful? he said. *You do?*

You don't?

What have I done, really?

An hour later, I came across the article that stuck with me. It wasn't a cleverly penned story about Silicon Valley. It wasn't trend analysis. It had been published by a small magazine that had since gone under. I could see in his tax return from two years back that he'd been paid fifty dollars for it. I wondered that you could put a price on such things.

As a young boy, I didn't know my father. He lived across the country, which to a child of five is the same thing as living in Australia or up at the North Pole. He didn't visit. He didn't write. He didn't call. If there were pictures of him in our house—pictures that somehow hadn't been ripped or cut up—I never found them.

He was not a subject my mother would speak of. My aunts would make eyes and tsk-tsk their tongues when I asked, and send me back to my mother. At seven, when I first saw drawings by Escher, they left me with the same feeling. All those pathways that went nowhere. I couldn't figure out where the stairs began that would bring me to the rooms I wanted to visit. They were always across a courtyard or some other broad expanse.

It was an unknowable chasm. A vast space. The distance from the earth to the farthest moons of Neptune. At eight, I decided that I hated him, that I would never seek him out, even if he were dying and begging to hold my hand, just once. It was a scene I replayed when I couldn't sleep at night. He was sick with cancer. He was wasting away. He had a month to live and all he wanted in life was to see me, and I, I would turn away.

But instead, it was my mother who died. Unexpected. Unplanned. Just like I had been, nine years earlier. And after my aunts made all the arrangements, I traveled across the country, which, as it turns out, is much different than going to Australia or up to the North Pole. And I met him. Sometimes, you forgive because you choose to forgive. And sometimes, you forgive because there is no other choice.

The ringing of my phone pulled me away. I wiped my eyes and answered.

"Sasha Gardner," I said.

"You sound stuffy. You're not getting sick are you?"

"Hi, Mom. I'm fine. How's Dad's ankle?"

"Healing. He's still wobblier than usual. We're going back to the hospital on Thursday to have it looked at and get a few tests done."

"Tests for a sprained ankle? Like what?"

"It's nothing major," she said. "Just some things the doctor suggested. What about you? Do you have an exciting week planned?"

"Not really," I said, glancing again at the piece I'd just read. "But I'm making progress on an audit."

"Anyone I know?" she asked.

"I doubt it. But he seems like a good guy."

"Oh really," she said. "How interesting." I could hear her smiling.

"Mother, please."

Once I was off the phone with her, I knew what I had to do. There was no more avoiding it. I needed another copy of his return. I was going to finish this audit. I was going to finish *something*. I took a breath and dialed, for the third time, the *Stockton Star*.

"Jonah Gray," he answered.

That voice. His voice.

"Hello?" he said.

"Uh, hi," I managed to say. I cringed. I hadn't really expected him to answer. Why hadn't I prepared a script to read from?

"Yes, hi," he said. I thought about his story of forgiveness. I tried to picture him as a little boy in Virginia. "Can I help you with something? Are you lost?" he asked.

I cast around my cubicle for something to hang on to. I needed a way in without giving him my name. Sasha Gardner was his vilified auditor. I didn't want to be her, not yet, at least. "Yes, my name is..." I glanced at the neatly labeled folders Jeff Hill had made for me. "Jeff...rine Hill," I said.

"Jeffrine?" Jonah Gray asked, in that voice that was like a deep, clear lake. He sounded sort of amused, like his curiosity had been piqued. Or maybe I just wanted to imagine that.

"Yes. I'm calling from—"

"How do you spell that?"

"J-e-f-f-r-i-n-e," I said. How did I know?

"That's an interesting name," he said. "I don't think I've heard it before."

"Jonah's an interesting name, too," I said. "Sort of."

"My mother had a thing for cetaceans," he said.

"Excuse me?"

"Whales. My mother liked whales."

His poor dead mother, I thought. "Ah," I said. "And you?"

"Do I like whales?" he asked. "Well, yeah. I guess. They're so big and slow and ancient. And closely related to the hippo. Pretty much the way I feel after a rough night. I saw one once when I was out on the Bay. I think it was a migrating gray. I mean, I didn't see the whole whale, but the blowhole. It was still pretty cool."

I was smiling by then. I liked that he seemed content to let the conversation wander. Clearly, he wasn't an efficiency-minded drone who immediately saw to his business and then hung up.

"Me, I like manatees," I offered.

"I'm sorry, Jeffrine," Jonah Gray said. "I think I interrupted you back there. I realize I don't know what you're calling about. Do I know you?"

"Uh, no," I admitted. I was embarrassed by my manatee confession. What had I been thinking? Why would I tell anyone that? "I'm calling from the Internal Revenue Service," I said.

I felt the cold begin to seep through the line in the pause that followed.

"Hello?" I said.

"Yes," he said. "I received a letter from a Ms. Gardner. Apparently she's auditing me. You know her?"

"Gardner?" I asked.

"Sasha Gardner. There can't be too many auditors with that name."

"Yeah. She's, uh, she works in this office."

"Should I be scared?" he asked. "Don't tell me—I got the worst one. It would be just my luck to get the worst one."

"No," I said, too quickly. "Sasha's fine. Actually, she's nice. And fair. And smart. You know, she's a person like anyone else. Just because she's an auditor doesn't mean she can't have nice, normal relationships." As opposed to Jeffrine, I thought, wincing. Apparently Jeffrine was a manatee-loving misfit.

"I shouldn't have been so judgmental," Jonah Gray said. "I try not to be. I guess her letter just arrived at the wrong time. But I trust you, Jeffrine. You've gotta trust a person who likes a sea-cow."

I smiled. "So you did get her letter. That's good. Well, not for you, I guess." Of course he'd received the letter. It was posted on his Web site. But Jeffrine might not know that, I reminded myself.

"No, not for me," he agreed.

"At least we know the postal system is working!" I hoped that Cliff, in the adjoining cubicle, couldn't hear me sound like a simpleton.

"To what do I owe the pleasure of this call, Jeffrine?" Jonah asked.

"Are you just confirming that I received the notice? Because I received it. Did I ever."

"Oh, right. No. Not exactly. Actually, I'm calling to request another copy of your tax return," I said. "A photocopy would be fine."

There was a pause and then, "Why?" he asked. There it was, his journalism background revealing itself. The ferreting. The curiosity.

"Just standard protocol," I said. I hoped that sounded official. I had decided on that phrase over lunch.

"Can't you make a copy? You must have my return somewhere in your offices. Go ask the infamous Sasha Gardner."

"Have you ever been audited before?" I asked, though I knew that he hadn't.

"No," he said. He sighed. "This is going to be a real chore, isn't it? Everyone's been telling me what I'm in for. I guess I didn't realize it would begin so soon. Where should I send it?"

I was relieved. "You can send it to me. The same address that was on the letter you received. The Oakland district office."

"And you said your last name was Hill?"

"On second thought, send it to my boss. Sasha—"

"Gardner. I know. So, does she live up to her name?" he asked.

"I'm not sure what you mean."

"Oh, you know, when I hear Sasha, I think—"

"A Russian boy," I cut in.

"Well, Russian, at least."

"I don't think that's her background," I said. "I once heard her mention that she was part gypsy."

"And of course, when I hear Gardner, I think—"

"Gardening," I finished. Based on my last name alone, everyone expected me to love the feel of dirt beneath my nails. I enjoyed the outdoors, and I had as much affection for trees and grass and other flora as the next person, but gardening to me had always seemed like a lot of effort for little reward. Of course, I wasn't going to tell Jonah that.

I heard him pause. "You know, that's a common misperception. Actually, the surname Gardner comes from a different root," he said.

"It does?"

"Don't sound so surprised, Jeffrine," he said. "There's no reason you should have known that."

"Right," I said.

"Most scholars think the surname Gardner comes from the Saxon for battle cry. I guess I wanted to know whether she was a fighter, a real warrior princess."

"It's not from gardening?" I repeated. "How strange. I always assumed it was." I wondered whether my father knew that.

"Like I said, it's a common misperception."

"Huh."

"So, is she?" he asked.

"A fighter? Not professionally. But she looks scrappy."

He laughed. It was a wonderful sound. "I'll send a copy of my return out tomorrow morning."

"Great. That's great. Thanks."

"Anything else?" he asked.

I wanted to say yes. I wanted to ask what had happened in his life, what had happened when he went to live with the father he'd never known. I wanted to ask why he'd left everything behind, left Tiburon, the Catalina, the *Wall Street Journal*. I wanted to ask him so many things.

"No, that's it," I said. I heard disappointment in my voice.

"I must say it's been an unexpected pleasure chatting with you, Jeffrine. Give a holler if you need anything else."

Chapter Nine

TWO AFTERNOONS LATER, I WAS ON THE PHONE WITH
Martina, who'd been unable to make my parents' anniversary party.
After two months of waiting, she had finally been assigned to a new
account—something to do with beef jerky—and had spent the
weekend at a brainstorming retreat. I took great pleasure in pointing
out that forty-eight hours of thinking up new approaches to dried
meat made my job look almost normal.

Martina and I were discussing where to meet for happy hour. The
Escape Room was closed for fumigation, and Martina had suggested
that we meet nearer to her work, at someplace called the Ball Bar.

"I've never been in, but one of my colleagues thinks it's a sports
bar. She thinks this because of the name."

"What do you think it refers to? Testes?" I asked this at the same
moment I noticed Jeff Hill waiting at the entrance of my cubicle.

He waved.

I cringed. I covered the mouthpiece. "I'll be right with you," I
whispered.

"Take your time," he said.

"Who are you talking to?" Martina asked.

I lowered my voice to barely audible. "New guy," I said.

"I can't hear you," she said. "Your mother is right. You don't enunciate."

"Did you watch the *news* last night?" I asked. "Did you see the story about that *guy*?"

"Oh, there's someone there," she said. "A news guy?"

"New," I said.

"Oh, new guy. The new guy is right there. Am I right?" She sounded pleased with herself.

I looked up again. Jeff was leaning against the gray-beige supports that stood in for walls. He was tall enough to enjoy an uninterrupted view across the entire sea of cubicles. He gave me a little smile, then pulled a brochure off the top of my bookshelf.

"You got it," I told Martina.

"Is he cute?"

I glanced at Jeff out of the corner of my eye, hoping that he wouldn't notice the once-over.

"Fine," I said.

"Fine like okay, or fine like 'damn, he's fine'?"

I looked again and considered the adjectives I might use for him. I felt certain that he'd catch on if I tried to work *obsessive* and *compulsive* into a sentence.

I covered the handset again. "Is it important?" I asked Jeff.

He shook his head. "Take your time," he said.

"Somewhere in between," I said to Martina.

"Is he standing right there?" she asked.

"Pretty much."

By that point I'd grown self-conscious. I didn't think that Jeff was listening intently to everything I said, but the conversation was no longer private. He'd overheard things before.

"I got the address. I'll catch up with you there," I told Martina.

"Ball Bar," she said. "Not to be confused with the Sac Shack." She was laughing at her joke as she hung up.

"Sorry about that," I said to Jeff. "I was on the phone."

"So I saw," he said.

I waited for him to continue, but he didn't. I looked around and shrugged. "Did you need something in particular? Can I help you with something?"

"Oh, no," he said. "I was just on your floor, so I thought I'd drop by and say hello. I guess you're going out tonight?"

"Yeah. With a girlfriend of mine."

"Is the Ball Bar a favorite of yours?"

"You know, I've never been," I said.

"You'll have to tell me how it is." He gave me a little wave and left.

Normally, I'd have been gone by five-thirty. But Martina didn't work government hours, so I dawdled, adding a little mascara and messing with my hair in the bathroom before returning to my cubicle for the rest of my things.

I could hear my phone ringing while I was still in the hallway, and I broke into a run to try to catch it in time. I fully expected it to be Martina, telling me that she was running late. I hated to sit at bars by myself, curled like a shrimp with my back to everyone else, waiting, fake smiling if I did make eye contact, bringing a book with me so that I'd have something to disappear into. A book to a bar? No wonder I'm still single, my mother would have said.

When I reached my cubicle, I lunged across my desk for the phone, knocking over a mug of pens and stack of Post-it pads.

"Sasha Gardner!" I said. It came out as a desperate almost yelp.

It wasn't Martina. In fact, the voice on the phone wasn't one I recognized.

"Why?" a man asked.

"Why?" I repeated. "Why what?"

"Why do this to the poor guy? He's been through so much, and now this."

"You know, I'm not the worst thing that could happen to Mr. Gray," I said. "I'm not some heartless—"

"You know how I met Jonah?" the man asked, cutting me off.

"How?" I settled into my chair.

"We were both in San Francisco. I was growing all these cacti. Now, those are succulents. They can't do with too much water."

"I know what a cactus is," I said.

"Well, it was raining like the dickens, and the building starts leaking all to hell, pouring down on my poor plants, only I was gone, see? I was out of town."

"Okay."

"So the water proceeds to leak through to the condo below. Turns out, that's where Jonah lived. He comes up to my place, figures out what's going on, that I'm out of town but those cacti are in there, and you know what he did? Do you know?"

"He cleaned up?"

"No, lady. He didn't just clean up. He spent all afternoon shuttling my plants into a dry room and turning on heat lamps. Even before he got his own place straightened out. And cacti, often they got these thorns."

"I know what cacti are like," I said. "Listen, I appreciate the story. I get that he's a good guy. But these audits are random. It's not personal."

"See, that's where you're wrong," the man said. "Everything you do in life is personal."

"Don't worry about it," Martina said. "Drink your beer."

"They keep on calling," I told her. "It's amazing how protective they are of him. I hate that they all think I'm the bad guy. I'm not the bad guy."

"You work at the Internal Revenue Service," Martina said. "Since when do you care what people think of you?"

"I don't know. Since now, I guess. I'm getting tired of it. I want to be out in the world."

"So quit. Go out into the world."

I froze. "Nah," I finally managed to say.

"No?"

"What else would I do?"

Martina frowned. "Anything, Sasha. Be an accountant somewhere else. Or not. Do something totally unrelated."

"Now doesn't seem like the best time."

"You say that every time we have this conversation."

"Have we had this conversation before?" I asked. I honestly couldn't remember.

Martina rolled her eyes and set her drink on the bar. "So tell me more about that new guy, the one who was in your office when I called."

I thought of Jeff Hill and wondered what Martina would make of him. "He's nice. He collects bugs. He's pretty serious. Unlike my audit. Did I mention how I was sitting alone in my cubicle, reading this article he wrote and totally cracking up—"

"Is he cute?" Martina asked me.

"He's tall and thin," I said.

"How on earth would you know that someone was thin from a tax return?" Martina asked. "God, don't tell me that you people are starting to ask for height and weight. As if the government didn't get personal enough."

"I was talking about Jeff Hill," I explained. "You'll recall that Jonah Gray lives in the geographically undesirable city of Stockton and I've never met him. I don't know if he's thin or tall."

"You sure seem obsessed by this audit. Way more than usual. I think you like him. And hey, didn't I say I thought you'd be a good match? Can I get some credit here? Wait, are you guys secretly dating?" Now she was interested.

"How did you get all the way to dating? I've talked to the man on the phone once. I actually told him that I like manatees."

Martina shook her head. "Why do you insist on making things so hard on yourself socially?"

"He started it with whales. And he's interesting. He had a great life that he up and walked away from."

"Was it some scandal? Now *that* would be interesting."

I shook my head. "I don't think so. He's a quality guy. I mean, I think he is. I'm pretty sure he is. I feel like we connect on some level."

Martina's eyes went wide. "I was right. You do like him!"

"I don't even know him. It's crazy, right?"

"No, you like him. You never say that shit about connecting."

It was true. I'd rarely been drawn to someone the way I found myself drawn to Jonah Gray. But why not? What was it—about Gene or any other guy—that hadn't drawn me in? Why was it so hard to find someone I felt at home with? I'd always believed that there was something less complacent about me, something that held out for more, if only I could find it. But when I heard Jeff Hill brag about memorizing Social Security number origins, I had begun to realize that maybe I was part of the problem.

Maybe I wasn't drop-dead gorgeous, but I was pretty enough to get hit on regularly and asked out by the smaller subset of guys who weren't repelled by my job. And anyway, there were plenty of average-looking people out there who had found someone willing to go the distance with them. Hell, the entire world was full of average-looking people— even actively unattractive people—who'd found someone to sleep beside and debate paint colors with and read the newspaper aloud to.

It's not like I couldn't find *someone,* I reminded myself. I'd found Gene (or rather, my mother had), and he'd been willing to read the newspaper with me on Sunday mornings. But he hadn't found *me.*

"I know it sounds cheesy," I said, "but I always find myself envying those couples that go around wearing matching track suits."

"Painfully cheesy," Martina agreed.

"But they're such a set. I've never felt like I've matched anyone to that extent."

"There you go, assuming that togetherness like that is always positive. Those couples remind me of trees that have grown all tangled together. You know how, in the spring, that tree in my yard looks like it has two types of flowers?"

"I like that tree," I said.

Martina rolled her eyes. "Well, it only looks like that because some moron planted two different trees way too close. Now they're all pressed up against each other and their roots are tangled. It's not healthy. For plants or people."

"Maybe everything would have been easier if I'd just stuck with Gene," I said. "I wouldn't be here, wondering whether I'm crazy and broken and destined to be alone."

"We're back to Gene? Gene drove you crazy."

"Maybe I just didn't give him enough time. Maybe I didn't give *us* enough time. Maybe we could have grown together and we'd be wearing matching track suits right now. Don't you ever wonder whether there was someone you would have done that with, but you broke up with him too soon?"

Martina frowned. "Me in a matching track suit? I don't think so."

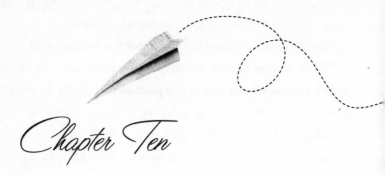

Chapter Ten

MAYBE IT WAS THE CONVERSATION IN THE BALL BAR OR maybe I was just impatient. The next day, I called him again.

"Jonah Gray," he answered, there at work at the *Stockton Star.*

"Hi, I called you a couple of days ago. My name is—"

"Jeffrine," he said. "I recognize your voice."

"You do? Right. I guess you must have."

"What can I do for you, Jeffrine?"

"I just wanted to double-check that you'd sent—"

"Oh, I sent it."

"Because it hasn't shown up yet. But it's probably stuck in our processing center."

"I imagine you get a lot of mail over there. The IRS probably doesn't rent the smallest post office box."

"I think we probably rent the post office," I agreed. "By the way, I read one of your articles. In the *Star,*" I said.

"You did, did you? Mind if I ask which one?"

I had reviewed them all at that point, so I just chose at random. "The one about the kids spray-painting those poor cows."

He laughed. "You read that? You must have been doing your homework. Soon, you're going to know all my secrets."

I smiled to myself but didn't admit that that was the point.

"You'll be glad to hear that the cows were all okay. Turns out there's a non-toxic solvent that gets paint off hair. Or fur. I guess it's cow hair, isn't it?"

"And horse hair and pony hair," I said.

"Maybe it's only fur after it reaches a certain length," he mused.

"Actually, there's no structural difference between fur and hair. Turns out it's just a human distinction."

"Really?" he asked. "Are you sure?"

"I've actually researched this topic before," I said, wondering how eccentric that would make me sound to him—or to anyone, for that matter.

"You researched that? That's one of those things I've always wondered about and you went and figured it out. You never know what's going to come in handy, do you?" he said.

Alone in my cubicle, I felt myself blush. "So what are you working on now? Can I ask or is it a secret?"

"What am I *supposed* to be working on for the *Star,* or what am I actually doing?"

"The latter sounds more interesting."

"Writing a letter to my sisters."

"You have sisters?" That was something he'd never mentioned in his writing, nor had they shown up in his tax return.

"Two. Two half sisters actually."

"Oh, shit," I said, realizing that I'd completely forgotten to follow up with Uncle Ed about dinner with Marcus the night before. His secretary had called with the details, and I'd written them down, then promptly set them aside.

"What?" Jonah Gray asked. "Is that going to affect my audit? They're financially independent."

"No, no, I'm sorry. It's not you. I just remembered something. I'm sorry. Your sisters—do they live in Stockton, too?" I asked. Uncle Ed could wait. I'd already missed the dinner.

"Oh, no. One is in Minneapolis, the other's in Boston."

"Sounds like you've got some wanderers in your family."

"Something like that. What about you?"

"Just brothers. Two. Well, two and a half. Oh hey, this might be your return now." I said.

From where I sat, I could see Ricardo making his way toward my cubicle, a thick envelope in hand. I stood to meet him, walking with the receiver pressed to my ear, around my desk, to where my cubicle opened into the hallway. In doing so, the phone cord pulled tight and jumped over my mug of pens, upending it.

"Dammit," I said. I was going to have to move that mug.

"Are you okay over there?" Cliff called through the wall.

"I'm fine, Cliff," I called back.

"I've got something for you," Ricardo said, holding out the envelope.

"Jeffrine, it sounds like you're busy," Jonah said to me.

"Yeah, I'd better go," I said. I didn't want to hang up, but I was afraid Ricardo would say something that Jonah might overhear. My real name, for example.

"Just let me know if you need anything else from me," Jonah said.

"Who are you talking to?" Ricardo asked.

I waved him away. "I sure will," I told Jonah. "It was nice to talk with you again."

"The pleasure was mine," he said, then hung up.

I looked at Ricardo. "What's up?"

"Just bringing you your mail," he said. "It's hand-addressed, so I thought it might be something interesting." He handed it to me and waited.

"What?"

"Well?"

"It's private," I said.

"You're no fun anymore."

"Was I ever fun?" I asked him.

He considered the question. "I think you could be. There's still hope."

The moment he was gone, I tore open the envelope and looked at the front page of Jonah's return. I dropped to my chair. He'd made a correction on the copy he'd sent. He'd crossed out the box he'd originally marked and marked "Married," instead.

I called Martina.

"I don't understand," she said. "You said he was single."

"He was. He said he was. He was originally. But between now and then—"

"You're saying he got married in the past week?"

"No. He's been at work all week. He's at work today. And anyway, this is last year's return. I don't know. Maybe he forgot he was married."

"That's not a good sign. Forgetting you're married isn't like forgetting to buy toilet paper."

"You think I don't know that?"

I suddenly felt myself teetering on the edge of really screwing things up. I'd forgotten my dinner with Uncle Ed and Marcus. I was being chastised by people I'd never met. I was making excuses to call an auditee and pretend to be someone I wasn't. And I had spent the last week focused on a man who wasn't available. I had always prided myself on my ability to juggle, but it seemed that balls were dropping all around me. They had rolled under couches. They had bounced down storm drains. I had lost all sense of rhythm.

I looked at the first page of his return again, at the copy he'd sent, as asked, front and center on my desk. There was the neatly printed name. The 229 of his Social Security number, 530 Horsehair Road. And now, *Married, filing separately.* If only Ricardo had destroyed another page instead. I could have remained happily ignorant.

"He was single two years ago," I said weakly. In each of the ten past returns Jeff Hill had looked up for me, Jonah Gray *had* been single.

"A lot can change in two years," she pointed out. "I seem to recall that you had a crush on some guy named Marvin two years ago. Where is he now? Do you even know?"

"Maybe I need to take the rest of the day off."

"I'm sorry," Martina said. "I know you had your hopes up."

"Plus he's got a dependent." I hadn't noticed that before.

"You've been mooning over this guy for a week, and it turns out he's married with a kid?"

"That's what it looks like."

"And that changes things?"

"Of course it changes things!" I'd seen the effects of infidelity within my own family. The very fact that I lived in California was an effect of it. That wasn't a minefield I planned to explore.

"Mr. and Mrs. Jonah Gray," Martina said.

"The Grays. Happy holidays from the Gray family."

"At least you're acclimating to the idea."

"What choice do I have? God, I can't even stand to look at his return anymore."

"So get someone else to finish it for you. You've done that before."

"Maybe," I said. "I mean, I'm probably no longer the impartial auditor he deserves. That's enough of a reason. Maybe Susan. The senior auditor title should grant me a few perks." Another call was coming through. "Will you hold on?" I asked.

"I'm a busy person, you know," Martina said. "I was deep into a research brief on the dried beef market when you called."

I put her on hold. "Sasha Gardner," I said.

"Sasha?" It was my mother, but her voice sounded as if it were moving through leaves, hard to catch.

"Hi, Mom. Listen, I'm on the other—"

"Sasha, I need your help." That got my attention. My mother didn't usually phrase requests so plainly. She was better at complex, behind-the-scenes manipulation.

"What is it? What's happened?"

I heard her take a deep breath. "Do you think you could come by the house tomorrow morning? Saturday?" she asked.

"Sure. Why? Did something happen?"

"I just…I need you to…I want to cover the pool."

"The pool?"

"I can't do it by myself."

"I thought you had the pool service do that. It's not even Labor Day."

"Your father and I…we're going to close it early this year. Bring your bathing suit. It's supposed to be nice out." Her voice sounded near to breaking, which was strange. She'd never been much of a swimmer.

"What time?" I didn't have any other plans, but it still felt like an inconvenience.

"How about ten?"

"You know, I've never put the cover on. I'm not sure how much help I'll be."

"Ten tomorrow morning," my mother repeated.

"I'll see you then," I said. "But I've got to go. Martina's on the other line."

I thought she'd say, "Oh, Martina," or "Give my best to that lovely girl," or something along those lines. But she didn't.

"Ten," was all she said. Then she hung up, just as Martina had, a while before.

I turned back to Jonah Gray's file, now thick with his completed return, the background information the Service had collected and his ten past filings. I gathered all the elements together and carried them over to Susan's cubicle. Susan wasn't the best auditor around, but she got her work done on time.

"What's this?" she asked.

"I'm reassigning an audit to you," I said.

"Why?"

"Because…because I think this particular return will be good training."

"Training?"

"There are a variety of deductions to assess."

"But I already have a full load."

"Then you can also consider this a time-management exercise."

"Did Fred Collins say something about my organization? Wait, is this because I called you a know-it-all?"

"Did you?" I asked, trying to look surprised. "This isn't personal,

Susan. It's about choosing the right auditor for the job. We need to work efficiently."

But back at my cubicle, I found it difficult to follow my own officious advice. I began a new return, but made no headway. I didn't care. My heart wasn't in it.

Chapter Eleven

AT TEN ON SATURDAY MORNING, I PULLED UP TO MY parents' house in Piedmont. Kurt's car was parked in the driveway, which rankled me a little. My mother hadn't said anything about inviting him down. My mother probably thought that I wouldn't be able to figure out how to cover the pool by myself or that Kurt would. Kurt, who couldn't even change a tire.

Inside, the house felt still, as if everyone were asleep. I headed for the bathroom to change into my swimsuit—I'd say hello afterward—and that's when I heard whispering.

It wasn't normal whispering. It was the tone you might use if you were pissed as hell but there was a kid nearby or someone was asleep or for some other reason, you were trying to keep your voice down. I realized after a moment that the whisperer was Lori, my sister-in-law.

"I don't want to hear it. I really don't," she snapped.

"But—" That was Kurt.

"Enough!" she said. Her shriek cracked the house's stillness. "We will discuss this at home."

I turned the corner and saw Lori in the hallway, her arms crossed. She was glaring at Kurt who stood a few feet away, in the doorway of the bathroom. The standoff broke as soon as they caught sight of me.

"Sasha, I didn't, we didn't—what a nice surprise," Lori said, moving to give me a hug and squeezing a little hard for comfort.

"I didn't know you guys were coming down this weekend," I said, choosing to ignore what I'd just overheard.

"Well, when Lola called," Lori said.

"About the pool cover?"

Lori frowned. "She said she needed Kurt's help moving furniture. It sounded important."

"Did you bring the boys?" I asked.

"Mom took them out for a few minutes," Kurt said.

I looked toward the bathroom. "Mind if I get in there?" I asked Kurt. "I want to swim while I still can."

Lori was gone when I emerged, but Kurt was waiting for me, across the hall in my former bedroom. I use the word *former* instead of *old* because the entire room had been redone in the previous year, re-redone to be precise. Anything that once defined it as mine was long gone, packed in boxes in the back of the closet or on shelves in the garage. Only a stuffed bear in a rocking chair alluded to the fact that a child had ever lived there.

Kurt sat in the rocking chair, the bear in his lap.

"What's up?" I asked.

"What an awful morning," he said.

"Mom asked you here to move furniture? Why didn't she ask Dad?"

Kurt shrugged. "I don't think Dad's even awake yet."

I looked at my watch and frowned. Our father was a habitually early riser. I didn't know whether he was born to the trait or whether it was a product of an accountant's focus on waste, be it time or money.

"What's so awful?" I asked.

Kurt took a breath. "I need to ask you something," he said. He dropped his voice so low that I had to lean forward to hear him. "If Lori asks you—I don't think she will, but if she does—tell her that you don't remember when I left the party."

"The anniversary party?" I asked. "Why?"

"Just say you don't remember."

"I *don't* remember," I said. "I know it was before Dad—"

"No," Kurt snapped. "Just that you don't remember. Nothing extra."

I sat up. "What did you do?" I asked.

He didn't answer. He stood, handed me the stuffed bear and left the room. I looked at the animal, then arranged it on the chair again. It wasn't mine, nor had it ever been.

Soon, my mother and the boys returned. I greeted three-year-old Jackie and five-year-old Eddie with hugs, then marched them off to Lori, who was in the kitchen making a snack. My mother and I followed close behind.

"I'm glad you could come," my mother said to me. She sounded better than she had on the phone, but she looked tense.

"I didn't realize you had asked Kurt and Lori over, too. I'm sure they could help with the pool cover."

"You know, I didn't even think of that," she said, sitting at the kitchen table.

Lori was in the midst of pouring milk for the boys. "I love that polish on you, Lola," she said.

My mother held out her hands and gazed at her fingernails. "Do you? I thought it might be a little dark when I saw it in the bottle," my mother said.

"No, it looks great."

At times like those, I wondered whether Lori and I were even the same species. She had been in the house for less than an hour and could simultaneously care for her children and talk manicures, all while smiling through whatever storm was passing between her and my brother. If I handled things half that well—well, I wouldn't have been behind at work, for one.

My mother caught me squinting at her hands. "Sasha," she said. "If you ever wanted to come with me to the salon, you know I'd pay for it."

"You've offered that before," I said.

"I'm sorry about earlier," my mother said to Lori. "I'm sure I was just confused. I wasn't paying attention to who left when."

"It's not your fault," Lori said.

"What happened earlier?" I asked. But my mother just shrugged and Lori pretended not to have heard me. "So Dad's still in bed?" I tried, when it became clear that there wouldn't be an answer to my first question.

"What? What are you talking about?" my mother asked.

"Kurt said that he thought Dad was still in bed. Is he feeling okay?"

"Oh, that. Of course," my mother said, settling back down.

"The ankle's okay?"

"Your father's ankle is nearly all better," she said. I thought her smile looked forced. I wondered whether my parents were also fighting. Maybe there was something in the air.

"Where's Blake?" I asked.

"He's got one of his pageants or something," Kurt said, walking into the kitchen. I noticed that Lori didn't look at him.

"It's just marching-band practice," my mother said, waving Kurt off. "You know that."

"Whatever," he said.

My no-longer-so-little brother had always been musically gifted and had recently risen from lead trumpet to drum major in his high school's marching band. Being drum major meant leading the band through its half-time twists and turns, using a whistle and working a mace, the giant stick that all the other marchers were supposed to keep an eye on. It was a rare honor for a sophomore to be chosen.

Kurt had been unimpressed by the news, deeming the marching band "a social wasteland" and wondering aloud why Blake hadn't gone out for basketball or soccer or even the newspaper. Even I hadn't expected Blake to embrace the marching band with such fervor. It seemed to me that most musical fifteen-year-olds would have headed for a rock 'n' roll outlet instead. But when I mentioned as much to my mother, she reminded me that the world of the drum major often included majorettes, a siren song for most boys Blake's age.

My mother turned to look through the sliding glass doors, out to the patio. "I really must spend some time tending the garden today," she said.

I followed her gaze and adjusted my bathing suit. "Maybe I'll get in the pool."

I dove in and once Lori had dressed Eddie and Jackie in swim trunks and water wings, they barreled in after me. Lori arranged herself on one side of the pool, her legs dangling into the water. Kurt sat on the side opposite in a lounge chair.

My mother busied herself by a grouping of planters. For a garden limited to pots and window boxes, she cultivated an impressive assortment of plants. She was always checking pH levels and adding fertilizer or bone meal and carefully pruning everything back before the basil could bolt or the tomatoes grew leggy. I never understood her willingness to tend each one so painstakingly, only to let it all wither come winter.

Before the start of every growing season, she always picked a single vegetable to try to cultivate, carefully choosing the most expensive or obscure heirloom varieties, the sort you'd never find in a supermarket.

"It's our family tradition," she liked to say, though what she planted was always her decision. Each year, it was something new. We ate more kohlrabi in one summer than most people eat in a lifetime. ("It's the early purple Vienna variety," I remember her pointing out, as if that would somehow make our tenth meal of the stuff novel.) One year, she'd grown Brussels sprouts. That particular year, she'd chosen a fancy breed of broccoli.

Now she sighed. "I'm afraid I've got loopers," she said.

I swam over and propped my elbows on the pool's edge. "I don't know if that's good or bad," I admitted.

"They're an evil sort of worm. At least, I think that's a looper. I keep meaning to bring one to the nursery, but with the anniversary party and then your father's ankle and—well, maybe this is not the year for broccoli after all." She shook her head sadly, but remained where she was, bent over her wan little plants, picking bugs off one by one. A thankless task, I thought, before swimming away.

My mother de-looped for a while longer, then carefully took off her gardening gloves and rose to her feet. She wiped the dirt from her lap, turned around and looked at us. I was still in the pool with the boys. Lori was sprawled across a towel, reading a magazine. Kurt remained in the lounge chair, brooding.

"I'm so glad you could come over this morning. I have to tell you something," my mother said. We all watched her, waiting. "Your father isn't well."

"It's not the flu, is it?" I asked.

"He's in the hospital," she said.

This was how I would find out, wearing a bathing suit, my fingers pruned and pale from the water, the sting of chlorine in my eyes.

"What are you talking about?" Kurt asked.

"Daddy's sick?" Eddie asked, looking at Kurt.

"Not me, honey. Grandpa is. My father."

"Grandpa's sick?"

"What's going on?" I asked.

"The cancer came back," my mother said. "It's in his brain now. Dr. Fisher believes he might have six months."

"Six months?" Kurt asked.

"Left," my mother said.

"What's in six months?" I heard Jackie whisper.

"Shh," Lori said. "Just listen."

"Is that why we're here?" I asked. I wished I were out of the pool, or at least wearing a shirt. It seemed as if I should have been wearing clothes, serious clothes, at such a moment. But I was frozen there.

"Why didn't you tell me?" Kurt asked.

"I just did," my mother said.

"Six months?" I repeated. "Are they sure? Can they be so sure?"

Anyone who has ever had a relative in remission lives in fear of this sort of news. The phone call from the doctor's office. The routine blood test, sure-it's-nothing, we'll-know-on-Monday call that comes in around lunchtime, as if it's an animate thing that knows just how to kill an appetite. I remember when we found out the first time. My father had had a fever that nagged on too long. Stage-three lymphoma, as it turned out.

But in a way, that initial announcement wasn't the worst because my family was so cosseted in denial. It was a wrong number, a mislabeled file, or else it was a technician's mistake, not cancer at all. It takes time for that stuff to sink in.

One night in January of that same year, I had found my father passed out on the floor of the hallway bathroom, vomit half in the bowl, half out. I thought we'd lost him, and only then did it occur to me that we might. Chemotherapy is literally a mix of solvents, like alcohol. After a time, it will wear away the most stubborn lacquer of denial, whether you're the one taking bitter medicine or your father is.

Only, he had beaten it. He had knocked those angry, replicating cells from his lymph system, and what the chemo didn't dissolve, a surgeon pulled out, leaving my father with fewer lymph nodes but a body no longer at war with itself.

I don't know why I had assumed that it wouldn't return. I think I figured he was so difficult to get along with, the cancer would eventually move on to a more amenable host.

"When did you find out?" Kurt asked.

My father, it seemed, had begun to lose his color vision about a month earlier. My mother said that he thought it was just a side effect.

"Of what?" I asked. "He hasn't been on chemo for four months."

"Don't be mad," she said. "It wasn't until it was nearly gone that he really noticed. And of course, he's been having those headaches."

"What headaches?"

"He didn't mention them?"

"What headaches?" I asked again, though the answer didn't matter. I thought of the deviled eggs he'd found too pale, the stumbling, his fall at the anniversary party, his irrational anger. So there had been headaches, too. It didn't change anything.

The phone rang.

"I'd better get that," my mother said.

"Just let it go," I said.

"It might be the hospital." She stepped inside the house. "He should be coming out of surgery soon."

"He's in surgery?" I called after her. I turned to Kurt. "Did you know about any of this?"

He shook his head. "I should have. I can't believe I didn't see it."

"It's brain cancer," I said. "Why do you think you would have been able to see it?"

"I can't believe you're swimming at a time like this," he snapped.

"Sasha," my mother called. "It's for you." She stood at the sliding door with the receiver in her hand.

"Who is it?" I asked, but she just shrugged. I pulled myself out of the pool and padded over to her.

"Aren't you going to dry off first?" my mother asked.

I grabbed a ratty towel from the nearest chair and patted my legs. "Surgery?" I repeated.

My mother handed me the phone. "Say you're in the middle of something," she said.

"I told you not to answer it," I said. "Hello?" I pulled the line tight and stood just outside the sliding doors. The last thing I needed was a lecture from my mother about wet carpet.

"Sasha, it's Ellen Maselin. Your parents' neighbor?" she said.

I covered the receiver and whispered to my mother. "Ellen Maselin."

"Why is she calling you?"

I shrugged. I didn't remember the last time I had said more than hello to Ellen Maselin. I barely knew the woman.

"Of course, Ellen. How are you?" I asked.

"I hope I'm not catching you at a bad time," she said.

I looked around the patio. Everyone was staring at me. "It's not great," I said.

"I won't keep you," she said. "I just called to say…well, you've seen my garden, haven't you?"

"I guess." I passed the Maselin's front yard whenever I visited my parents. Was the Maselin house the one with the flowers that reminded me of old ladies' swim caps? I thought my mother had called them hydrangeas.

"Well, I'm a bit of a fanatic. Oh, you know, I like to keep up, when and where I can. I read. I take courses. I even use the Internet."

"Okay," I said, not sure where she was going.

"What does she want?" my mother whispered.

I waved her off. I couldn't explain what I was doing on the phone, in my bathing suit, numb from the news of my father's terminal diagnosis.

"I'll cut to the chase. I understand that one of your audits this year is a man named Jonah Gray," she said.

My mind whizzed to a stop. Had I heard her correctly? "Jonah Gray?" I repeated.

"Oh, Jesus," Kurt muttered. "Not that guy."

"Who's Jonah Gray?" my mother asked. "Do I know him?"

"Let me just say," Ellen went on, "neighbor to neighbor, that I do hope you'll take it easy on him. He's a remarkable gardener. And so generous with his time and his advice."

In the August sun, I felt myself growing cold. The water from my bathing suit dripped down my legs, like insects racing across my skin. I wanted to know more about my father, not about the merits of the married Mr. Gray. Not just then, in any case.

"Mrs. Maselin," I managed to say. "You realize that I can't discuss such matters with anyone but the person being audited. It's a privacy issue." It wasn't exactly true—especially with Jonah's own open discussion of the audit. But it would get me off the phone more quickly.

"Oh, of course," Ellen said. "I just thought, since Ian mentioned that he saw your car, I thought I'd give a call."

"I'm going to have to go now," I said. "You take care."

"You, too. Hi to your parents for me."

"Sure," I said and stepped inside to hang up the phone.

"What was that about?" my mother called. "Try not to drip on the carpet."

"When can we see Dad?" I asked.

The front door slammed and a few seconds later Blake loped around the corner, twirling a Popsicle stick. Blake was the tallest of us Gardners, taller than my father by age thirteen, and now, at fifteen, just beginning to grow out of gangly.

"What are you doing here?" he asked.

Before I could answer, my mother squeezed past me and planted herself between Blake and the door to the patio. "Your sister came to help with the pool cover," she said.

"What?" I asked.

"Is that Kurt and the boys?" Blake asked, craning his neck to see past her.

"I hope you're not ruining your appetite with Popsicles," my mother said.

Blake frowned. "They're, like, thirty calories each," he said.

"Why does he know the calories in a Popsicle?" I asked my mom.

My mother shrugged.

Eddie ran inside just then and barreled into Blake. "Uncle Blake!" he shrieked.

"Hey, kiddo," Blake said, lifting him up.

I turned to my mother. "I take it you haven't told him about Dad?" I whispered.

She took a deep breath. "We didn't want to worry him before we knew more."

"You know more now," I said.

"Don't do this, Sasha," my mother said. "Your father and I are his parents. We decide. You're his sister."

It struck me that my uncle had said the same thing to me at the anniversary party. Only about Marcus. Which reminded me that I still hadn't called Ed to apologize for missing dinner.

"Grandpa's sick," Eddie said, loudly enough for everyone in the room to hear him clearly. "Six months."

"What? What are you talking about?" Blake asked. He looked from Eddie to me and my mother.

"He's got six months," Eddie said. "That's half a year."

"Shouldn't we be getting ready to go to the hospital?" Kurt called from the patio. Lori had Jackie out of the pool and dried off.

Blake carefully lowered Eddie to the ground. He looked at my mother. "What's going on? Is it true?"

"It is true," my mother said.

"So why is Eddie telling me about this? Why didn't you tell me? Apparently you invited Sasha and Kurt over to tell them, but you couldn't even wait for me to get home? What the hell?"

"Your father and I didn't want you to worry," my mother said.

Blake looked exasperated. "But you could tell a three-year-old?"

"It just kind of worked out that way," I said.

"Jackie knows, too," Eddie said proudly.

Blake shook his head. "You know, sometimes I feel like I'm not fully a part of this family."

"Don't say that," my mother said sadly. "You're a very important part."

The lot of us crammed into my father's car. My mother's usual car was a late-model luxury sedan. It didn't matter which make or model; she never kept a car long enough to grow attached. She'd pick out something on a one-year lease, then trade it in a year later for whatever was newer and more expensive. As luck would have it, her lease had expired earlier that week, and news of my father's recurrence had trumped her car-shopping plans, so she'd turned in her used car without bringing home another.

At the other automotive extreme sat my father's ancient Mercedes. For years, he had driven the same diesel station wagon we referred to as "the Truckster." Butter-colored and always smelling slightly of gas, the Truckster seemed to run on knocks and shudders.

"Do you want me to drive?" I asked her, when we were out in the driveway.

"Is that thing even safe?" Kurt asked.

"I've already got the car seats in there for the boys," my mother said. "Get in and let's go."

Uncle Ed was already at the hospital, talking with Dr. Fisher, as the rest of us swarmed into my father's oncologist's office. We stared at them expectantly.

"I told them," my mother said.

"Actually, she told the rest of them, and Eddie told me. Eddie is five," Blake snapped.

"A lot can change," Dr. Fisher said. "We don't know everything about cancer. We're learning more all the time."

"You said the same thing the first time," I said. "Can't you give us any specifics?"

"Sasha, be polite," my mother said.

Dr. Fisher said that my father's surgery had gone as smoothly as brain surgery goes. The surgeon had shaved his head and made quiet incisions and brief explorations, then sewn him up again. When we arrived, he was still unconscious but recuperating.

"Jacob's metastasis is relatively aggressive," Dr. Fisher said. "I'm recommending a course of radiation to start immediately. Chemo will follow. But the brain is difficult."

"I want him to get the best care possible," my mother said.

"Of course," Dr. Fisher said.

"He wants to be at home, in his own home. He's going to be cared for at home."

I wanted her to stop saying *home*. You repeat a word too many times and it loses its context. I was already unsure what *home* meant.

"You're going to need help taking care of him," Ed said.

"Already?" I asked. "Is it that bad?"

Dr. Fisher rooted around a pile of papers on his desk, then handed us all copies of a brochure. "This is that twenty-four-hour home-nursing service I mentioned before," he said to my mother. "They're excellent. It's likely that his sensory and motor skills will deteriorate first. That's just the nature of where the lesions are. That's why we want to start the radiation as soon as possible."

"Can I sign up now?" my mother asked.

"Give it some thought. Talk it over. They're not cheap," Dr. Fisher said.

"Cost doesn't matter. I want Jacob to have the best."

"Would you excuse me, please?" Uncle Ed said. He stood and headed for the door.

"Where are you going?" my mother asked, but he didn't answer her.

I turned to Dr. Fisher. "There must be examples of people beating this."

"People beat every kind of cancer," he said.

"Okay then," I said. "I don't see why we're not focusing on that."

"But at your father's stage...well, it would be statistically remark-able."

"Oh, damn," my mother murmured.

"What?" I asked.

"I forgot your father's health care folder. He wanted me to give it to Ed. Sasha, will you take your father's car and go get it?"

"It's a folder?" I asked.

She nodded. "Marked Health Care. It's probably in your father's study."

With car keys in hand, I left Dr. Fisher's office and shuffled down the hospital hallway. I could barely remember when the oncology department was unfamiliar territory. I'd grown to know its twists and turns, where the closest bathrooms were, where the soda machine was, the quickest route to the cafeteria. I hated that I knew it so well, and that I would now have the opportunity to get reacquainted.

At the end of the hall, I saw Uncle Ed talking with a man I didn't recognize. He could have been anyone—patient or the family member of a patient or a colleague. Maybe he was the surgeon who'd just peered into my father's brain. Maybe he would know something more specific.

As I headed toward them, Ed looked up, then nodded. The man—I could see that he was younger than Ed, maybe even younger than I was—turned to look at me. Then he shook Ed's hand and walked off. He had disappeared around a corner by the time I reached Ed's side.

"Who was that?" I asked.

But Ed didn't answer. "Where's your mother?"

"Still with Dr. Fisher," I said. "I'm headed back home to get Dad's health-care file for you."

"Ah, right. Jacob mentioned that. Thanks."

"Do you have any idea when Dad will wake up?" I asked him.

"Apparently, he just did. He's still groggy, but I'm sure he'll want to see you when you get back," he said. "Sasha," Ed began.

"I know," I cut in. "I totally spaced on dinner last week. I was having the worst day at work. A guy I was auditing—"

"I'd like to try again," Ed said.

"What do you mean?"

"I'd like to bring Marcus around again. For dinner."

"Again?"

"It's just dinner," Ed said.

"Why?"

"Because he's family. If it was a good idea before this news about your father, it's got to be even more important now."

"Did you ask Mom?"

"Just you and me and Marcus. Nothing fancy. How's this week. Say, Wednesday?"

"Soon. Wednesday seems really soon," I said, but I didn't have the energy to fight him. "Sure, okay," I agreed.

"I think you're going to like him," Ed said.

"Sasha?" It was my mother, hollering down the hall from Dr. Fisher's office.

"Over here," Ed called, waving.

She hurried over. "You haven't left yet. Good," she said. "Lori asked whether you could bring Eddie with you. He doesn't like the hospital. You know how five-year-olds are."

"Not really," I said.

"Do me a favor and also bring your father's insurance card back, when you come. It's in that folder where he keeps all his policy information. I want to get him signed up for that in-home service."

In the process of buckling Eddie into his safety seat in the Truckster, I handed him my purse and the twenty-four-hour nursing brochure from Dr. Fisher. During the ride home, my purse slid off his lap, upending itself in the foot well behind the front passenger seat. He held tight, however, to the multicolored brochure Dr. Fisher had handed out. Eddie had just learned the basics of reading and was eager to practice.

"Care in the com...comf...fort of your own home," he read.

"That's great, Eddie," I said, checking him in the rearview mirror.

He kept reading, his lips moving as he sounded out the words. "How do you pronounce q-u-a-l-i-t-y?" he asked.

"Quality."

"What does that mean?"

"Um, something that's good," I said.

"Quality he...heel...heelth?"

"It's probably *health*. What's the next word?"

"Care," Eddie said.

"Yeah, *health*. *Health care* means, well, it has to do with keeping yourself from getting sick," I said. We were on Banner Hill at that point, almost back to my parents' house.

"I'm getting sick," Eddie said.

"Oh, sweetie—I'm sorry to hear that. Do you think you're getting a cold?"

"Sometimes car reading makes me need to throw up," he said.

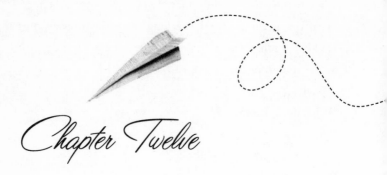

Chapter Twelve

I PULLED INTO THE DRIVEWAY AND HAULED EDDIE from my father's car as quickly as possible.

"Here we go," I said. "Just breathe deep. Is it better now that we've stopped?"

Eddie nodded.

"Why, you're not Jacob." I looked up to see Ian Maselin heading toward us.

I forced a smile. "No. Just borrowing the car." I hurriedly scooped up the contents of my purse from underneath the car seat.

Mr. Maselin took his time walking over to us. He was out with his dog, an obese golden retriever named Buddy. Eddie shied away, but I knelt down and let Buddy lick my hands.

"You're spending a lot of time out here," Mr. Maselin said.

"I guess so."

"You must not be dating anyone." He smiled.

"Not right now, no," I said.

"Did my wife reach you?"

"Earlier, yeah."

"I couldn't give a hoot about plants myself. Never saw the point of getting my hands that dirty. But it keeps Ellen out of trouble."

It bothered me that Ian Maselin and I shared an indifference for gardening. I didn't want to have anything in common with him.

"Good thing I'm not a jealous man," he went on, "or I'd be worried about that fellow she goes on about. Your mother's got a green thumb, doesn't she? I'm surprised she doesn't know about him."

"She does now," I said, watching Buddy sniff one of the Truckster's back tires and lift his leg.

"I'm going to pick that rose and watch her as she grows in my garden." Ian Maselin was looking at me as if he expected me to start singing along. "No? Tom Jones again. 'Spanish Harlem'? Great song. *There is a rose in Spanish Harlem,"* he sang.

"I'd better get this little one inside," I said, motioning to Eddie.

"You should stop by some time and see the new wine cellar," Ian said. "Anytime you'd like. Come on, Buddy boy." I felt Ian Maselin's eyes on me as I led Eddie away.

"Who was that man?" Eddie asked as we reached the door of my parents' house.

"That was Mr. Maselin," I said. "We don't like him."

I brought Eddie into my father's study and set him up with a pen and a ledger pad, the sort I colored on as a girl. Then I opened my father's filing cabinet and found his medical folder.

Glancing inside, I couldn't help but admire the way he had tracked the total cost of his first bout with lymphoma. A CPA to the core, every reimbursement amount was noted, every aspirin, every doctor's visit, every test. I hadn't realized just how expensive his cancer had been. The tally came close to a million dollars.

At the bottom of the page, I saw that he had subtracted the total from one million. I smiled. Clearly, he'd been thinking the same thing. Like father, like daughter.

But on the next page, the details of his insurance policy caught my eye. One million was not just a round number but the lifetime limit of my father's health insurance. That's why he had compared it against the total cost. He had used up almost all of his coverage.

Alarmed, I scrambled to call the insurance company. A woman there confirmed what I was afraid I had read.

"What about upgrading his policy?" I asked.

"You could look into it," the woman at the insurance company said, "but it's a little late for that. In cases like this, it'll get real expensive, if they allow it at all."

"Eddie, do you still have that paper you were reading me in the car?" I asked.

Eddie brought over the brochure and I scanned the text. Home care was cheaper than hospital care, but it was clear that the nursing service would quickly use up everything that was left. And who knew what the brain surgery had cost? And now radiation? I thanked the woman and hung up the phone.

"Time to go back?" Eddie asked.

"Yeah. I guess so."

I dropped Eddie in the cafeteria, where my other nephew, brothers and mother were having a snack, and my mother pointed me toward the room where my father was recuperating from his surgery. Peeking inside, all I could see were his feet and the backside of an attendant who leaned over the bed, making some sort of adjustment. A curtain blocked the rest of my view, and I was afraid

that if I explored any further, I might see my father in an uncom-
fortably exposed state. The cancer and the brain surgery were
enough. I didn't want to barge in when he was naked.

Backing away from the door, I bumped into Lori.

"So you and Eddie are back," she said.

"Yeah. Everyone's in the cafeteria."

"I'm sorry the boys and I didn't make the party last Saturday," she
said. "Sounds like it was a good one."

That struck me as a strange thing for her to say, there and then,
but it was like Lori to try to put people at ease with small talk. "I'm
sure my parents understood," I said. "Pink eye isn't much of an anniversary present."

"Kurt said that he left," she began. Then she bit her lip and looked
away. It dawned on me that she wasn't engaging in small talk. She
had a very specific goal.

I waited. I wondered about the gap between what Kurt had told
her and what she'd heard from my mother. But Lori seemed to steel
herself. She stood a little taller and gave me a smile. Forced, but still
a smile.

"You have enough to deal with right now," she said.

I glanced back toward my father's room. The attendant had not
yet emerged. "So how's it going in Stockton?" was all I could think to
ask.

Lori's smile eased into something more genuine. "It reminds me
of Iowa, actually," she said. "Very green. Nice, real people. Gets
rural awful quick."

I nodded.

"Your brother hates it," she said.

"No, he doesn't."

She looked at me, almost grim. "I think he does."

I didn't know what to say. I hadn't expected Kurt to like Stockton—he maintained an air of vague disdain no matter what his address—but I had expected him to make the best of it.

"Kurt mentioned that you have a friend in town," Lori said.

"He did?"

"I'm forgetting what he said. Someone who works at the paper? A reporter?"

"Jonah Gray," I said. "He's not a friend, exactly."

"The man you got the phone call about? I guess I got it wrong," she said. "Why did I think it was someone you liked?"

I shrugged. I didn't want to get into it. Just like she didn't want to get into whatever was brewing between her and my brother.

"Anyway, I hope we'll get you out for a visit before too long," she said. She nodded toward the room. "The nurse just left, if that's what you were waiting on."

"That guy was a nurse?" I asked.

Inside the recovery room, my father was awake, but he looked awful. On his shaved head perched a bandage and over that, what looked like a thin sock.

"Don't look so worried," he said. "I'm not going to die this instant."

I was relieved to hear him speak. His voice sounded the same, that Virginia drawl laced with exasperation.

"How do you feel?" I asked him.

"Fine," he said. "That is, for someone who's had a little brain surgery." By the way he smiled, I could tell he was floating on pain-killers. I wished I'd been offered some, too.

"I don't think there's such thing as a little brain surgery," I said.

"I hope we have good weather for the next six months. But what can you do?" He shrugged.

"Not this," I said, shaking my head. "I thought I could, but now I don't think I'm going to be able to. It's going to be so hard."

"Oh, come on now. Chin up. Be a big girl."

"At least try to act like you care," I said.

He patted the bed and I went to sit beside him. He looked more subdued than before. "Why wouldn't I care? I don't want to leave your mother. Or you or your brothers."

"You barely have any insurance left," I said. I pulled the folder from my bag and put it on the bedside table. "But you already know that. Is that what you wanted to share with Ed?"

He smiled. "You want to see something scary, check the financial records in the same filing cabinet. If you'd worked with me, you'd already know this stuff. But it can be our little secret."

"What can be?"

"I'm tapped out." He tapped me lightly on the nose as he said it.

My stomach soured. "You're not serious."

He sighed. "Getting sick, not working, that gets expensive. And all these trips your mother wanted to take. Celebrating my return to health. And the Tahoe condo upkeep, the greens fees, your mother's needs—she's got her needs," he rattled on.

"Dad!"

"Don't worry, your mother will be fine."

"Mom isn't sick. What about you?"

"Dr. Fisher assures me that I won't be fine. But all the money in the world isn't going to change that," he said.

"I'm sure there's stuff we can do. He mentioned radiation. And chemo."

That got his attention. "I don't know how much of that I'll be up for," he said, suddenly sober. "Look at this place."

I considered the false wood grain of the night table, the industrial vinyl of the chair by the window, the antibacterial curtains. I wondered how many people had died in the same bed where my father now lay. I didn't want him to spend the rest of his life in that room any more than he did.

Chapter Thirteen

I DIDN'T KNOW WHAT I WAS SUPPOSED TO DO, OR FEEL, after that. It hadn't sunk in, or maybe it had but I couldn't feel it yet. That seemed the most likely scenario, as I don't quite recall where the next few days went.

We were all at the hospital on Saturday, and before I knew it, it was Wednesday morning, and I was finally returning to my bungalow in Oakland. What a relief to get back to my life, or get away from my life, or probably both. What I knew for sure was that I was looking forward to changing out of the shorts and shirt and bathing suit I'd left the house with on Saturday.

Finally back, I pulled the mail from my overstuffed mailbox and opened the front door. And then, I gagged.

I'm no neatnik, but I've always been reasonably finicky when it comes to my kitchen. A stack of newspapers might mean that you're behind on your reading, but a stack of dirty dishes means bugs and mold. I have nothing against collecting, as a hobby, but my attitude is that whatever you amass oughtn't require refrigeration. Hummel figurines are one thing. Hamburger is quite another.

Four days earlier, I had locked up my house, leaving trash in the trash can, breakfast dishes in the sink, coffee in the coffee-maker and a nice fat salmon steak defrosting on the kitchen counter. Still believing I would only be attending to a pool cover, I had only planned to be gone for an hour or two. By Wednesday morning, that salmon steak had reached a state quite distinct from thawed.

Once I was able to keep from retching, I pushed my way inside and threw out everything I thought might be contributing to the stench—dishes included—all while trying to hold my breath. I could almost taste the rotten fish when I tried breathing through my mouth. Had I realized what I'd be walking back into, I might have stayed away for another week.

When the garbage was double-wrapped and safely outside, I opened every window, then dropped to the couch to sort through my mail. Most of that belonged in the trash, too, but one hand-addressed note stuck out of the mix. I recognized Gene's handwriting.

I wanted to make sure that you're okay, he wrote. *Your box is getting full, so I guess you haven't picked up your mail for a few days. Maybe you're on a much deserved vacation?*

I had to smile. The previous four days hadn't felt like a vacation, even though I'd struck out on Saturday morning with a bathing suit in my purse.

On Saturday afternoon, coming back from the hospital, we had again pressed into my father's old station wagon—my mother driving, Kurt in the front seat, me, Lori and the kids crammed in the back, with Blake in the way back. Perhaps it was because the cramped quarters reeked of fuel and motor oil and age. Perhaps it was our agitation from the news of my father's diagnosis. Either way, everyone scattered as soon as we got back to the Banner Hill house.

Blake had stormed off to his friend Barney's house, still angry that he hadn't been treated like an adult—or at least the same as me and Kurt. Kurt and his family quickly retreated to Stockton, though he and Lori still seemed to be on the outs. My intention had been to return to Oakland that afternoon, but my mother asked me to stay the night, so that the two of us could keep each other company. Then she proceeded to spend most of the evening on the phone, informing her friends and various relatives of our newfound situation.

Actually, I didn't mind the time alone. I sat out on the deck and watched the dusk turn to nighttime. You can't really share grief. You might be sad side by side with someone else. You can show and receive sympathy. But at the core, everyone's sorrow is their own company, like a shadow or a bad date you can't shake. No one was going to come and rescue me from it, so I thought that I might as well sit a while and get to know its personality. I had a feeling we would be companions for some time.

On Sunday, as I readied myself to leave, my mother knocked on my bedroom door. "Honey, I hate to be an inconvenience, but could I borrow your car for maybe an hour? I have some papers to sign at the hospital."

"Can't you take the Truckster?" I asked. "I was sort of hoping to get home, at least for a change of clothes."

"I had Duncan come get it last night."

"Duncan?"

"Your dad's mechanic. You know him. Remember, I tried to set you two up a few years back?"

"You got rid of Dad's car?"

"I didn't get rid of it. I'm having it overhauled. If your father's going to be driving it in his condition, I want it running safely."

"Fine. My keys are in my purse."

"If you want a change of clothes, go ahead and dig through my closet." She came back in a few moments. "Where did you say your keys were?"

"They should be in my purse."

She handed me my purse. "I don't think so," she said.

I dug through, listening for the familiar clang. "They always end up at the bottom. They can be hard to find," I explained, my hand in the bag, feeling around. Finally, I gave up and poured the contents of my purse onto the bed. I pawed through. No keys.

"Can you remember where you last had them?" my mother asked.

"I haven't needed them since I got here yesterday," I said, patting down my pockets. "I must have had them then." I went outside and crawled around on the ground beside my car, but found nothing. I searched behind the bed and dresser in my former bedroom, under the couch cushions, everywhere.

"Never mind, dear. I'll ask your uncle Ed to give me a ride," my mother said. "You just stay and look."

At some point that afternoon, I realized that my keys were most likely in my father's car, under the front passenger seat, where my purse had disgorged itself when Eddie and I came back to get Dad's medical folder.

"I'll go get them tomorrow," I told my mother, once she was back home that evening.

She frowned. "Not tomorrow. Duncan is closed on Mondays."

"Closed on Mondays? Why?"

"Because he's open on Sundays, I guess. I never asked him why."

"So we don't have any working cars?" I said, now exasperated. "Aren't you supposed to be getting a new one?"

"Do you need to go somewhere?"

"I was hoping to get home."

"Sasha, dear, you are home."

"Back to Oakland, I meant."

"Do you want to take a cab? I can pay for a cab."

I thought about my father's insurance situation. The day before, I had delved further into his financial filing cabinet. He hadn't been kidding when he'd described himself as nearly broke.

"I can wait," I said. I wasn't going to be the daughter that leveraged her father's medical care for a cab ride.

On Monday, I called in sick and sat in my father's study. Before long, I was at his computer, and soon after that and against my better judgment, I found myself back on Gray's Garden. There'd been a healthy amount of chatter in the preceding few days and I found myself welcoming the diversion it offered. Some postings voiced concern over a new form of black rot. Others discussed the emerging menace of Sudden Oak Death. Someone with the screen name "Clematis_cutie" had asked whether it was true that sourdough bread deterred slugs (apparently it doesn't). "Lindasmom" wondered whether it was possible that mulch made from cocoa beans could poison dogs (apparently it can).

But the liveliest discussion remained Jonah Gray's impending audit, now just two weeks away.

Just act all unpredictable when you get in there. Those people can't handle it if anyone isn't an automaton, like they are.

Or pretend you don't speak English very well.

Women like it when you use humor. Get her laughing.

Now you're assuming that she's a woman. LOL!!

I know the type. Pissed-off, frigid, man-hater, humorless, bean counter.

That's where Jonah stepped in. *Hey there,* he wrote.

No need to get mean. We're talking about a real person here who is just doing her job. Besides, as my date with the IRS approaches, I've been trying to be open to the positive side effects of this experience. It has forced me to contemplate the financial, professional and personal choices I've made. It has prompted me to revisit past decisions and think about why I did what I've done. I'm a different person now, and as I look back, I am awed by the mountain range I've slogged through to be here. As for Ms. Gardner, maybe we'll all be surprised. Maybe she'll be delightful. Maybe she'll even be understanding. I know what you're thinking, faithful readers—that poor Mr. Gray has begun to go round the bend. Or else I've decided to plead temporary insanity. Don't think it hasn't crossed my mind!

I wondered how much headway Susan had made with his file. I found myself regretting that I'd reassigned it to her. Why had I been so compulsive? I wasn't a compulsive person. Hell, I was the opposite. But this guy—or the whole situation—brought out an emotional reaction in me that I wasn't accustomed to. Why had I worried so much about my impartiality? Given my father's diagnosis, a friendly audit would surely be a welcome distraction. And yet

I'd gone and transferred his case to Susan. So he was married. Did that mean he wasn't worth knowing? I tried to remember whether Susan had any plants in her cubicle.

My father's study overlooked the back patio and the pool. From where I sat, I could see my mother patiently picking bugs off her broccoli plants. I looked back at Gray's Garden and clicked to the form Jonah provided, the one that allowed anyone to join the fray. Even better, no e-mail account was needed. Just a screen name.

My mother is having issues with broccoli, I typed. *She thinks it's loopers or something. Any easy suggestions? I know next to nothing about gardening.* I smiled to myself as I signed off, *J-E-F-F-R-I-N-E.*

On Tuesday, the Truckster was ready. My mother called me as she drove it out of Duncan's shop. "It's practically purring," she said.

"That's great. And my keys?"

"Safe and sound. I've got them in my purse," she said. "I figured you'd want to stick around until I brought your father home from the hospital."

My mother had spent a lot of energy on my father's homecoming. She had caterers prepare a week's worth of his favorite meals. She had put new linens on the bed. She had bought bouquets of fresh flowers for every room. No expense had been spared, which of course had me agitated.

I'm not saying that my father didn't deserve some TLC, but it seemed apparent to me that he hadn't come clean with my mother about their financial situation. At least, I wanted to think that my mother wouldn't have gone to such extravagant lengths had she known better. I had also checked with Dr. Fisher about the costs of my father's radiation therapy, due to begin the very next day. And I had double-checked my calculations, twice. They couldn't keep this up. Their funds were nearly gone.

As soon as the front door opened, I could hear her chattering on about the home nursing service.

"Won't it be wonderful knowing that someone will be here, twenty-four hours a day if we need it, to keep an eye on you?" she asked. "And these people are professionals." She sounded relieved— then again, my mother had always taken comfort in the prospect of spending money. It was part of the problem.

For some reason, it irked me just then, as if she were trying to buy her way out of his illness. Wasn't she willing to take care of him at all? Sure, I hadn't exactly offered, but he'd certainly accept her help before he accepted mine.

I followed their voices into the kitchen and found my mother pulling a bottle of champagne out of the refrigerator.

"It's eleven in the morning," I said.

"Your father's home," my mother said. "Time to celebrate!"

"Should he even be drinking? He's on some pretty heavy painkillers."

"Jacob, you're not planning on driving anywhere, are you?" my mother asked. "So it's fine, dear."

"Dad, you've got to tell her," I finally said.

"Tell me what?" my mother asked. She was smiling, as if she thought I might have news of a trip or a party.

"The insurance, your finances," I said. "The fact that there's no money."

"What are you talking about, Sasha?" my mother asked.

My father began to push himself away from the table. "Maybe no champagne for me," he said. "I'm a little tired."

"Now," I insisted. He was already losing strength. It only took one firm hand to keep his chair from moving. "It won't get any easier," I said.

"Sasha, I will not have you treating your father that way in his fragile condition. The man just had brain surgery, for goodness sake!"

"You can't afford the in-home nurse," I told her.

She looked at me as though I were still a child. "Maybe this service costs a bit more than you're comfortable with, but it's important."

"Fine. You can choose. It's either the home-care nurse or the radiation therapy. Not both, and don't say that you'll pay out-of-pocket, not with Dad not working, not if you want to stay in this house after—" I realized I had said enough. I felt like a heel.

My mother looked at my father, who looked at the floor.

"So it's true," she said, when he didn't look up. "But the help," she murmured. "Jacob, why didn't you tell me?"

"I didn't think it would come back," he said. "And when it did, you seemed so worried."

"Oh, for heaven's sake," she snapped. "So what does that mean, that the two of us are stuck in this house for the next, however long? Is that the way you envision it?"

"I haven't envisioned—" my father began, then stopped.

"I'll come on weekends," I said. "I can help. And Blake is here. I'm sure Kurt will pitch in when he can."

"It's not the same. These are trained nurses. We're not equipped to do what they do." She turned to my father. "How could you let this happen? Didn't we have a deal?" She shook her head and left the room, the champagne unopened on the counter.

My father looked at me. "That's why I didn't tell her," he said. "You really think it's better now?"

"What about using some of the money in her trust?"

"No."

"Don't you think she would want you to?" I asked.

"It's off the table, Sasha. Your mother stuck it out with me. I'm not going to leave her in the poorhouse."

"Cutting back and making a few compromises isn't asking her to—"

"I was to provide a life without compromise," he said. "That was the deal."

"Come on, how realistic is that?"

My father just looked at me. "What would you know?"

I spent the rest of the day keeping my opinions to myself, skimming leaves from the pool and wishing that my mother had given me my keys back before she'd roared off in my father's car. In the afternoon, when my father was asleep and the house was quiet, I found my way back to Gray's Garden.

He had written back. In the discussion area, I noticed a new thread about loopers.

With such an unusual name, I can only imagine you to be the same Jeffrine I had the pleasure of speaking to a while back. I'll keep the circumstances of those conversations away from prying eyes. So your mother has loopers. Or at least, her broccoli does. Well, since you're not much of a gardener (I won't hold that against you, yet), you might not know that broccoli is a member of the brassica family, which means that it started out as a wild cabbage...

He went on at some length about the pests that prey on plants in the cabbage family, then he suggested ladybugs and a bacterial spray. The answer itself didn't mean much to me, though I printed it out for my mother. But he had remembered me—or, he had remembered Jeffrine, which would have to do for the moment.

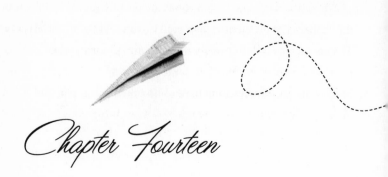

Chapter Fourteen

I KNOW THEY SAY THAT ABSENCE MAKES THE HEART grow fonder. But sometimes, absence can also reveal the waning of once fond feelings. Time passes and it's a surprise to realize that you haven't missed him, or her, or the place or the job that once felt like a match. Believe it or not, I used to look forward to going to work. Every audit felt like a new challenge, tested me, pushed my understanding of the tax code to new levels. I never knew who I would meet, what life I'd be investigating or what I would learn from it.

As I stepped back into my cubicle on Wednesday afternoon, the fourth floor *sounded* the same as ever. The ringing of phones, the flutter of paperwork, the hum of voices trying to maintain a modicum of privacy in a cubicle. But the rush and promise of those sounds were lost on me. I no longer worried about my mounting pile of unanalyzed audits. I didn't care enough to worry. I looked around my cubicle and felt nothing but an itch to get out of there.

I was clearing off my desk, readying to visit Fred Collins, when my phone rang. I considered letting voice mail pick up, but I realized that the call might contain news of my father. I grabbed the receiver.

"Yes," I said.

"Finally you pick up the phone. I've been calling for the last three days. I want to talk to you about Jonah Gray," a man said.

I closed my eyes. "Why am I not surprised?"

"I want to tell you something. I had this cycad, see, and it was dying. Dying! You know how much a cycad'll run you?"

"I don't," I admitted.

"A pretty penny, is how much. Tens of thousands, can be how much. I get so worried and I don't know who to turn to, and a lady at the nursery says, have you talked to Jonah Gray? And I says, who the heck is Jonah Gray? So she gives me his number and I phone him up, oh, I was in a state. I phoned him up on a Friday night. Poor guy, he works all week, and still he takes my call, listens to what's going on, says he'll come by. He lives two hours away if a minute. But he makes the drive so's he can look at the cycad up close."

"That's awfully generous," I agreed.

"That's what I'm getting at," he said. I waited for him to continue, but he didn't.

"So what happened?" I finally asked.

"Oh, it was dying."

"Couldn't he do anything about it? Couldn't he save it? I thought he worked magic with plants."

"Well, he does. Sometimes. But every plant's got a lifetime, just like a person. Some are long, some are short. But there's only so much you can do to extend it. He knew that. Other people, they kept telling me to fight it. Add this. Add that. Jonah talked to me about how old the plant was—and how California probably wasn't even a state when it was young. That'll give you perspective, huh? And it made me think, 'I gotta let it go.' I just thought you ought to hear that."

"Thanks," I said.

"You probably think us plant folks are loony-tunes, carrying on about greenery like this," he said.

"No, I don't," I told him. "I'm not sure that it matters what you care about. Maybe it's the caring itself that matters."

When he heard about my father's relapse, Fred Collins was very understanding. He assured me that he would distribute all the pending files on my table to other auditors around the department. "You concentrate on other things."

"They're going to hate me," I said. "All that extra work." As I said it, I realized that I was trying to make myself sound concerned.

"It's the least we can do for a lifer like yourself."

"Except one," I said. "There's one case that I passed to Susan, but I'd kind of like it back."

"Are you sure?" Fred asked. "This isn't going to be easy. Don't feel you've got to do it on my account."

"Just the one," I said, writing down Jonah's Social Security number. "I'd like to finish it."

"Suit yourself. I'll let her know."

The elevator couldn't come fast enough. I didn't want to run into anyone else I knew, didn't want to be forced into small talk or see any of the auditors who were now going to have to shoulder my workload. Then the doors opened.

"You're back!" Jeff Hill said. He smiled broadly, as if he were thrilled to see me.

"I was just heading out," I said.

"So you're not back."

"Not quite." I stepped into the elevator. He made no move to get out. "Going down?" I asked.

"Sure," he said. "How was your vacation?"

"I wasn't on vacation."

"Oh," Jeff said. "Well, you missed an exciting few days in the archive department," he said.

"Really?"

"I guess that wasn't a very good joke," he said. "I meant it as a joke."

"Oh, right." The doors opened onto the lobby and we both stepped out.

"I suppose I shouldn't keep you," he said. "Though the idea is tempting."

"I need to get going."

"I've been meaning to ask whether you'd want to grab dinner some night next week. You'll be back next week, won't you?"

"I should be."

"Got any evenings free?"

"I imagine I do," I said. I had lost all sense of what my life looked like. All I knew was that I wanted to be out of the building, and saying yes seemed like the quickest route.

"Well, great. How's next Thursday? Shall we aim for next Thursday?"

"Next Thursday should be fine."

"I've been driving by this one restaurant for a while now, but I've never been in. It's called Hunter's. I hear it's good."

"Hunter's," I said. It was the same restaurant where I was due to meet Uncle Ed and Marcus that very evening.

"Have you been there before?"

"No," I said.

"Do you know it? Is it clean? Would you rather go somewhere else?"

"No. It's fine. Thursday. Hunter's. It all sounds just fine," I said.

When the doorbell rang an hour later, it was Martina. She gave me a big hug made awkward by the large cardboard box she was holding.

"Sweetie, I'm so sorry. How are you holding up?"

I shrugged. "I'm okay. Shouldn't you be at work?"

She pushed the box into my hands. "I brought you something."

"I can see that. What is it?"

"To keep your energy up," she said.

I opened the box and saw that it was filled with individually wrapped servings of beef jerky. "You brought me meat? This is your new account?"

"It's a new concept in jerky. I made sure you got all five flavors."

"I appreciate the gesture."

Martina sniffed the air. "What's that smell?" she asked, wrinkling her nose.

"Smell?"

"Bad fish, maybe?"

I nodded. "It's a long story. It's not so bad in the bedroom. You want to come and help me decide what to wear?"

She shrugged. "What impression are you going for? What's Marcus like anyway?" she asked, following me toward my closet.

"He's got to be twenty-five, twenty-six now. I should know when his birthday is," I said.

"But what's he like? Is he anything like Kurt?"

"I don't know. I've always imagined him as one of those guys who's kind of mad underneath, even when he's smiling. He's not going to tell you, but you'll feel it."

"Really?"

"Of course, I haven't actually seen him since he was eleven."

"Eleven? Then how can you—"

"He's got every right to resent us," I pointed out.

"But if he wants to have dinner—"

"Uncle Ed is the one who was pushing dinner. For all I know, he strong-armed Marcus into it."

"But is he smart? Is he funny?"

I shrugged. "He's never really applied himself, as far as I know. I don't know if that's because he's lazy or irresponsible or just one of those guys who thinks the world owes him a favor."

"At least you're looking on the bright side."

"Well, why has he shown up now?" I asked. "Why move all the way to California? What does he want?"

"You're worried about your father. That's why you're being like this."

"Maybe."

Martina smiled.

"What?" I asked.

"So many questions. Didn't I say that you were like that reporter? Whatever happened to him?"

"I stopped thinking about him because he's married. You know that."

"Really. You stopped thinking about him." I could tell she didn't believe me.

"He thinks my name is Jeffrine," I admitted.

Martina frowned. "Is he an idiot?"

I shook my head. "If there's an idiot in this situation, it's got to be me."

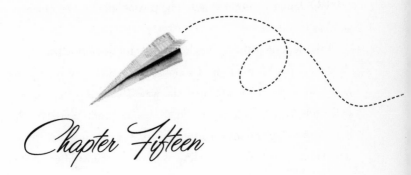

Chapter Fifteen

LOOKING THROUGH THE FRONT WINDOW, I COULD SEE them sitting at the bar. It was easy to make out Uncle Ed's broad back and his familiar tweed sport coat. But I stared at the young man beside him. I knew it had to be Marcus, though I couldn't see his face and wasn't sure I would have recognized him anyway. I could see that he looked leggy and narrower than Ed, more wiry. He wore a leather jacket and jeans. He had dark hair. But that was all I could make out.

I'm related to him, I thought, staring at his back. What would that turn out to mean?

I took a deep breath, walked to the restaurant's main door and stepped inside.

Like Jeff Hill, I'd driven by Hunter's plenty of times but never eaten there. It was a woodsy place with a lot of game on the menu. It was supposed to be good, but I'd never felt any impulse to go inside, perhaps on account of a childhood attachment to Bambi. Hunter's was split in half with the dining room to the left as you entered, and the bar, where Ed and Marcus waited, to the right.

"Welcome to Hunter's! May I help you?" the hostess chirped as soon as I entered.

"I'm meeting people. They're waiting for me in the bar."

She pointed to my right. I suppose there was no way she could have known that I already knew the way. That was the conundrum of her job. Was she helping people, or was she simply cluttering their lives with redundant information and greetings immediately forgotten? Then again, I wondered, how was my work any different? One could argue that the hostess's effect was, at least, minimal and benign.

"Sasha, you remember Marcus," Ed said.

Marcus turned around.

"It's you," I said, recognizing the young man I'd seen talking with Uncle Ed after my father's surgery. "You were at the hospital when we first heard about Dad."

"Hello, Sasha," Marcus said. "I'm glad you could make it this time." He didn't sound like he was seething. In fact, he sounded like my father. The same cadence exactly.

"I'm sorry I missed you last week," I said. "Work has been a little unusual of late."

I found myself studying the different parts of his face—eyes, nose, ears—trying to distinguish which attributes came from our shared father and which must have come through his mother.

I thought that we had the same lips, my father's deep cleft below the nose. The same straight-arrow hair, though his was wildly spiked while mine hung limp. But his eyes had to be hers. While I had my father's blues, Marcus's eyes were a dark, deep brown with long lashes, the sort only men seem blessed with. He had a nose that took a slight turn halfway down, the sort of flaw that added to his appeal, as if before the break he might have been too pretty. His unkempt hair and two-day beard only made him more striking.

"I think I remember you," Marcus said. The coffee-colored gaze seemed neither friendly nor cold. Just curious. "Nice to meet you again, either way."

"I hope so," I told him.

The hostess came in to announce that our table was ready.

"I see you found your party," she said.

That seemed obvious, but I wanted Marcus to think that I was nice. "Sure did," I answered, as perkily as I could.

She brought us to our table. I watched her smile linger on this man who was both a stranger and my half brother.

When Marcus took off his leather jacket, I saw that his arms were lined with tattoos. They began just above his wrists and extended at least as far as the start of his short sleeves. I picked out a flower, a frog, an ornate Celtic knot before I felt him catch me looking. He didn't attempt to cover himself up, but I focused on maintaining eye contact all the same. Even then, a little tattoo on his neck, just at the cusp of his collar, proved a challenge not to look at. Maybe that was the point.

"Can I get you anything to drink?" our waitress asked. Her eyes were also on Marcus.

I ordered a beer. Uncle Ed raised the scotch and soda he had brought in from the bar.

"Just a club soda," Marcus said.

"You want lime with that?" the waitress asked.

Marcus shook his head.

"Lemon? Anything?" She seemed reluctant to leave.

"No, thanks. Just club soda. Just plain."

"I was surprised when Ed told me what you've been up to," I said to him. "I mean, that you were nearby. When did you leave Georgia? You know what I just learned? That Georgia was the first colony to cultivate grapes. And yet, does anyone drink Georgia wine? Is there even a wine industry down there?"

Marcus frowned. "I'm from Florida."

"But weren't you in Georgia at some point?"

"Only for six months," he said. "Never by choice."

I nodded. I wished I could remember the details of his stay in jail. "So how do you like Sacramento?" I asked, changing gears.

He shrugged. "It's fine. Quiet. Friendlier folks on average than Floridians. At least, the Floridians I ran with."

His comment reminded me of my mother's excuse to Kurt and me, that California kids were nicer than Virginia kids. It struck me that she had invented that pretext because of the young man to my right.

"That reminds me," Ed said. "I have to tell you guys this story about my trip to Mexico last month. I was on the beach and—"

Marcus cut in. "Is this that guy with the prosthetic leg?"

"Did I already—oh, of course, I told you. Yeah, that crazy leg." Ed laughed.

"What?" I asked.

"No, if I've already told it," Ed said.

"That was crazy strange," Marcus said.

"I still can't get over it," Ed said. "Every time I see a pair of red sneakers." He shook his head, grinning broadly.

"I don't think you've told me," I said.

"I'll tell you later. It's a long story. Remind me."

I felt as if I were still standing outside the restaurant. Sure, it was nice how easily Marcus and Ed got along, but I found myself wondering whose family I was visiting. I studied my menu. I took a swig of beer and waited for the waitress to take our order. I looked around the restaurant and watched the hostess eye Marcus as she seated a party of five. When Marcus excused himself to wash his hands, maybe five minutes later, I turned to Uncle Ed.

"You've certainly buddied up to him."

"What are you talking about?" Ed asked.

"It seems like your loyalty would be with your sister, with Mom. Especially now."

"Loyalty?"

"Loyalty."

"And what, precisely, did Marcus ever do to your mother?"

I hesitated. "Well, fine, so it wasn't Marcus, it was—"

"Exactly. It wasn't Marcus. The answer to that question is 'nothing.' But because of bad luck, he doesn't get a father? He doesn't deserve to know his relatives? It was your father's own actions that started this, remember. That boy's just the result of them."

I sat with that for a moment. It felt true.

"Listen, Sasha," Ed went on. "You don't ask for much. You've never needed a lot of tending. I respect that. Marcus is the same way. So he screwed up for a few years. He's headed straight now. That's what matters to me and what should matter to the rest of you."

"What about his mother? He's got that whole side of his family."

"He's got a half sister eight years younger who's back in Florida with her dad. Eloise Johnston died about three years ago."

Marcus returned to the table then. "Are you two talking about me?" he asked with a smile.

I looked down at my napkin and shrugged. Ed took a sip of his scotch.

"That was supposed to be a joke," Marcus said. He turned to look at me. "You have no idea what to make of this, do you? I can tell that you don't think much of me."

In that sentence, the drawl was gone and his enunciation was as crisp as a news anchor's. I couldn't pretend that I hadn't heard him or needed him to repeat the question. I knew I could have taken Marcus's statement literally—did I think of him much? It was true, I didn't. Or at least, I hadn't before the anniversary party. But that wasn't what he meant.

"What do you mean?"

His eyebrows rose in mock surprise. He knew I'd understood.

I had to say something. "I don't know you well enough to—"

"Nah," Marcus said, leaning back in his chair and waving off the uncertain beginnings of my answer. "You're wondering who I am and why the hell I'm here. You're trying to figure out what I want. Whether I hate you. Whether I'm just planning to fuck things up. Isn't that right?" He didn't sound angry, just matter-of-fact.

"Something like that," I agreed.

"At least you own up to it. Can't say the same for the rest of your immediates. Blake's cool though," he said.

"You met Blake?"

Marcus looked at Ed, as if unsure how to answer.

"Your father and I took Blake and Marcus to a baseball game. This past spring," Ed said.

"So Blake knows about—"

"It was just a baseball game," Ed said. "It wasn't a therapy session."

"He's got a great head on his shoulders," Marcus said. "So much to say."

"He's a good kid," I agreed.

"He's not a kid," Marcus said. "Sure he's only fifteen, but he knows what's going on. I think about all the shit I was into at that age."

I was embarrassed. I knew Blake wasn't a kid. And I didn't want to follow my parents' example by treating him like one.

"Sasha," Ed said. "There's a reason I insisted on this dinner."

"Other than us meeting each other?" I asked.

"I think I mentioned that Marcus recently completed his degree," Ed said.

"Oh, right. Congratulations."

"In nursing," Ed said. "He's an RN."

I must have looked surprised.

"What of it?" Marcus asked.

"Nothing," I said. "That's great. When I saw you in the hospital, you weren't wearing a uniform."

"I don't work there," he said.

"And that would explain why."

"He's an excellent nurse," Ed said.

"You don't need to pile it on," Marcus told him. "All she's going to want to know is whether I'm qualified."

"Qualified for what?" I asked.

"When your father was first diagnosed, last year, I told Marcus," Ed said. "It seemed a fitting time to reconnect."

"I took some specialized classes," Marcus said. "To get my qualifications up."

"Qualifications?" I asked. I looked from Marcus to Ed and back again.

"Marcus has offered to help," Ed said.

"Jacob," Marcus said. "The home nursing."

I suddenly got it. "You can do that?"

"That's what I'm saying," Marcus said.

"Marcus has offered to provide the sort of in-home, round-the-clock care Jacob's going to need. Your father and I have discussed everything. The insurance. Their financial situation. It's the exact same care. It's a gift, Sasha," Ed said.

"You haven't mentioned this to my mother yet, have you?"

"Frankly, I wanted to gauge your reaction first," Ed said.

"Where would you live?" I asked Marcus. "You can't commute from Sacramento." Even Stockton was closer.

"It's in-home care," he said. "I'd expect to stay in their home."

"Yeah, right. My mother—"

"Will realize that this is the best way to keep Jacob comfortable. Don't you think we can help her realize that?" Ed asked.

"You mean me."

"I'll do my part," Ed said. "I think you and Kurt can both appreciate how much Marcus's help would ease the burden."

"Dad isn't a burden," I said, feeling indignant all of a sudden.

"And Marcus has offered to help keep it that way," Ed said.

"Why?" I asked.

Ed looked at me strangely. "What do you mean, why?"

But Marcus nodded. "She means, why would I offer."

"Right. Why would you want to move in with people who never invited you in before?"

"Now, Sasha," Ed began, "I don't think that's quite accurate."

"No? When did we invite him into the house? When did we ever? It's crazy that he'd want to come now. Isn't it? Tell me why it's not crazy. You don't see me offering to move into some stranger's house to help out around tax time."

"It's not the same," Ed said.

I hated that he sounded so serene, when I felt anything but. The suggestion—that Marcus move into the Banner Hill house—was ludicrous. Anyone who understood my mother's feelings about Marcus would have thought the same. And yet, the suggestion had a certain reasonableness and logic to it.

"She's right," Marcus said to Ed. "I've never been invited over. Not once." He turned to me. "And I can see how you'd be wondering why I'd even offer. I mean, I have every reason to be angry. What if I take it out on our father?"

I hadn't actually traced the thought that far. I was mostly imagining him trying to have a conversation with my mother, a woman who had effectively banned his name from her home. But it did bring up the question of care. Why hadn't I thought of that first?

"I want to hear you explain it," I said, deliberately vague.

"I don't hate you, if that's what you're worried about. I don't really care about you one way or another, at this point. But I wouldn't mind a chance to know my father to some extent before he dies."

I nodded. "But this is really generous," I said. "I mean, you'd be giving up income for, you don't even know how long."

"It's not going to be that long," Ed said softly.

I bit my lip and looked out the restaurant's front windows, at pedestrians wandering by. I nodded, to this fact and to the whole idea. Although Marcus's offer was by far the most economical, this wasn't only about economics. I trusted Ed, and he was the one who had said that you don't punish the child. In this equation, it seemed to me, most of us were children.

"Dad's okay with the idea?" I asked.

Both of them nodded.

"Then we'll have to hear what Mom says."

Chapter Sixteen

"NO," MY MOTHER SAID. "NO.YOU'VE GOT TO BE KIDDING. That boy? In our house? Jacob..."

The following evening, Thursday, I had invited myself to my parents' house for dinner. Ed had invited himself, too—ostensibly, we were both there to check on my father. Blake was out at band practice and Kurt couldn't get away from Stockton.

My father shrugged. "I thought it sounded like a reasonable option," he said.

"My own brother." My mother glared at Ed. "I can't believe you'd do this. Sasha, is it me or is this crazy?"

They were all looking at me, waiting. I didn't want to be there. I would happily have traded places with Blake, happily been treated like a kid and kept clear of the hard decisions. Everyone probably has those moments, when they realize they are no longer children, moments of maturity that tend to sneak up on you. This was one of those.

"It would make things a lot easier financially," I began, hesitant. "On the other hand, it might be stressful. For you, the rest of us, probably even Marcus himself."

"More stressful than having to deal with Jacob's cancer alone? Than not being able to afford a treatment that Dr. Fisher recommends?" Ed asked.

"You've got an agenda," my mother said. "You want him here. You could pay for that in-home nurse without batting an eye, but you won't."

"Lola, that's not fair," my father said.

"Oh, please. He's got more money than God."

"You're exaggerating. Besides, I won't take Ed's money," my father said. "I told him as much."

"So it's about pride," she said.

"Yours or mine?" my father asked. "Marcus's offer is generous and—"

"And what?" she demanded.

My father hesitated.

"And what?" she asked again.

"And it's fair." That was me speaking.

My mother looked at me, her expression a mix of hurt and surprise. Then she turned back to Ed and my father.

"I see how you two arranged this. I'll have that woman's son in my house, or else I'm the bad wife, right? That you would do this to me, now of all times." She shook her head and looked down at her hands. "Why is this happening now?" Her voice began to quaver.

"Because I got sick," my father said, placing a tentative hand on her shoulder.

My mother looked up with sudden vigor. "How did that boy even know you were sick?"

"We've been in touch," my father said.

Her mouth dropped open, but she seemed to have forgotten how to speak.

"Not often," he added. "It's not hard to reach me. We've been in this house for a long time."

"What is it with you damn Gardner men?" my mother muttered, as much to herself as to anyone. She rose to her feet and left the room.

"Actually, that went better than I expected," Ed said.

I found her later, a dark shape on the patio. "That solution you recommended really worked," I heard her say.

I racked my brain. What solution had I recommended? Did she think I'd come up with the idea to bring in Marcus? I could barely see her, but I picked out the glow of an ember. I hadn't seen her smoke since before Blake was born.

She exhaled. "The loopers. I sprayed it on my broccoli and they're all gone. Where did you find that?"

"Maybe I just knew it," I said.

She laughed, a harsh sort of hiccup. "Right."

"It was from that Web site Ellen Maselin likes," I admitted. I didn't confess that I had become a regular reader, too. Where else would I have learned about grape cultivation in Georgia?

"Can you imagine having that boy in this house? And responsible for your father?"

"He's twenty-six now," I said.

"I thought he was in prison."

I didn't answer. I knew that Ed had detailed Marcus's nursing qualifications to her.

"What do you think he's like?" she asked.

I froze. I was torn between sharing my impressions and the knowledge that admitting our dinner at Hunter's—admitting that I could describe him with some accuracy—would get me into trouble.

I was saved by my mother's own train of thought, still moving. "I'll tell you what he's like. I bet he's just like his mother."

"I don't think I met her," I said.

That wasn't precisely true. I did have one memory of Eloise Johnston. I was probably four or five, and in my father's office, coloring on a ledger pad. A woman had walked in and bent down to ask what I was drawing. The rhythm of her voice was the same as my dad's, and as she bent, her black hair fell around her face, so that she had to pull it back with one hand. Then she stood, and I watched as her red shoes crossed the carpet. I had never seen red heels before. They looked terribly exotic.

"She was a piece of work, I'll say that for her. Always after something."

"And you figure Marcus—"

"Fruit doesn't fall far from the tree," my mother said.

"I don't know. You and I have our differences," I ventured.

"Fine. We'll bring him here and you'll see. Ed will see. It'll be a disaster, I'm telling you. It's like asking the fox to guard the henhouse, as your father would say. But how do I refuse?" She sucked one last time on her cigarette, then stubbed it out.

"Does, uh, Blake know?" I asked. I realized that I didn't know if Blake was aware that he even had a half brother, much less that it was Marcus. That was how little we had spoken of him in recent years. Sure, they'd been to a ball game, but Ed could have introduced Marcus as a colleague or friend. I hadn't noticed any big resemblance between Marcus and Blake that might have created suspicion.

"He knows," my mother said, her voice flat. "Your father told him. I thought he was too young for it, but now…" She petered off, then stood and turned toward her garden, a series of black shapes in the nighttime. I wondered whether she knew exactly which amorphous shadow corresponded to which plant. I had a feeling that she did.

"I never knew that Gardner—our last name—doesn't come from garden," I said. "It comes from a Saxon word about war. Did you know that?"

"Is that right?" She didn't sound interested. "I only married into the name. That's more your concern."

"Back in the den, you said something about Gardner men," I said. I had been wondering whom else she was referring to. We'd never been close with my father's father—especially not after the move to California. And he had no brothers.

My mother sighed.

"Is it anything I ought to know?" I asked.

"Apparently Kurt didn't get back to Stockton until Sunday morning. After the anniversary party. It's a drive, but it's not that long a drive."

"And Lori thinks——" I began.

"Lori knows," my mother said. "A wife knows."

Chapter Seventeen

AT WORK ON FRIDAY, MY MIND KEPT DRIFTING. Marcus's tattoos. My mother's cigarette. Rotten salmon. Kurt at the anniversary party staring at the waitress's legs. The new scar on my father's scalp. Loopers. It was a mess in there.

A slap of papers jarred me back into my office. I looked up to see Susan standing before me, hands on her hips. She had dropped an armful of file folders across my desk.

"Satisfied?" she asked.

"I'm sorry?"

"Listen, Sasha. I was as sorry as anyone to hear that your father is ill. Truly. That's got to suck. But first you give me this talk about time management and hand me this file. Then I get started on it, and now you want it back? How am I supposed to read that? Do you hate me or something? Are you trying to get me fired?"

"No! No. Of course not. It's not you, Susan. It's the return."

Susan frowned. I could tell she didn't believe me. And why would she? When had a single return ever meant more to me than any other?

"I've got to go. It's all in there," she said. She turned on her heel and left. As she did so, the pile of papers shifted, sending half of the sheets to the floor.

Down on my knees, on the hard industrial carpet, I began to gather Jonah Gray's life back together. Pages of previous returns were mixed with bank statements from the past year, IRS work sheets and various tax schedules. Even out of order, I was glad to have him back.

I was looking forward to the opportunity to leave my family and its messiness behind, even for a few hours a day. Instead, I could spend time exploring the life of a man so genuinely upstanding and generous. Whatever had happened in his life in the previous July, whatever had prompted him to leave so much behind, at least it was unrelated to what was currently whirling about my own family. As such, Jonah Gray's audit seemed like a life raft.

Peeking out from beneath my bookcase, one slip of paper caught my eye. It was a notification of a stock sale—the liquidation of Jonah Gray's entire account, to be accurate—from the previous year. But that didn't make sense. When I had scanned through his return the first time, I had noticed that he'd kept his stock accounts untouched when he moved from Tiburon. I remembered thinking how that made sense, especially if you were moving to a city called *Stock*ton. Okay, maybe I am a kook, but that was the mnemonic I used to remember that he hadn't declared any stock sales. The notification I had just found made clear that he should have. Not declaring the capital gains amounted to tax evasion.

I dropped the paper and leaned back against my bookcase, shaking my head, exhausted. Enough. I was beat from the night before, from the days before, from the news of Kurt's dalliance, from the idea of Marcus moving in, and from a gnawing sense that

I should have been the one to offer. Now, Jonah Gray had lied? Was there no safe harbor left?

I brought my hands up to my face and let the tears come, crying for how small I felt and because I wasn't doing more for my father and because I couldn't. Because people didn't like what I did for a living and because Kevin at the Escape Room never came back and because I'd pushed Gene away and everyone at work thought I was a freak and what the hell was so wrong with me anyway? And because I'd found the one piece of paper I didn't want to find, the one that revealed a side of Jonah Gray that I would have given anything not to see. Why couldn't I have overlooked it? What use was my mind if it only made me miserable?

It felt like the last straw. He was married, but perfectly willing to flirt with me on the phone. He skipped out on his life in the Bay area—and no one had been able to provide me a reasonable explanation for that. He had plastered my name on his Web site, as if it were some digital dartboard for strangers to hurl insults onto. And now he had evaded paying capital gains taxes. How much more proof did I need that it was time to forget this guy?

I looked up to see Jeff Hill walking down the hallway, his head bobbing above the cubicle walls.

"Jeff!" I called out.

He stopped immediately and turned around, arriving back at my cubicle as I scrambled to my feet.

"What if we went to dinner tonight instead of next Thursday?"

"Tonight?" he asked. He seemed a little uneasy with the idea. Or maybe he was thinking about all the germs that I'd picked up while on my office floor.

"Do you have other plans?" I asked. It suddenly felt very important to accelerate our dating schedule.

"No. I guess not. Do you still want to try Hunter's?"

"Perfect."

"Say, seven?"

"Also perfect," I said, giving him my best smile. "I'll meet you at Hunter's at seven. And that's a definite affirmative."

He looked at me as though suspicious of my sudden enthusiasm. Then he nodded. "I'll see you then," he said. "That'll be nice."

As soon as he left, I called Martina.

"Have you even tried the jerky yet?" she asked.

"Speaking of jerks, I'm done with Jonah Gray. Just so you know. Done. Absolutely done." I told her about the stock sale I'd found. "All these people have been on me about what a hard a year he'd had. How awful it has been at 530 Horsehair Road. Well, he's not the only one who's had a hard year."

"I think maybe you're upset about more than this journalist guy," Martina said.

"I tell you, I'm done with him. I don't know what I thought I saw there, but forget it. Forget him."

Martina didn't respond.

"What?" I finally asked.

"Nothing. I'm just surprised to hear you go from sixty to zero so quickly. I figured this guy was going to mean something, since I've never known you to be so drawn in to an audit. I'm sure you know what's best. You just aren't usually so, well, compulsive."

"I'm not usually dealing with tax cheats either."

"Well, you are, actually. But I agree that you're not usually interested in them romantically. Did you say 530 Horsehair Road? And that's Stockton, right?"

"Why?"

"I'm just looking up his zip code."

"Oh, no. I don't want to play that game. He's not my boyfriend."

"Did I say that he was?"

"And he's not some hottie you met at a bar." Whenever Martina would meet a guy—whether at a bar or party or while traveling—she made sure to ask his zip code. Some people were interested in a person's job or background or astrological sign. For Martina, zip codes were her measure of compatibility. As a marketing professional, she loved how people cluster in groups—those who drive similar cars, read the same magazines, watch the same television shows, attain the same levels of education. It was fascinating, if a little scary, how much she could determine about the character of a relatively small swath of land.

"Why does it matter?You don't like him anyway, right?" I heard her typing and after a few seconds, I heard her say "Huh, that's interesting."

"What is?"

"Does he hunt?"

"Hunt?"

"A lot of people in that zip code hunt."

"He gardens," I said.

"There's a high likelihood that he drives an RV."

"An RV?" I asked.

"My grandfather drives an RV," Martina said, sounding a little defensive.

"Well, this guy is only a couple years older than we are. I don't know what he drives."

"Maybe a tractor."

"A tractor?"

"They've got a lot of farmers in that area. He probably eats dinner early. Is he Filipino?"

"I don't know. I don't think so."

"There are a lot of Filipinos there, too."

"Ricardo's Filipino. He's from Stockton."

"I told you, this stuff is better than palm reading."

Begrudgingly, I found myself wondering whether Jonah Gray was like the other people in his zip code. That would have meant, as Martina explained, that he was a hard-rock music fan. That he watched daytime television and game shows, belonged to a veterans' club and bought collectibles by mail. And that he was more likely than people in other areas of town to own a pet bird.

Don't get me wrong, all those traits were fine, but they didn't exactly describe the men I'd been drawn to in the past.

"It doesn't matter anyway," I said. "He's married with a kid and a tax evader to boot."

"Then it doesn't matter if he has a bird," Martina agreed.

That night, right at seven, I met Jeff in front of Hunter's. As we walked inside, I found myself looking toward the bar. It seemed remarkable that only a few days before I had been introduced to Marcus in there.

"The dining room is this way," the hostess said, seeing me glance in the opposite direction.

"Oh, I know," I said.

"When I asked you, you said that you hadn't ever been here before," Jeff said.

"Just once. Earlier this week, actually."

"That's how I remember you," the hostess said. "You were here with that adorable guy. The one with all the tats."

I felt Jeff Hill watching me.

"Marcus," I said, to both of them. "Family stuff."

"Wow, I would *not* have guessed that," the hostess said, bringing us to our table. "You guys were, like, totally different. Tell him to stop in again. He was totally hot."

"My half brother," I explained to Jeff.

We sat and Jeff immediately began centering the salt and pepper shakers and his utensils. He looked up at me. "You don't mind, do you?"

I didn't mind. I didn't find it particularly sexy, but I didn't mind. "Do what you need to do," I said.

"So how many brothers do you have?" he asked.

"Three," I said. It was the first time I'd included Marcus in the count.

"But one's a half brother. So really, two and a half."

"Which rounds to three," I pointed out.

As I watched Jeff read the menu, I wondered whether our date was a bad idea. As a rule, I avoided office romances. Of course, Jeff wasn't a coworker in the manner that another auditor would have been. The archive department was two floors down. But the rule had provided a ready excuse when I'd been asked out by Lance (whose breath would have kept me from saying yes anyway), by Brad (funny, but he'd never shut up) and by Troy (who had asked out every woman on the floor within a week of taking the job).

So why had I said yes to Jeff? I wondered, as I watched him frown at the entrées. Was it because he was new? Because Ricardo thought he might be right for me? Because everything else felt so fragile and foggy and he was so steady and evident?

Jeff closed his menu and set it on the table. "I'm so glad you agreed to come to dinner," he said. "I want you to know that I don't usually date people I work with. I never once dated a cop when I worked for the Oakland P.D."

I smiled. Maybe I would find that we had other things in common, too.

"So, I'm going to get the venison. What about you?" Jeff asked.

"I was thinking about the linguini," I said, closing my menu.

"Pasta in a game restaurant?" he said. "The duck looks good, doesn't it? Why don't you try the duck?"

"Okay, maybe the duck," I said.

"You look great in that color by the way," Jeff said.

I looked down at my blouse. "In this blue?" I asked.

"What color would you call that? Sort of a whitish blue?"

"Um, light blue?" I said.

"You should wear it more. It makes your eyes look really beautiful."

Jeff looked at the hostess, who was headed back to her podium by the door.

"Our hostess isn't happy in her job," Jeff said. "It figures. Can you imagine having to be nice to people all day?"

"Why do you think she's unhappy?" I asked. "She's been smiling each time I've seen her."

"But look at her when she's not with a customer. She doesn't smile then. She stops smiling as soon as she's alone."

If I leaned back in my chair, I could see her, standing near the entrance to both the bar and the dining room, waiting for the next party of two or three or four to arrive. Jeff was right. She was slumped against the wall, picking at her nails, her expression grim. But as soon as the door to the restaurant opened, her posture straightened and a smile pasted onto her face.

"I see what you mean," I said. "That's too bad."

"How's that bad? She could be an actress," Jeff said. "She's very good at showing people what they want to see. Most people can't make the transition so quickly."

"Do you always analyze restaurant staff?" I asked.

"I like figuring out what people don't know they're telling me," Jeff said. "I was really shy as I kid," he went on. "People barely talked to me, so I sat and watched a lot. You know, when I wasn't collecting insects."

"You don't seem shy," I said.

"I'm better now at asking for what I want," he said. He smiled at me.

"So what have I told you?" I asked. I found myself nervous to know.

"Something's going on with you," he said. "Everyone talks about you like you're the most on-the-ball person in the office, but you're not, are you? Not right now at least."

I felt my eyes begin to well up. I shook my head.

"I mean, that's fine. I don't need to know why. I respect your privacy. But you asked, and well, I could see it."

"What gave me away?"

"Your desk."

"My desk?"

"It's been cluttered since I first met you. I don't think it usually is."

"It's not," I said. For some reason, it was important that he believed me.

"I didn't think so, because you don't have piles."

"Piles?"

"See, there are messy people, but you're not one of those. You don't leave old food containers around. Then there are cluttered people. But really cluttered people usually have some organizing principle that you can see if you look carefully. You know, defined piles, stacks of reading, overstuffed file folders. But you don't. Your bookshelves are neat and organized. Your photographs don't have any dust. It's like you've only let your desk go in the past month or so."

"All of August," I said. "It's true."

"I hope I didn't upset you," Jeff said. "You asked."

"So what's your desk like?" I asked, though I had a feeling I knew. I looked at the salt and pepper shakers, precisely arranged.

"It's organized and clean," he said, "but you knew that."

The rest of dinner was surprisingly easy. Jeff seemed relaxed— at least, as relaxed as I'd ever seen him. He told one or two decent jokes. He asked about my friends. He held definite opinions, but they tended to complement my own, and it was a relief to be with someone who wasn't scared of making decisions.

He walked me to my car after dinner, and there, under the fluorescent streetlights, he leaned in. Though I hadn't quite made up my mind about him, about what I wanted or didn't want to happen, I found myself kissing him. It was nice, actually. He had made the decision for the both of us, and it was reassuring to feel someone's arms around me, so solid and certain. Reassuring isn't necessarily the wrong reason.

Back at home though, I didn't sleep well. At first, I thought it might be the beef jerky, the smell of which had leached through the cardboard box to permeate my bedroom. But even after I relegated the stuff to the hallway, I tossed in my bed.

I liked Jeff. Sure I did. And his world fit my own so neatly. He had no issue with my job. His car was paid off. I felt confident that he'd never leave dirty dishes in my sink. And his eye for detail and head for facts made me feel better about my own. And after a successful date, after you'd found yourself curled into the crook of the guy's arm, leaning in and kissing him back, didn't it make sense to drift off imagining what you might be at the cusp of? So why was I still thinking of Jonah?

Chapter Eighteen

THAT SATURDAY, I ARRIVED AT MY PARENTS' HOUSE AT three, to see how my mother was handling things. Marcus was expected for dinner that evening.

"You didn't need to come early," my mother said. "I don't feel like I have to bend over backwards, for this person of all people."

"I'm not saying that you should."

"Maybe I'll just run the vacuum," she said, glancing around the living room.

"You want me to do that?" I offered.

"If you'd like."

So I vacuumed, and when I was done, I found my mother in the kitchen, leaning into the refrigerator with all her weight and scrubbing the shelves. When she emerged and noticed me waiting, she smiled self-consciously.

"You're wondering why I'm doing this," she said.

"Sort of."

"I threw out last week's lamb chops and some of your dad's old limburger, and then, well, I don't know. It had to get done at some point."

She had stacked all of the perishables in a pile on the counter. As I looked closer, it was clear that each condiment bottle and jar had also been rinsed.

"Is there anything else you want me to do?"

"Just sit. I'll get this food back in the fridge and we're finished," she said.

But we weren't finished. All afternoon, she kept noticing things—a spiderweb in the top corner of the ceiling, dust along a windowsill, a pair of Blake's shoes hiding beneath the TV-room sofa. The same things that had gone untouched for weeks that Saturday were deemed unsightly.

At six, Ed brought my father back from radiation therapy. "Someone's been cleaning," my father said.

My mother cut her eyes at him. I imagined she might have liked to say, *Yeah, you asshole, I've been cleaning up for the son you had when you cheated on me.* I was fine with the idea that my mother might yet be angry at my father, even though his mistakes were more than a quarter century in the past by then. Had I been in her shoes, I probably would have wanted to say something biting. But the fact was my dad had cancer. He was going to die. Neither of us said anything.

When the doorbell rang, right at seven, my mother jumped a little, then settled back against the couch. She made no move to answer the door, and her look told Blake to remain seated as well. I thought about Ed's comment—about who was being punished in this situation. I didn't want to be part of the Gardner cold shoulder, so I hopped up and went to let Marcus inside.

"Hello again," he said. He wore a black sweater that covered his tattoos, his hair was neatly combed, and he was clean-shaven. I found myself wishing that my mother had met him before, so she could have appreciated how much he'd cleaned up for the occasion.

Maybe Ed had advised him to make the effort. Or maybe Marcus felt compelled to look nice for this visit with relative strangers. Maybe he had done it for my father, to make the smallest waves possible. I had to remind myself that Marcus and my father actually had a relationship now.

Or maybe Marcus wanted the evening to go well, needed it to, even more than we did. Whatever time my father had left was all that Marcus would get before he was orphaned for good. I heard Ed saying, "Don't punish the child." I realized this was what he meant by that.

"Everyone's in the living room," I said, motioning for him to follow me there.

Ed did the introductions. "Lola, this is Marcus Johnston."

"Good evening," Marcus said. "Thank you for inviting me over tonight."

"Is that what I did?" my mother asked.

Ed cleared his throat.

"Dad! Can you come in here?" I called down the hallway.

"You have a lovely home," Marcus said.

I respected his determination.

Finally, my father appeared. My mother looked at him, then turned back to Marcus and smiled more graciously. "Why, thank you, Marcus," she said. "I don't believe you know my youngest son, Blake."

"Hey, man," Blake said, quickly standing to shake his half brother's hand. It was clear that my mother wasn't aware of the baseball game, though I supposed it didn't matter now. Suddenly, the same subjects that had been tucked away throughout Blake's life were standing in the middle of the living room.

"And of course, this is Sasha," my mother said.

"I'm glad you could make it," I told him. And I was.

"Well, it smells wonderful in here," Ed said.

"It's the pot roast," my mother said. "I trust you eat beef?" my mother asked Marcus.

"Yes, ma'am," Marcus said.

She took a deep breath. "You might as well call me Lola," my mother said.

I watched Marcus walk over to my father. There was no question as to whether they were related. Though Marcus's darker coloring was his mother's, his bearing and voice came straight from my dad. It was funny to hear how their accents matched.

"How are you today?" Marcus asked. "That radiation can really tire a guy out, can't it?"

My father nodded. "It wears me to pieces," he said.

"Any disorientation afterward?" Marcus asked. "Feeling sort of wobbly?"

My father nodded again.

"Is it better after you rest?"

"Usually."

"Then keep on resting. Don't let the bear get you yet. You've got some running still to do."

"Blake, help me get the table set for dinner," my mother said, standing and moving toward the kitchen.

"Aren't we waiting for Kurt?" Ed asked.

"He's not coming," my mother said.

"But he told me he was coming," Ed said.

"And he told me that something came up."

Blake dragged himself off the couch and followed her into the kitchen. "We're eating in the dining room?" I heard him ask.

"Of course," my mother said.

"What do you mean, of course? We haven't eaten in there since…" He paused. "Easter?"

"Oh, it hasn't been that long," my mother said.

"Has, too."

It was true. The formal dining room was usually reserved for special occasions. It was a stiff, closed-off room, with an air that carried the tang of silver polish and mothballs.

"Well, there are six of us tonight," my mother said. "You want to try to fit around the kitchen table?"

"I'm just saying," Blake said.

Considering that my father had cancer and that Marcus was getting to know a side of the family that had previously rejected him and that Blake was still sore about being the last to know, the conversation that Saturday was remarkably benign.

"I suppose you like being a nurse, then?" my mother asked Marcus.

"I do. Very much," he said.

"You're going to take care of Dad?" Blake asked. "What can you do?"

"I haven't gone all feeble yet," my father snapped. "Give the old guy a little time."

"Come on, now. He didn't mean any harm. I know y'all are concerned," Marcus said. He turned to Blake. "I can make sure he remains as comfortable and pain-free as possible, for as long as possible."

I looked at Blake and thought he seemed older than fifteen. I wondered whether this past summer would turn out to have been the last one of his boyhood. I wondered whether he had any inkling.

My father turned to me. "Your brother said you've developed a thing for one of your audits."

I was taken aback. For six years, my father had made it a point to be uninterested in my work. I wondered if he was bringing up the subject to try to keep the family tension at a more manageable level.

"Which brother said that?" I asked, eyeing Blake suspiciously.

"Kurt called a couple days back," my dad said. "Don't do anything stupid."

"A thing?" Ed asked. "Do you need it looked at?"

"It's not a thing," I said to him, then turned back to my dad. "I'm not doing anything stupid. I'm not doing anything."

"Who's the audit?" Marcus asked.

"He's nothing. I mean, he's not nothing—"

"So he's something," Ed chimed in.

Maybe we were all punchy from the stress of that dinner. I didn't appreciate being the target, but I was willing to play along for a short while, if it got us through alive.

"He's neither nothing nor something," I said. "He's just a guy I'm auditing. It was weird, is all. He's from Virginia and he had the same kind of sailboat as we did. But it's nothing important."

"Sasha, you like someone? A man?" my mother asked.

"Why is this my life?" I sighed. There was no way I was going to fan the flames by mentioning my recent date with Jeff.

"Kurt said she did," my father said.

"That was before," I said. "Can we drop it?"

"His name is Jonah Gray," Blake said. "I talked to Kurt when he called, too."

"Jonah Gray?" my mother asked. "The gardener?"

"I thought Kurt said he worked at a newspaper," my father said.

"He's a wonderful gardener, Sasha," my mother said.

"Don't start. I've got gardeners coming out of the woodwork to tell me that."

"Just keep your eyes open," my father said.

"They are open. Open enough to notice that he was dodgy with last year's taxes."

"I find that hard to believe," my mother said.

"Well, he didn't declare any stock sales, yet stocks were sold. Figure that one out."

"I'm sure there's a reasonable explanation," my mother said.

"You've got to declare," my father intoned. "You've got to report."

"Besides, he's married. And filing separately, so he's probably hiding the sales from his wife."

"You don't know that," my mother said. "Don't prejudge the man."

"That's her job!" my father hollered.

"I don't know what I know anymore," I said.

"Sasha's got a crush," Blake sang.

I had tired of being the target of my family's inquisition. I was all for pretending, for Marcus's sake or my father's or everyone's, that everything was *Leave It to Beaver* easy around the Gardner dinner table. Hell, we were all doing it. But I was going to share in the ribbing, too.

"Blake's got a girlfriend," I said.

"Shut up," he said. "I do not."

"Then where'd you get the hickey?" I asked, pointing to the bruise on his neck.

"You have a hickey?" Ed asked. "Is it your first?"

"What are we talking about now?" my father demanded.

"Blake's friend kissed him a little too hard," my mother explained.

"Mom!" Blake looked as if he might implode.

"Where?" my father asked.

"What, dear? Isn't that what a hickey is?" my mother asked.

I laughed and caught Marcus's eye. He'd been watching us in silence. "See what you've been missing?" I asked.

"What's burning?" my father suddenly barked. "I smell something burning."

"Do you?" My mother rose from her chair. "Oh, dear. Don't tell me I left the oven on." She hurried into the kitchen.

"I don't smell anything," Blake said.

"Something is burning," my father said again.

"I heard you the first time," Blake said. "Jeez."

My mother returned from the kitchen, frowning a little. "Well, the oven's off, thank goodness. You had me worried. Do you still smell it? Maybe the neighbors are grilling."

My father sniffed the air again. "I don't smell anything," he said.

Marcus put a hand on my father's arm. "It might be that the radiation therapy is affecting your sense of smell. It's a harmless side effect, just a little disarming when it happens."

My mother turned to Ed. "Is that true?" she asked.

"That would be my guess, too," Ed said.

"Would someone show Marcus to the spare room?" my mother asked. We had finished eating by then. "I understand he's going to be staying over."

I looked at Marcus. "You're staying over?"

"What spare room?" Blake asked.

"Your sister's old room," my mother said.

"That's where you're going to put him?" I asked. It wasn't my room anymore, and she had a right to do with it what she wanted. But still. "Why not Kurt's room?"

"Kurt got a little touchy when I suggested it. Anyway, your room has more privacy," my mother said. "I don't really care which room he takes." She kept her eyes down as she spoke, very carefully smoothing out the napkin on her lap.

"So long as he's not touchy about me sleeping in his old bed if I need to stay over," I said.

Finally, my mother raised her eyes. She looked straight at Marcus, her face expressionless. "Well, which would you prefer?" she asked him.

"It really doesn't matter to me," Marcus said.

"Go ahead and take mine then," I said, afraid that there would be some sort of showdown between them. I got up from the table. "Here. Follow me. I'll show you the way."

Chapter Nineteen

I DIDN'T SLEEP IN KURT'S OLD BED THAT NIGHT, BUT happily dozed in my own, back in Oakland. Bright and early though, I was back in Piedmont. I felt obligated to make sure that everyone else had survived the night, too.

They had, and over breakfast, the idea of a picnic trip to Stockton took root and then shape. It was Sunday, the weather was fine, and though others may have been content to visit Stockton, I wanted the real reason Kurt had skipped dinner. I suspected that it had been some sort of protest.

My mother called Lori to coordinate, and then my parents, Blake, Marcus and I packed up and headed out to the driveway.

"Whose motorcycle?" Blake asked, his eyes wide.

"Mine," Marcus said.

"Wicked cool," Blake said. "Are you going to ride to Stockton on it? Mom, can I ride with Marcus?"

"No, you may not," my mother said. "You'll ride with your father and me."

"You don't want to come in the Truckster?" I asked Marcus, as he reached for his helmet. My mother had remained without a car of her own, her first nod to a budget in years.

"I've got to bring a couple things down from Sacramento," he said. "Figure I'll head there straight from this picnic."

"Are you okay to ride up there all alone?"

"You can ride with me," he said. "If you're so worried."

It wasn't an offer I expected. "I don't have a helmet."

"I carry a spare."

"No fair," Blake said. "She doesn't even like bikes."

"I like bikes," I said.

"I meant motorcycles, not bicycles."

"Blake, would you get in the car, please?" my mother asked.

"Sorry, man," Marcus said to Blake. "Maybe next time. What about it, Sasha?"

I'd never ridden on a motorcycle or even on a moped for that matter. "Have you ever gotten into an accident?" I asked. It seemed like a reasonable question.

"A car hit me when I was seventeen."

"And since then?"

"You don't have to ride with me," Marcus said. "I was just offering."

"No, I will. I will." I said it as much to myself as to him. "What do I need to do?"

I pulled on the helmet, and he showed me how to climb on, where to put my feet and how to avoid touching the hot exhaust pipe. There was room on the seat behind him, and a backrest I could lean against. Once I settled in, it was surprisingly comfortable.

My mother got out of my father's car and walked up to me. "Are you sure you want to do this?" she whispered. "Are you sure it's safe?"

I wasn't sure of anything at that point, but I didn't want Marcus to think that I didn't trust him or wouldn't take any risks.

"I'm already on," I told her. "It'll be fine." In truth, I was uneasy. I was that person who always offered to drive, so that I'd be certain to arrive on time and leave on time and take the right routes and I wouldn't get stuck somewhere I didn't want to be. That person didn't ride on the backs of motorcycles.

"You be careful with her," my mother admonished Marcus.

"We'll see you there," I said. Marcus accelerated out of the driveway and I felt the thrust of the motorcycle push me back into the seat. "You and my mom seem to be surviving each other so far," I said, yelling toward him as the wind whipped my face. Riding on the back of Marcus's motorcycle was more fun than I wanted to admit.

"She reminds me a little of my mom," Marcus yelled back.

"You're kidding."

"Not in every way. Mine was a lot more demonstrative."

"To you, I'm sure," I said.

"To everyone. Of course, I never saw her at a comparable time. You know, losing a husband."

"She never remarried?"

"She never married," he said, correcting me.

A bug hit me in the thigh. I flinched from the sting of it.

"You scared?" he asked.

"No," I yelled into the wind. It was true. I felt as if I was flying. There was something so freeing about letting someone else worry about the road ahead. Why hadn't I done it before? "It feels like you know what you're doing," I said.

"I could have a death wish. You think of that?" he asked, pulling up to a stop sign. He turned around and looked at me. "This whole thing could be a trap."

"You said you didn't hate me," I said.

He gave me a quick smile, then he turned back to the road and didn't take his eyes off it until we arrived in Stockton.

We met at a regional park across town from where Lori and Kurt and the boys now lived. Winding into the parking lot, I spotted their car, and then saw Kurt and Lori spreading a cloth over one of the picnic tables. Jackie and Eddie sat on the sidewalk, running model cars over sticks and leaves.

Marcus pulled his motorcycle into an empty parking space in front of where the boys were playing. I watched as they looked up at the growling machine. Eddie poked Jackie and the two let go of their cars.

I waved at the boys as Marcus parked the bike and cut the ignition.

"Hi Eddie! Hi Jackie!"

Eddie pulled Jackie closer.

I jumped off the bike and stepped toward them. Now, Eddie pulled Jackie to his feet and the boys began backing away. I realized they didn't recognize me with the motorcycle helmet and sunglasses.

"It's okay. It's me. It's Aunt Sasha!" I pulled off the gear and finally got a smile.

By this point, Kurt and Lori had spotted us—or at least spotted two adults talking to their children—and were hurrying in our direction.

"What were you wearing?" Jackie asked.

"That was a motorcycle helmet," I said.

Eddie squinted up at Marcus. "Who's he?"

"This is your uncle Marcus," I said.

Marcus squatted down and held out his hand. "Which one of you is Eddie?" he asked.

Eddie raised his hand.

"I see," Marcus said. "So which one of you is Jackie?"

Jackie raised his hand and giggled.

"Uh-huh," Marcus said, scratching his chin. "So who is Marcus then?" he asked.

"You are!" the boys yelled in unison.

"Smart kids."

Kurt and Lori were watching us, waiting, so I tapped Marcus on the shoulder. "I should introduce you," I said.

Marcus got to his feet and held out his hand. "Kurt," he said. "I'm Marcus. I don't think we've ever met."

Kurt nodded and shook his hand.

I wondered whether they were sizing each other up. I knew I was. Side by side, I could see that they shared my father's jawline and the shape of his face. But I could pick out few other traits in common. Marcus was both taller and thinner than Kurt, and frankly, better looking.

"This is my wife, Lori," Kurt said to Marcus.

"Hello, Marcus," Lori said, extending her hand. "I understand you'll be helping out with Jacob."

"Trying to," Marcus said.

"That's all we can ask," Kurt said.

"Sometimes we can ask for more," Lori said. The comment seemed directed at Kurt.

"Can I lend a hand getting ready?" Marcus asked. "Got anything left in the car?"

Lori smiled at him. "You really sound like Jacob. Your voice and everything."

"I'll take that as a compliment," Marcus said.

Kurt pulled me away. "Can I see you for a minute?"

"Ouch. Gentle," I said, following him.

"Where do you get off introducing him to my kids as their uncle?" Kurt said, when we were far enough away. He looked genuinely confused. And angry.

"He *is* their uncle."

"Oh no, he isn't."

"What is your problem, Kurt?"

"Well, for starters, maybe you forgot already but our dad is dying."

"You don't get to be an ass to the rest of us because Dad is sick. It's not as if you're the only one who's freaking out about it."

"Oh, I'm the one being an ass."

I looked around the park. "You see anyone else?"

Kurt turned away and mumbled something I couldn't hear. I said as much.

"I said," he spat, as he turned back toward me, "that it doesn't feel right."

"What doesn't feel right?"

"Anything. This whole thing. Dad being sick. Marcus showing up out of the blue."

"It wasn't out of the blue. Dad got this ball rolling a while ago. In every way."

"Well, it sure is convenient for Marcus. He moved in awfully quick."

"So this is really about Marcus. Not about Dad," I said. "Go ahead. He can't hear you."

Marcus and Lori were at the picnic table, uncovering various containers of potato salad, coleslaw and greens.

"He's a stranger, Sasha. Some stranger is going to be taking care of our father. Think of the influence he'll have. Think of all the ways he can wheedle in."

"He's not a stranger to Dad. And I didn't hear you chiming in to offer. You want to take a leave of absence from your job to spend the next six months in a sickroom?"

"I can't," he said.

"I know. We all know you can't."

Kurt leaned against the side of his car and looked at his shoes. I went and stood next to him, close enough that I could feel the warmth of his body down my left side.

"Did *you* offer?" he asked.

I shook my head. "He wouldn't want my help."

"That's not true," Kurt said.

"No?"

Kurt shrugged. "I don't know. Maybe. He does get snippy with you."

"Tell me about it."

My dad's old Mercedes began winding through the parking lot. For the first time ever, we were all there, all four of my father's kids in the same place at the same moment. As Blake and my parents began to climb out of the car, Kurt stalked off toward the picnic table. I amended my thought. Maybe we were all in the same physical location, but not the same place.

While the rest of us took seats around the picnic table, Blake roughhoused with the boys. He gave them airplane rides, pony rides and allowed himself be tackled and dragged to the grass.

"Eddie, Jackie! It's time to eat. Leave your uncle alone," Lori called, as the boys tried to keep Blake pinned to the grass. Blake was laughing so hard that his eyes were tearing. Eddie whirled around to answer his mother just as Blake looked up, and their bodies collided, Eddie's elbow with Blake's nose.

"Dammit!" Blake yelled, as blood began to gush.

"Mom!" Eddie screamed.

But it was Marcus who sprang into action, rushing to Blake with one of Lori's ice packs already in hand.

"Just sit tight and let's aim to keep the swelling down," Marcus said, his voice calm and steady as he led Blake to the picnic table.

"Oh, my baby boy," my mother said.

"I'm not a baby," Blake managed to say, sounding cottony.

"Is it broken?" Lori asked.

"Hard to tell just yet. Could be."

Blake groaned. Marcus took a closer look.

"It doesn't look like it's out of alignment. Sure is a spouter, though," Marcus said.

Blake groaned again.

"Eddie, come here and apologize to your uncle Blake," Lori said.

Eddie dragged himself over to the picnic table. "Sorry Uncle Blake," he said.

"It's okay," Blake said. "It was an accident."

"Thanks for helping, Uncle Marcus," Eddie said.

"Any time," Marcus said.

Kurt got up from the table and moved away.

"How about you eat something now," Lori suggested to Eddie, who dutifully began to pick at his lunch plate. Jackie, on the other hand, insisted that he wasn't hungry.

"Here, Jack, let's practice our throws," Kurt said, tossing a football to his younger son.

Jackie happily retrieved it, and Kurt kept tossing, a little farther every time. I watched as one of my brother's throws flew high over Jackie's head.

"He's only three," Lori called. "Give him a break."

Jackie ran to get the ball, but no sooner had he touched it than he started screaming. In an instant, Lori was on her feet, racing toward him.

"What happened? What's wrong?" she called out, but he kept wailing. It took a full ten minutes of shrieking to ascertain that a bee must have alit on the colorful foam ball and stung Jackie's hand as he reached for it.

"I've got to get out of this heat," my father suddenly announced as Jackie's whimpers continued in the background.

"You want to rest in the car? I'll put the air-conditioning on," my mother suggested.

"Maybe for a few minutes," he said.

"Can I help?" Marcus offered.

"He's fine," Kurt said, waving him off as he and my mother helped Dad away.

Marcus looked back at me. "So," he said. "What's your complaint?"

"My complaint?"

"Are you sick? Sunburned? Spider bite? Maybe some food poisoning?"

"I'm sorry. This day was supposed to be relaxing."

"If everyone's doped up by the end of it, it might still be." He smiled a little and pulled a pack of cigarettes from his back pocket.

"I didn't know you smoked," I said.

"I've got to figure that you don't know most things about me."

I'd grant him that. "But you're a nurse," I said.

"So?"

"Aren't you supposed to be healthy?"

"Jacob's an accountant. Isn't he supposed to keep better track of his money? Just because you know how to do something doesn't mean you always do it."

"Fine," I said.

Marcus lit a cigarette and inhaled. I noticed that he smoked the same brand my mother used to.

"What are your bad habits?" Marcus asked.

"I didn't mean to say it was a bad habit," I said.

Marcus waved me off. "Over-apologizing, maybe?"

"Not usually, no."

"Because you're never wrong, I'll bet. Then what?"

I looked around the picnic table. Amid all the turmoil, I'd stayed in the exact same place. "Sitting back and waiting maybe," I said.

"That's your bad habit?" He flicked his ashes onto a half-eaten plate of potato salad. "Jesus, you could stand to develop a few more. Cigarette?"

I shook my head. "What about riding on the backs of motorcycles?" I suggested.

Marcus nodded. "Speaking of which, I'd better get on the road."

"When are you coming back to Piedmont? When do you think you'll get started with, you know, Dad?"

"Probably tomorrow or the next day. Why?"

"So I'll see you next week?"

He stubbed out his cigarette. "I guess so." A few moments later, Marcus had gathered up his things and left.

I, too, had grown tired of Gardner family day. It felt as if we weren't a family so much as a group of isolated individuals in orbits that barely intersected. I turned to Eddie, who'd been sitting at the edge of the picnic table, watching everything. He hadn't yet bounced back from his role in Blake's bloody nose, and after hearing Jackie's bee-stung shrieks, had wound himself into a little ball and looked as if he were willing himself not to cry.

"I see that your mom brought her bike," I said to him. "You ready for an adventure? Just you and me?" It was a smile worth seeing. I got the kid bundled into the bike trailer and we were off.

I was definitely more in a mood for fields than family. Whenever an intersection presented a clear choice, I veered in the direction that looked more rural. That led us past crops I didn't recognize, past orchards, past fields already stripped of their harvest.

"Are you okay back there?" I called.

Eddie smiled, his little helmet knocking back and forth.

It was a beautiful day, blue sky above and dark gray asphalt below. I sped up and the discrete greens in the fields blurred into one. I ascended a hill, pushing hard to maintain my speed with the trailer behind me, legs pumping, heart racing, lungs burning. It was good to feel something so searing. At the crest, out of breath, I saw a rickety country store and coasted to a stop in front of it. I got off the bike, heaving.

An old man sat in a chair outside. "Can I help you?" he asked.

I nodded, but couldn't speak. I put my hands on my waist and bent down, trying to catch my breath.

"You're outta breath," the man said. I nodded again and looked up. Behind him, a painted sign revealed the store's name and address. I recognized the zip code as the same one Martina had researched for me. This was Jonah Gray's neck of the woods.

I glanced at the old man, trying to gauge if he looked more like an RV driver or a bow hunter. Mostly, he seemed like the kind of person who'd lend a hand if you ran out of gas or lost your wallet.

"Am I anywhere near Horsehair Road?" I asked, at last able to speak.

"Sure are. You're not but a quarter mile off. What you'll do is keep heading down this here road and you'll see it. On the left."

"Thanks."

"You know someone on Horsehair, do you?"

"Gray?" I said, reluctant to offer anything more.

"Oh sure," he said. "Helluva year. Hope he's feeling better."

I headed back to the bike.

"What's horsehair?" Eddie asked.

"The name of a street," I said. "Wave at the nice man, okay?"

The man at the grocery was spot-on. Horsehair Road was barely a quarter of a mile farther. The area looked as if it had begun as a single farm, before being subdivided for a housing development. In the first block stood a number of newer homes, the landscaping still sparse around them. It was the sort of neighborhood that might be pretty, given fifty years and enough rainfall.

I continued down the road. The newer houses sported addresses in the one hundreds, so 530 Horsehair had to be a few blocks more. I pedaled as if I knew where I was going. And I did, sort of. But what business did I have there? It was wildly inappropriate, my father would have been quick to point out, to visit the home of someone I was auditing. And with my nephew as a witness. Yet I kept going, and within a minute or so, the newer development had fallen away, and I found myself at the end of the road, at the edge of a long, gravel driveway that led to an older farmhouse—530 Horsehair.

I glanced at Eddie and wheeled the bike around, retreating a few yards. Then I turned around again. I wasn't sure what I was there to see, but whatever it was lay at the end of the driveway. I had ridden on the back of a motorcycle, for goodness sake. I could do this. Jeffrine could do this. I stopped at the edge of the road and dismounted.

"What are we doing?" Eddie asked.

"My thoughts exactly," I said. He looked confused. "We're exploring," I told him. "Didn't I promise you an adventure?"

"Is it safe to get out?"

There were no cars visible, either along Horsehair Road or in the driveway of the farmhouse. "I think it's safe," I told him.

Eddie picked his way out of the trailer and stood beside me. I clicked down the kickstand and tucked the bike beside the mailbox.

"Do you want to take your helmet off?" I asked, but Eddie shook his head. "Maybe that's best," I said.

He gazed into the field of corn that lined the road. I pulled out my cell phone.

"Who're you calling?" Eddie asked.

"Just…someone," I said. I dialed the phone number for the *Stockton Star* and requested Jonah Gray's extension. I knew from reading his Web site that he often worked Sundays, preparing for Monday's paper.

"Jonah Gray," he answered.

I hung up. He was at work. That was all I needed to know.

"Your friend wasn't home?" Eddie asked.

"Nope, not home." I offered Eddie my hand and we stepped onto the driveway, toward the house. The corn, on either side at shoulder level, waved in the light breeze.

"Where are we going?" Eddie asked.

"Just down a ways," I said. I squeezed his hand. The trust he had in me made me want to cry. Of course, I wouldn't have brought him there had I thought that any harm would come of it. Whatever Jonah Gray's issues were—with his stock sales or gardening—I felt certain he posed no danger to small children. Indeed, he had devoted a whole section of his site to poisonous plant identification.

At the end of the drive, the corn petered out, and a scrappy, slightly uneven yard spread up to the farmhouse. Between the drive and the yard sat a thick stump, maybe two feet high. I wondered if that was all that remained of the sixty-five-year-old black oak that Jonah had declared lost a year earlier. Off the front of the house, a wide porch extended, with a bench swing and an American flag that fell limply from a wall-mounted pole. The place looked as if it had seen a lot of living, not all of it easy.

"What are we looking for?" Eddie asked me.

I didn't answer. I didn't know how to explain it to him, or what I would say were Mrs. Gray to spot us poking around her lawn. I concentrated on walking as though I belonged there.

I noticed Eddie frowning.

"What's wrong?" I asked.

"It's boring. There're no toys," he said.

He was right. I looked around the lawn and porch, and saw that nothing on it pointed to the life of a child. I knew that Jonah had claimed an Ethan Gray as his dependent. But given how recently Jonah had married, I realized that Ethan was likely an infant, not yet old enough to enjoy an outdoor jungle gym or soccer goal. I wondered why he never mentioned a son on his Web site.

"What's that?" Eddie asked, lurching toward the back of the house.

I liked that he believed that I knew where I was going. He tugged me around the side of the farmhouse, past the huge stump and back toward an area out of sight from the driveway. Behind the house, the lawn grew more lush, with a flagstone walkway and bird feeders strung between a pair of tall trees. At the edge of the lawn stood a shiny glass-walled greenhouse.

Eddie ran up to it and peered through the windows. "At the zoo, they had a place like this for butterflies," he said. Then he pushed away from the glass and wiped his hands. "It's just plants," he said, not trying to hide his disappointment.

"Plants can be cool, too," I said.

He shrugged, no longer as willing to believe me.

"Did you know that the oldest living thing on earth is a plant? Well, a tree. Right here in California."

"No way."

"It's true. There are bristlecone pines in the White Mountains that are four and a half thousand years old. That's like forty-five centuries. That's like dinosaur old."

"That's old," Eddie said.

"In a way, plants are like very quiet, green animals."

"Like a snake?"

"Sure. A vine is like a snake, right?"

"But snakes move."

"Yes, but, well, you like bananas, right?"

"I like bananas."

"Some banana trees can grow an inch a day. It's true. The farmers who grow them swear that they can hear them creaking and stretching."

"Scary," Eddie said. "How come you know so much about plants?"

"I don't, actually. But I've been reading a lot about them recently."

I wished I could identify what was growing inside the greenhouse. Through the glass I saw rows of hanging ferns, flowers as big as grapefruits, spiny cacti, thorny palm trees, slick-looking leaves in the shape of hearts, trees that looked like miniature willows, trays of moss and grass and what appeared to be water lilies. There were bags labeled Potting Soil and bags labeled Loam and Mulch and Peat and Sand. There were gardening gloves and trowels and pruning shears and little rakes. It looked like a magician's storehouse.

"Hello there," a man said.

I jumped at the voice and wheeled around, searching for its source.

An older man headed toward us, down the path alongside the house. He limped and listed a bit to the left. Eddie immediately took my hand and tucked in behind me.

"Hello," I said. I wasn't sure what to do next. I was obviously trespassing. Front yards were one thing. Backyards were something else entirely.

I figured I could outrun the man, should it come to that—but I was loath to panic Eddie, and I had to assume that carrying a five-year-old would slow me down. As I stood there, considering my escape path, I noticed that the old man hadn't demanded to know what I was doing there.

"I haven't seen," he said, then got stuck on the word. "Seen, seen." He seemed to be struggling to pick the right one. "You. In years."

"Excuse me?"

"You're a Potter girl," he said.

"This is my aunt," Eddie said.

"No, I'm…" I started to say but petered off. The man was too old to be Jonah Gray, but that didn't mean that I wanted to explain myself. "We were biking and we got a little lost," I said. "Then we saw the greenhouse."

"We're lost?" Eddie whispered.

"You live…you live there. Across that field," the man insisted, pointing through the corn.

"She lives in Oakland," Eddie said.

The old man didn't appear to have heard him. "What's your name, little one?"

"Eddie," he said. He no longer seemed scared.

"Do you live here?" I asked.

"This is my home," the old man said. "I'm not going anywhere. I don't have to. I've paid…paid, paid…bills."

"It looks like you're quite a gardener," I said.

He looked at the back lawn, then shook his head. "Allergies."

I wanted to ask him more—who he was and if Jonah's wife or son were around, but I didn't want Eddie to realize how little I knew. I'd gone far enough and I didn't want to push it. It was time to return to my own family.

"We should get back. Our family is waiting."

"Your family," he said. "You say hello. For me."

I could tell that he still meant the Potters. "I will," I promised.

"How's your father?" the man asked.

"He's okay," I said. It didn't seem to matter whether I was answering for my own father or for the unknown Mr. Potter.

"Don't blame him for getting old," he said. "It happens. To the best of us."

"I won't," I assured him.

"Don't be a stranger. I'll mix lemonade next time. Always nice to have the company of a young lady and gentleman," he said, his words at last running smooth.

"See you," I said, though I didn't actually expect that I would again. Eddie and I made our way back up the driveway. The man waved and turned back toward the house.

"He was nice," Eddie said.

At the end of the drive, I strapped my nephew into the trailer, then climbed back onto the bike.

"There you are," my mother said, seeing us arrive. "I was beginning to worry."

"We had an adventure!" Eddie announced.

"Is that right?" my father asked. "An adventure?" He was back at the table, less wan than when we had pedaled off. He patted the bench beside him and Eddie sat down.

"We met a man with a limp, only he wasn't scary and I didn't point," Eddie said.

"How considerate," my father said.

I looked at my father. The old man had been right—I couldn't blame him for getting old or sick. It just happened.

"Do you need anything, Dad? A drink? Something to eat?"

He reached out and I gave him my hand.

"Nothing," he said.

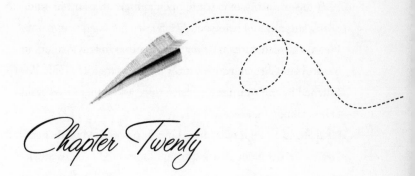

Chapter Twenty

ON MONDAY MORNING, AS THE MAILROOM ATTENDANT made his rounds, a letter landed on my desk. The return address read 530 Horsehair Road.

A bolt of panic. Had the old man figured me out? Had he realized who I was and tracked me down? Did Jonah Gray know that I'd been snooping around his house?

But then relief. The letter had been postmarked that past Friday. It was in the mail before I'd gone to Stockton and trespassed. I breathed a little easier.

Dear Ms. Gardner, Jonah Gray had written. I recognized his handwriting from his return.

I don't mean any disrespect when I say that I'm not exactly looking forward to my upcoming interview with you, but I am not writing only to tell you that. It was just brought to my attention that certain readers of a Web site that I maintain have taken it upon themselves to contact you on my behalf. I want to apologize for any inconvenience this may have caused.

It was probably an error in my judgment to post the initial notification letter I received, the one that included your name. Please know that it was never my intention for my readers to harass you. Gardeners are simply a passionate lot. While I'm touched by their initiative, I have since asked them to refrain from calling you about my audit.

It's been a tough year in the Gray household. My father suffered a stroke about a year ago, and I uprooted back to Stockton to take care of him. I'm not quite sure why I'm telling you this. Perhaps to explain that I haven't been taking care of everything else as well as I might have. But he's my father and you do what you've got to do. Apparently, in this phase of life, that means trying to keep him comfortable, safe and in his own house. Who knew such basic needs could be so difficult to fulfill?

Ethan Gray was no child, I suddenly realized. It all made sense. Ethan Gray was Jonah's father; 530 Horsehair was Ethan's house. The unexplained medical expenses, the donation to the VFW, even the AARP membership dues that I'd found confusing—they slipped into place in this now more rational universe.

That was why he had left Tiburon, left his job, sold the boat. He hadn't run away. He had run toward. He had run to help his father.

I thought about the old man in the garden, about his limp (from the stroke), his halting speech (aphasia, I could now deduce), his determination to stay in his home. This was the father Jonah Gray hadn't known as a child, the man he had both hated and found a way to forgive. For a second time, Jonah had upended his life to go live with him. Strange how a simple explanation can change one's perspective.

There wasn't much more to Jonah's letter.

But my family issues aren't your concern and are not meant as an excuse. My audit interview takes place next Wednesday. Whatever the result, it'll be over after that.

Yours, Jonah Gray

I looked at my calendar. Heaven help me, he was right. I'd forgotten that his interview was on Wednesday, just two days away. I searched for Susan's documentation on the Gray return, but that seemed to be one piece of his file she hadn't returned. Even if I did nothing else for the next two days, it would be a push to finish my analysis in time.

"Knock, knock."

Jeff and Ricardo were standing, like a bar chart, one tall, one short, at the entrance of my cubicle.

"Oh, hi. What are you two doing?" I asked.

"Are we still on for dinner tonight?" Jeff asked.

"Dinner?" I repeated.

"It's that meal at the end of the day," Ricardo said. "I'm sure you know some obscure fact about its history."

During the course of our initial date at Hunter's, Jeff had mentioned going out to dinner on Monday. I'd just forgotten it, but now, here it was, the Monday in question. No wonder the guy requested definite affirmatives. Maybe I was a flaky Californian after all.

"Seven o'clock tonight?" Jeff asked. "That's what you'd suggested."

"Where are you two lovebirds going to go?" Ricardo asked.

I ignored him. "Seven o'clock," I agreed, though it meant that I wouldn't be able to work late. There was always Tuesday night.

Jeff gave me a big smile before leaving. But once he and Ricardo were gone, I felt myself frowning. Jeff was a nice guy. And I had enjoyed kissing him at the tail end of our first date. But I wondered what that simple action had gotten me into.

I supposed that I had already made my choice. I was going on my second date, and after that, perhaps a third. I'd sworn to Martina that Jonah Gray was behind me and my date with Jeff was meant to prove that. But now I wondered why I'd been so quick, going from sixty to zero, as Martina said, in just a few minutes. If only Jonah had written me a few days earlier.

My phone didn't ring for the rest of the day. It rang only twice all told. Once was my mother, and once was Martina, asking which flavor of jerky had been my favorite. The calls from irate and protective gardeners in Jonah Gray's army had stopped coming in. He'd called them off, all right. And I was surprised to find myself a little sorry that he had.

Throughout the day, as I prepared for Jonah's audit, my mind wandered back to Stockton, peering in the windows of that old farmhouse, focused on a man whose world wasn't even mine to reach for. I couldn't stop imagining how our conversation would go on Wednesday. What would he say? What would I say? How would his laugh sound in person? Would his eyes light up? Would we speak of Roanoke? Or the Catalina?

And even if he turned out to be a jerk, a bore, evasive or defensive, that, too, would be something. As he had written in his letter, whatever happened, it would all be over and done with soon enough. And all that had drawn me to him—the phone calls, the postings, the life revealed in his returns and his words—all those things could be packed up and put away, and I could get on with it, with the rest of my life.

Chapter Twenty-One

IT WAS JUST ANOTHER FACE-TO-FACE. I TOLD MYSELF that I wasn't hungry. That's why I hadn't been able to eat breakfast. I needed new clothes. That's why nothing I pulled from the closet looked right. I drank too much coffee. That's why my heart started pounding when the receptionist called to say that my eleven o'clock appointment had arrived.

I made my way to the lobby, focused on my breathing. I wanted to portray steady. In charge. Sane. Not a man-hater or a bean counter or a trespasser. But when I surveyed the reception area, my heart sank a little. No one in there looked the way I thought Jonah was going to look. Though I still hadn't seen a picture of him, the act of combing through a man's financials always created a clear mental image. I figured I'd know him when I saw him. But there in the reception area, I wasn't sure what I saw.

Three of the people waiting were men of around Jonah's age. One sat with his eyes closed, head leaning against the wall behind. He was dressed entirely in denim—shirt, jeans and cowboy hat, all the same deep-rinse indigo. I hadn't figured Jonah Gray to be an all-denim guy, and if he were to wear jeans, that they would be faded, with smudges of dirt permanently ground into the knees.

The second guy was dressed nicely enough. Smart, flat-front twill pants and an ironed button-down. But he was twitchy, nervous. He wiped his palms on his pants again and again, smoothing out a wrinkle that wasn't there. He looked around the room, caught my eye and quickly looked away, and all the while, his knees bumped up and down to an uneven beat. That didn't square with my impression of Jonah either. The overgrown house. The relaxed and steady tone of his voice. The way he wrote about gardening through the dusk, lost in the smell of dirt and roots and leaves, until he realized that he was pruning by moonlight. Could this possibly be the same guy?

And then there was the third man. He sat still, quiet, unassuming at first glance. But a silent anger seethed from every pore, from the clench of his jaw and the way he held tight to a can of soda, squeezing the round-ness from the aluminum. He barely moved, but the undercurrent of rage that radiated from him was so bitter, I found myself stepping back.

"Jonah Gray?" I said, too quietly to be heard. I didn't want any of the three of them to stand. And yet, I had to know. "Gray?" I said more loudly.

A woman stood. "Here," she said.

I watched her approach, wondering whether someone was playing a trick on me. Was Ricardo in on this?

"I'll be representing Mr. Gray today," she explained. "I'm his CPA. My name's Linda." She looked more like a pageant winner than any CPA I'd ever seen, with coiffed hair and perfectly arched brows.

"He didn't come with you?" I asked.

She looked around the waiting room, then back at me. "No," she said. "He's not required to. But you must know that."

I was relieved and disappointed at once. I motioned for Linda to follow me. "So Mr. Gray decided to send a professional," I said, as we headed for my cubicle. "He's not scared of me, is he?"

"Excuse me?" Linda asked.

"Nothing," I said. It was a question that I wasn't sure I wanted answered.

"Do you know what I'm going to ask about?" I quizzed her, once we were sitting at my table, each of us with our papers arranged.

"I have an idea," she said.

"In Jonah's—I mean, Mr. Gray's—last return, he neglected to declare some significant capital gains from the liquidation of a retirement account."

"It was a lot of money," Linda said, nodding.

"Are you admitting that your client knowingly filed a fraudulent tax return?"

"Fraudulent, no. Inaccurate, sure. And that's not the half of it."

That wasn't the way most CPAs spoke to me. They didn't get chummy. They stuck to the facts and gave away as little information as possible. And apparently she wasn't finished.

"Poor guy," she said. "He was totally fucked over. Excuse my French. But royally fucked."

That definitely wasn't the way most CPAs spoke.

"Fucked?" I asked. As luck would have it, Fred Collins was passing my cubicle at that moment. He stopped, took a step back and looked inside.

"Royally," Linda said, offering him a Miss America-quality smile.

Fred smiled back, looking more confused than anything. He edged away.

"Here's the long and short," Linda went on. "Jonah's wife, Pilar, she's Argentine. Never really took to the States."

"It sounds like you know him pretty well," I said. Why did I say that? What did I care how well the pretty CPA knew him? The man was married.

"I've been friends with the Grays for a long time," she said. "Anyhow, Ethan—"

"Jonah's father? With the stroke?"

She looked at me as though she didn't appreciate being interrupted. "Right. He had the stroke last July. Plowed, full bore, into that poor oak tree before he could get to the hospital. Thank goodness a neighbor found him. That's when Jonah convinced Pilar to move to Stockton. Temporarily, of course. So Jonah could take care of Ethan. Well, Pilar, I only met her once or twice, but I mean, San Francisco was way too stifling for her. So you can imagine her reaction to Stockton."

"And the stock sales are related to the move?" I asked, in case Fred lurked nearby. I hoped to sound at least somewhat professional.

"Let me finish so you get the full picture. So Pilar left."

"Pilar left?" I repeated. "You mean, Jonah's separated?"

"Not separated. Divorced. I think it was final last month," Linda said. "She left about four, five months after they moved to Stockton. Left Jonah, left the States, hightailed it back to Argentina."

"So Jonah's _not_ married?" I asked, making sure that I understood. "Because his return said single and then married and I just didn't know—" I was afraid to feel relief before it was warranted.

"What did I just say? He's divorced. She left in January, just after New Year's. Poor guy—he was a wreck. Came home from work one day and poof, she's gone. Not only that, but she had cleaned out his investment accounts back around Christmastime. The girl faked a whole, happy holiday season just to buy herself enough time to get home. It's the sort of thing that gives women a bad reputation. She should have been an actress."

I was reminded of the hostess at Hunter's. Some people were very good at faking it.

"The thing was, if she had told him she was unhappy, Jonah would probably have given her the money."

"Of course he would have," I said.

Linda looked at me strangely.

"I mean, who wouldn't, right?" I tried to sound less giddy.

"Anyhow, with the move to Stockton and forwarded mail and all the hell with Ethan and the new newspaper job, he didn't put it all together for a few months—after he'd filed. He didn't think he had any stock sales to report. Talk about your marriage penalty."

"I'll admit that I was surprised when his replacement return came back with the Married box marked. He never mentions his wife."

"You've spoken to him?" Linda asked. "He told me that he wrote to you, but he said that the two of you had never spoken."

I felt my cheeks go red. I couldn't admit that I was Jeffrine. "No," I said.

"What do you mean, never mentions her?"

"On his Web site," I said.

"Oh, that. Right. Man, the people who follow that are so crazy about him. It's cute. A little weird, but cute."

"I bet he's got a beautiful garden," I said.

Linda seemed to remember where she was. "Anyhow, I've worked out a payment schedule, to cover what he owes plus penalties." She handed me a sheet of paper. "I told him that we might be able to ne-gotiate something a little more amenable."

"Maybe—"

"But he wanted to make sure everything was paid in full. Believe me, he wants this whole thing behind him. This audit has been nothing but a reminder of Pilar and a terrible year."

"I hope it hasn't been *that* bad," I said.

Linda looked at me as if I were unhinged. "Being audited by the IRS? Hello? You've got to realize that it's a nightmare."

"I guess." I felt like a total dork. I wanted her to say, "You're right. He should have come in person. You and he would really like each other." But she wasn't going to say that. She wasn't the unhinged one.

"So why do you think she left?" I asked, pretending to look at her proposed payment schedule.

"Pilar?" Linda paused for a moment before answering. "I wouldn't tell him this, but I think there was someone else. There had to be. Don't get me wrong—she was plenty jealous that Jonah would drop everything to take care of his father. He even donated this beautiful little boat he had to the people who helped Ethan after the stroke, when he could barely get a word out."

"How is he doing?"

"Jonah?"

"No, the father. Ethan."

"Better. Being at home has helped. And having Jonah there to take care of him."

"Were you surprised that he would just pack up and move to Stockton like that?"

Linda frowned, as if she was thinking about it. "He's not very close with his sisters, so Ethan is really the only family he has," she finally said.

"But after what happened when Jonah was a kid—"

"How do you know that?" Linda asked abruptly.

"Research," I said.

"I'm always surprised at what you people can dig up. Ethan wasn't the greatest father around. Not at the beginning. But they both came around. I think they're a lot alike, actually. So when Ethan had the stroke, it wasn't really a question of 'if' but 'how soon.'" Linda stood. "Anyway, here's my card."

Linda Potter
Certified Public Accountant
Stockton, California

"Audit a specialty"

"You're a Potter girl," I said, more to myself than to her. But of course, she was standing in front of me.

"I'm sorry?" She looked almost alarmed. "Do you know my family?"

"No," I said. "It's just something I say. You're a Potter girl. I'm a Gardner girl. It's nothing."

She looked at me for what seemed like a long time. "I trust you'll let me know your thoughts on the payment schedule and if you need any additional information," she finally said.

I had nothing to lose. "He's one of the good ones, isn't he?" I asked.

"Who?"

"Jonah. I mean, Mr. Gray."

Now I'd surprised her. She sputtered a little before answering. "He's one of the best. Why?"

"Numbers tell you a lot, but they can't tell you everything," I said. She smiled. A CPA could appreciate that.

I didn't hear from Linda Potter again. My job was to sign off on the facts of the audit. Restitution was handled elsewhere. And so, once she left my office, I sat at my desk, not sure what to do. Could it really be over?

"Of course you'll move on," Martina soothed, over beers that evening at the Escape Room.

"Of course I will," I said. "I guess I should be glad that my first impression was accurate."

"You sound really glad."

"I mean, I pegged him pretty quickly. I knew he seemed like a good guy. All those people couldn't have been wrong. Of course, now with the audit over, I don't have any reason to contact him again."

"No reason."

"Are you just repeating me?" I asked. "That's obnoxious."

Martina blinked. "I'm not sure what you want me to say. I'm not sure you ever really wanted to meet him. Or anyone, for that matter."

"How can you say that? Why wouldn't I want to meet him? And I've met Jeff, haven't I? I've got a third date with him on Friday."

"But you've always got a reason why it doesn't work. And it's never your doing. It's your job or the work thing or bad timing."

"Sometimes it *is* my job. You saw how quickly Kevin ran out of here when he saw my business card."

"So get a new job. But you won't, because you don't like change any more than Gene did. Why else would you keep agreeing to meet me here?"

"The Escape Room is convenient," I said. "And it's comfortable."

"What's comfortable about it? The bathrooms are gross. The peanuts are stale. And have you ever actually found a date in here?"

I had to admit that I hadn't.

"I think you like knowing what you're going to find in here and that no one's ever going to challenge you. God knows, you're in little danger of meeting anyone here who might matter. And if you do, you chase them away."

"You're saying there's something wrong with me."

"There's nothing wrong with you. You just need to let go a little. Put yourself out there. Dive in. Call him. Or don't. But don't let an audit decide. An audit is not fate."

Chapter Twenty-Two

I THOUGHT ABOUT WHAT MARTINA HAD SAID AS I drove to Piedmont the next day. I thought about a lot of things—how Jonah had managed to forgive his father, how Marcus had managed to forgive ours, what movie Jeff would suggest we see later that night (a third date established over the course of our Monday dinner).

Marcus and Blake were sitting in the kitchen when I arrived, finishing lunch. Blake was explaining what tattoo he wanted to get, and Marcus was advising Blake to wait a few years, or at least until Marcus was out of the house, so that he wouldn't catch hell for it.

Marcus and Blake were getting along famously. Blake lit up when he hung out with Marcus—and even when he spoke about him. I had called earlier in the week and caught my littlest brother on his way out to band practice.

"He's so cool," Blake had said.

"And he's good with Dad?"

"Oh, yeah. As far as I can tell. I'm not a doctor."

"And what about with Mom?"

Blake had hesitated. "They're not usually around at the same time."

"How so?"

"You know, Mom usually runs errands while Marcus is checking on Dad. Or when he brings Dad to an appointment, Mom will stay home. Or he'll go out and Mom and Dad will watch television. Marcus says that there should always be someone with Dad because he's having trouble with his balance."

"That sounds like a good idea," I'd said.

Indeed, when I came in on them in the kitchen, one of the first things Marcus asked was whether I'd be around for the evening.

"Actually, I have a date," I said. "Do you need me to be around?"

"No, I can reschedule."

"What about Blake?" I asked.

"I've got a dress rehearsal tonight and I can't skip it. Who's your date? The garden guy?"

"You don't know him."

"What happened to the garden guy?" Blake asked.

"Nothing happened."

"That's too bad," Marcus said. "I've always found gardeners to be good people."

"Really? Thanks," Blake said.

"He said gardeners, you dope, not Gardners," I said.

Blake laughed, realizing his mistake. It was the first time I'd heard that sound since before my father's diagnosis. It made me wish that I saw Blake more. But the school year had just begun and with it, his sophomore year. Marching-band practices were already taking their toll in the evening hours, and once football season began, in just a couple of weeks, performances would keep him tied up on weekends. And though he didn't talk much about her to me, Marcus had told me that Blake's spare time was often spent with Nancy, the baton-twirling hickey bestower.

My mother appeared in the kitchen at that point. "Sasha, could I see you in the bedroom?"

"Sure," I said, letting her guide me out. She pulled me down the hallway quickly. "Did I do something wrong?"

"It's your father," she said.

When we rounded the corner into the master bedroom, I saw my father on my parents' bed, his eyes closed. At first glance, he looked asleep. Then I noticed that his face was constricted, as if he were in pain.

"What's wrong with him?" I asked.

"I think maybe it's a seizure," my mother said. She reached out to hold his hand.

"I'll get Marcus," I said, turning to leave.

"He looks better now. I'm sure he'll be fine."

"But he's all knotted up. What if it's serious? We should tell Marcus."

"First help me move him into the hallway," my mother said.

"What are you talking about?"

"I feel strange having that boy in my bedroom."

I couldn't believe that I had heard her correctly. "He's not a boy, Mom," I said. "He's a nurse. He's Dad's nurse. And he lives here now."

"I don't feel right about it," she said.

"Then you move Dad. But move him out for good, because Marcus will eventually have to come in here. You heard Ed. It's only going to get harder."

"That brother of mine," she said. "He had this all planned. Getting Marcus in this house. He knew I couldn't say no."

"Is Marcus doing a good job?"

My mother didn't answer.

"Well? Has Dr. Fisher said that Marcus *isn't* doing a good job?"

"No," she finally said.

"Stop making this about you then," I told her and went to get him.

By the time Marcus was able to examine him, my father had begun to regain consciousness. Still, Marcus called Dr. Fisher, who recommended that Dad be taken to the hospital for tests.

"I can bring him," Marcus offered.

"No, we'll all go," my mother said.

So Marcus and I got my father settled into the Truckster, then came back inside to see what was keeping my mother.

"Blake, are you ready yet?" she was calling down the hall as we walked in.

"For what?" I heard Blake yell back. He was still in his bedroom.

"We're all going to the hospital," she said.

"I'm not going," I heard him say.

"What?" My mother glanced at Marcus before marching off toward Blake's room. I could hear her knock on his door. "May I come in, please?" she asked.

They were in Blake's room for a few minutes, before the door opened again. A moment later, she appeared in the front hall, alone. Her face looked pinched. "Blake will be staying here," she said, her voice clipped. "We might as well go."

"Is everything okay?" Marcus asked.

"It's fine," she said. "Apparently his practice is more important than his father."

"Do you want me to have a talk with him?"

"No thank you, Marcus. My son and I will have a longer discussion later."

In a romantic relationship, sometimes you can peg the beginning of the end. There was the fight I had with one of my college boyfriends, the one we never quite got over, about who would clean the hibachi we had bought together. During the fight, I had grown so angry that I told him to go screw himself. We stayed together for a month or two afterward, but we never recovered, not truly. Weeks later, when he finally called it quits, I knew that hibachi fight had done the damage.

With my dad's cancer, that first round of seizures woke us all to the fact that six months may have been optimistic, that we may already have been in the home stretch. My parents had been planning one last trip to Europe, but by the time my father was discharged, three days later, they no longer spoke of it. Dr. Fisher sent my mother home with hospital-bed brochures in her purse and a poster that mapped the human brain, so that we could visualize the region where new lesions had been found.

When Marcus, Mom and I returned that evening from checking my father into the hospital, Blake was dressed in his drum-major uniform, waiting for the honk of Nancy's horn to spirit him away to practice. He looked as if he'd been crying, though I knew he'd never admit as much to me. I was glad, at that moment, that Marcus was staying in the house and that he'd be there when Blake got home. I'd never been an angry fifteen-year-old boy. I didn't know what to say.

I called Jeff and begged off the movie. "It's not a good time. I'm just going to stay here and watch television or something," I told him.

"You're not all alone, are you?"

"My mother and Marcus are here."

"Marcus. Right. The tats man. You don't have any tattoos, do you?"

"No," I said. "Would that be a problem?"

"Maybe we could do something tomorrow night," Jeff suggested. "I'd love to see you."

In the den, I drank a beer and Marcus sipped club soda. I could hear my mother in the kitchen, but I couldn't muster the energy to offer assistance. Maybe she wouldn't join me and Marcus in the den, but that was her choice.

"How's my old room treating you?" I asked.

"It's fine," Marcus said. "That stuffed bear is a little creepy."

"Hey, it's not mine."

"Blake said it wasn't his."

"My mom bought it when she redecorated in there. I figure it's supposed to symbolize children."

"Are you kidding?" Marcus asked.

"How could I make that up? I imagine it's pretty different here than your place in Sacramento."

"A bit."

"What sort of place do you live in up there anyway? Do you have roommates?"

"Why? Do you think I live in some rat hole?"

I felt my cheeks redden. "I just realized I didn't know what you gave up when you moved down here."

He softened. "Not much," he said. "I've got some friends. I ride around on the bike. I hang out."

"You got a girlfriend?"

He shook his head.

"Really? You?"

He just shrugged.

"Boyfriend?" I asked, realizing all I didn't know.

"You got it right the first time," he said, smiling a little at my discomfort. "There was this physical therapist where I was working. But now I'm down here, and it wasn't a serious thing anyhow. I take it you're dating this Jeff guy?"

"I don't know. It's only been a couple of dates."

"But do you think you'll start dating him? I'm sure he wants to."

I shrugged. "The garden guy, he moved from Tiburon to Stockton to take care of his father. Maybe I should have been willing to make that effort."

"And leave your job? That doesn't make any sense. What's wrong with the guy's father?" Marcus asked.

"Stroke."

"That's hard, too."

"Why aren't you mad?" I asked.

"At you?"

"At my—at your dad. At our dad. How can you just forgive him? I grew up with the guy and haven't managed that."

"I didn't just forgive him."

"But you're here," I pointed out.

"It took a long while and a good deal of convincing. And he made some overtures. And Ed."

"That didn't seem weird? That it was my mother's brother who...you know." I petered off.

"Ed's definition of family is expansive."

"He rounds up," I said, nodding.

"Jacob did a lot of apologizing. I know that was hard for him," Marcus said.

"He's not very good at it," I agreed.

"And he asked me to come."

"He did? I thought it was Ed's idea."

"Guess again. He knew the strain it might cause, would cause. But he asked me to consider it and I did."

"When did you decide that you wanted to be a nurse?"

He looked over at me and narrowed his eyes. "Why?"

"I mean, you were working construction before."

"I've always liked to work with my hands," Marcus said.

"And I guess the surfaces are softer in nursing."

Marcus nodded. "Usually."

It struck me how differently he and I were trained to approach people. For Marcus, understanding someone professionally was literally a hands-on process. He touched, he poked, he injected and held in his arms both the sick and exhausted, as well as all sorts of emotional viscera that hid itself from view in nearly every other environment.

My job required me to approach people from afar, studying the trails of their lives, the wakes that they left in passing before I ever met them face-to-face. I didn't think I could do the sort of work Marcus did. It seemed like something that would get on you and not wash off.

"When did you decide to become a tax auditor?" he asked.

People outside the Service were always asking how I ended up there, as if they took comfort in knowing that there was a reason, something comprehensible like an accounting internship or genetic predisposition. "I blame Dad," I said. "I grew up rifling through his trash can and making collages from old 1040s. I always figured that was the start of some inescapable march toward the IRS."

"But if you'd ended up an artist, you could have said the same thing," Marcus said. "Jacob must love that you work there."

"Have you ever heard him say that?"

"No, but it's so similar—"

"Not to him, it isn't. I guess he had this idea that I'd go into business with him but—"

"But you were sane and avoided it?"

I smiled. "Something like that. I get the feeling he's never forgiven me."

"You didn't ever want to do something else? Maybe something that helped people?"

"I like to think that I help people."

"Really?" He choked a little on his drink.

"In the broad scheme of things. My job is about fairness. I pay. You pay—well, I assume you do."

"I pay," Marcus said. "You think I don't pay my taxes?"

"I didn't say that."

"I mean, it was only for, like, two years that I didn't. Now I pay."

"I want us to get along," I said to him, suddenly, without thinking.

Marcus looked surprised. He stared at the television set and said nothing for a while. Then he turned to me with the slightest smile. "We do get along," he said.

"What about you and Mom? Or you and Kurt?"

"Wanting something doesn't mean getting to have it. That might be news in this neighborhood, but it's something I learned pretty early."

"You wanted to be here. You got that."

"I'm glad I can help," he said. "But this wasn't what I wanted. Believe me."

Chapter Twenty-Three

I HAD TOLD MARCUS THE TRUTH—I HADN'T EXACTLY planned on dating Jeff Hill. But it happened. Jeff had such an active mind. Maybe he wasn't the most easygoing guy around, but he was attentive. He never forgot when we were supposed to meet. He'd notice if I was having a hard day—maybe my posture told him, or the tone of my voice—and he would make a point to stop by with a soda or a bouquet of flowers. He'd notice if I came to work late or seemed tired or overwhelmed by some new hiccup in my father's health. And upon noticing, he would always offer assistance. Not that there was much he could do, really. My father's decline was steady.

What's more, Jeff was always up for seeing a movie, any movie, even one he'd never heard of. I found that I didn't mind that he insisted on bringing his own food and was particular about where in the theater we sat.

And so, after we'd been dating for three weeks, and after he'd suggested it—more than a few times, actually—it seemed appropriate to introduce him to my parents.

He arrived at Banner Hill right on time, with flowers for my mother, a handshake for my father and a respectful peck on the cheek for me.

"Where's Blake?" he asked. "I've heard so much about the little guy."

"There's a football game tonight," my mother said.

"You never told me he played," Jeff admonished me.

"He doesn't. Marching band," I told him. "You remember."

"That's right. Drums?"

"Drum major," my father corrected.

Marcus came back from a run as the four of us were sipping a round of cocktails in the living room.

"And this is Marcus," I said. "Marcus, I've told you about Jeff. Now here he is in the flesh."

"Oh sure," Marcus said. "Nice meeting you."

"So this is the famous Marcus," Jeff said. I could see him looking at the colors and swirls that ran down Marcus's bare arms.

"I don't know about famous," Marcus said.

"Are you joining us for dinner?" I asked.

I saw Marcus glance quickly at my mother. "I don't know," he said.

"Of course you are," my father said.

"Of course he is," my mother agreed, if less enthusiastically.

Marcus and my mother seemed to have reached an uneasy détente in the previous couple of weeks. Maybe they'd just grown accustomed to each other, but whatever the reason, I'd noticed that my mother no longer left the room when Marcus entered. At least, not immediately.

"What are you drinking, Marcus?" Jeff asked, heading for my parents' bar.

"Some water would be great. Thanks."

"Nothing a little more powerful? It's Friday. You've got the weekend ahead of you."

"Just water," Marcus repeated. "I work weekends."

I made my way over to Jeff and whispered in his ear. "I don't think Marcus drinks," I told him.

"Oh, I'm sorry." Jeff turned around. "You don't drink?" he asked.

"Not alcohol, no," Marcus said.

Jeff handed him a glass of water. "I'm surprised. By the looks of you, I would have thought—well, can I ask why not?"

"You can," Marcus said. "But it's not something I talk much about."

"Fair enough."

"Okay then," my mother announced, standing to shepherd us into the dining room. "Who's ready to eat?"

Halfway through dinner, it became clear that my father was poking at his meal, without eating it.

"The chops don't do it for you?" my mother asked.

"I'm not hungry," my father said. "Y'all keep on eating. Go ahead. Eat."

"You're not feeling nauseated, are you?" Marcus asked.

Jeff looked alarmed and perceptibly pushed his chair back from the table, as if he were imagining my father vomiting across it.

"I'm just not hungry," my father said. "Lola dear, it all looks great."

"You can't even see it," my mother said.

"Dad stopped seeing in color around the time he started with the seizures," I told Jeff. "Now everything's gray to him. Isn't that right, Dad?"

"I can smell the colors," my father said.

"Speaking of colors," Jeff said to Marcus. I could tell that he wanted to move the discussion off food and nausea. "I couldn't help but notice your tattoos. That's quite a collection."

Marcus looked at his arms and nodded. "Are you a fan of the art form?"

"Do they actually call it an art form?" Jeff asked. "I mean, here in the States?"

"Some people do," Marcus said. He looked as if he was wondering where Jeff was headed. I was wondering the same thing.

"I could never get one. I don't like needles," Jeff said. "You're not worried about the needles?"

"I'm a nurse," Marcus said. "I'm not scared of needles."

"Not the prick. The cleanliness."

Marcus frowned. "I'm not shooting up, if that's what you're getting at."

"Oh, no, that's not—" Jeff began.

"So Jeff, I understand that you work in the file room," my father cut in.

"The archives, actually," Jeff said. He sounded relieved to discuss work.

"Archives," my father repeated. "Aren't archives mostly collections of old files?"

"There are some files in there, yes."

"Like I said, the file room."

"It's a bit more than that, actually," Jeff murmured.

"Dad," I said. "Please."

"Who wants dessert?" my mother asked.

"Jeff and I will clear," I offered, standing and motioning for Jeff to follow me to the kitchen. "What was that about?" I asked him, once we were out of earshot.

"What?"

"Why were you digging at Marcus?"

"I wasn't. I was just interested."

"It came off a little like digging."

"Just look at him and look at the rest of your family. It's like that game, which one of these things is not like the other."

"He's my brother, Jeff. It doesn't matter what he looks like."

"Well, half brother. Besides, you're the one who told me that your mother and Kurt don't even want him here."

"He's taking good care of my father. That's all you need to remember."

"I didn't mean to make you mad. I never want to make you mad."

"Why don't you give Jeff a tour of the house?" my mother suggested after dessert.

"I'd enjoy that," Jeff said.

"There's not much to see, really," I said as I led him down the hallway. "You saw the dining room, the kitchen, the living room where we had drinks. That's the den. That's my father's study. Bathroom." I pointed to the door of my old bedroom, which was cracked open. "That's where I used to sleep," I said.

"So this is where it all began," Jeff said. He opened the door a little wider. Then he frowned. "What's with the motorcycle boots?"

"Marcus is staying in here now," I said.

"The decor doesn't look anything like you," Jeff said. "Except maybe that stuffed bear."

"My mother redecorated when I went off to college."

"Are you serious?" He looked appalled. "My mother would never dare touch my room."

"Clearly, my mother doesn't see it as taboo. But it doesn't matter. I've got my own house now."

"But it's the principle, baby," Jeff said. "You must have been so hurt."

"No. Not really. This is Kurt's room, over here. This is where I sleep when I stay over."

"I notice that your mother didn't redecorate in here."

"Kurt has always been a little possessive about his room."

"So you sleep in your brother's bed?"

"It's not like we haven't washed the sheets." I said.

"But where does Kurt sleep?"

"He hasn't visited much since Marcus moved in. He calls, but I don't think Lori wants him staying overnight anywhere."

"Not even at his parents' house?"

"I thought I mentioned…there was that issue recently…my brother had a fling with a waitress at my parents' anniversary party."

"That's unforgivable," Jeff said.

"I guess that's up to Lori."

"Not really. Infidelity is a breach. Of trust. Of their vows."

"Don't get me wrong, I think he's a heel, too. But I figure it's not my place to say what they can and can't work out. If Lori feels that the boys will be better served by her staying…"

"Well, I think it's unforgivable," Jeff said.

"You said that." I decided not to remind him that the embodiment of my father's infidelity was camped out in my old bedroom. He was disturbed enough by the tattoos.

After Jeff's earnest thank-yous to my parents, I walked him out to his car.

"Thanks for coming," I said.

"Thanks for inviting me."

"Are you going—"

"Shh. Do you hear that?"

I listened. "The singing?"

"Someone is definitely singing."

"I think that's our neighbor."

At that moment, Ian Maselin rounded the corner with Buddy. *"Oh, I love my Rosie child,"* he was singing. *"You got the way to make me happy."*

"Neil Diamond tonight," I said. "Usually he sings Tom Jones."

"Cracklin' Rose, you're a store-bought woman—oh, Sasha. I didn't see you there," Ian said, cutting off. He brought Buddy to the edge of the driveway.

"Hi, Mr. Maselin," I said.

"Who's your friend?" he asked.

"This is Jeff," I said. "Jeff, this is Ian Maselin. And Buddy."

"You can really carry a tune," Jeff said.

"Well, Mr. Diamond makes it easy. That song requires almost no range."

Ian Maselin had been a semiprofessional piano player in his youth, and at his annual holiday party was known to demand that his guests take part in sing-alongs while he pounded the keys. In earlier years, I'd been roped in, as had Kurt and my mother.

"So, Jeff," Ian said. "Are you Sasha's special someone?"

"Mr. Maselin, really, I—"

"I like to think I am, sir," Jeff said.

"And you came to meet the parents. Good for you. That mother of hers is really something. Did you see the garden?"

"I guess I didn't get the full tour, no," Jeff said.

"Lola's got quite a green thumb. My wife is always saying."

"Jeff was just leaving," I said.

"Say no more," Mr. Maselin said. "Unless you're passing out good-night kisses. No? Well, come on, Buddy. Let's get a move on." Ian and Buddy wandered off. Not too long after they had disappeared from sight, the singing started up again.

"I'll take a good-night kiss," Jeff said. He leaned in, and I wanted to be there. But my mind was a mess. I was dating Jeff, so I was supposed to want to kiss him. But I was also irked with him, with his clumsy reaction to Marcus, with the way he had clearly judged my family lacking in some essential way. I was the only one allowed to judge my family.

At the same time, I wondered where I was going to find the energy to put it all in perspective. I didn't think I had it in me. And most of all, I was tired and just wanted to forget all about the evening. I just wanted to be dating Jeff—well, I was moderately sure I wanted that—and that meant kissing him long enough to let the rest of my life drift away. My father's illness, my mother's sour attitude, my older brother's resentments. I took a breath and met Jeff's lips with my own. I concentrated on kissing him back. But I couldn't shut out Ian Maselin's baritone voice as he made his way down the street.

"Cracklin' Rosie, make me a smile. Girl if it lasts for an hour, that's all right. We got all night. To set the world right. Find us a dream that don't ask no question, yeah."

Chapter Twenty-Four

ALL IN ALL, I THOUGHT JEFF'S INTRODUCTION HAD
gone well enough—at least until the next day. My mother and I were
out on the patio. Out of the blue, she stopped her pruning and
looked over at me.

"Whatever happened to that nice man you were auditing?"

"Nice man?"

"The gardener."

"Oh, Jonah Gray?" I said. I knew that she knew his name.

"That's the one."

"Nothing. I audited him, and then he got his life back."

"Oh, sweetie, don't be so self-deprecating. I'm sure being audited
by you isn't the absolute worst thing in the world."

"Thanks for the vote of confidence."

"Why don't you give him a call?"

"What? Why? Why on earth would I ever do that?" I asked.

"Why wouldn't you?"

"Because he doesn't know me. And I don't know him. And I was
his auditor. What good could ever come of it?"

"Pay attention, Sasha. Real, fundamental connections are few and far between in life," my mother said. "Didn't you say that he had a sailboat just like that one your father once bought? That's a start."

"Besides, if you'll recall, I'm dating Jeff now."

My mother sniffed and focused on her gardenias.

"I thought you'd be relieved to see me with a man," I said.

"You did, did you?" She kept on pruning.

I waited, watching her. "You might as well say it," I finally said.

"Say what?"

"You don't like him. You don't like Jeff."

"I didn't say it. You did."

"But it's true, isn't it?"

"He's fine, dear."

"Why don't you like him?"

My mother put down her shears and looked at me. "You live your life the way you want to live it. I don't want to interfere."

My expression must have prompted her to revise.

"Okay, honestly, I'd love to interfere. I just want you to have the best, dear." She didn't say that she thought Jeff was something less than that. She didn't have to. "I'm afraid that your father's illness has begun to teach me some hard lessons," she said.

"Like?"

"Oh, I don't know. How the best thing often isn't the easiest. I know I've pushed you toward a lot of different relationships because they were there and because I don't want you to be alone all your life. But you're special, Sasha. You ought to hold out for special, too."

I knew how much my mother enjoyed her meddling, so I was surprised to hear her admit that it might have been ill-advised. She really must have been doing some hard thinking. "You don't think Jeff is special?" I asked.

"Not in the way I mean, no."

That next week brought more of the same from Ricardo.

"So, how's it going with Jeff?" he asked.

"Fine," I said. "It's going fine. Why wouldn't it be?"

"There's a ringing endorsement."

"Really. He's nice and smart. And he makes me feel normal."

"I wonder if it's too late to set him up with Susan instead."

"What a terrible thing to say," I told him. "You don't like us together?"

Ricardo waved me off. "Whatever happened to that guy with the Web site? You stopped talking about him."

"Because I started dating Jeff," I said.

"Do you keep in touch with him?"

"I don't keep in touch with anyone I've audited. No auditor does."

"What about Collins?"

"Fred Collins? I don't know what you're talking about."

"I liked that bean guy," Ricardo said. "He got you all revved up."

"Maybe," I agreed.

"He was different and different is good," he said. "For you. I mean, you're already different, so it makes sense."

"That's exactly what Jeff lets me forget," I said.

After Ricardo left, I sat there, staring at my phone a while. I told myself not to think too much before picking up the handset. I told myself that I could always hang up. I told myself I just wanted to hear his voice.

He answered. "Jonah Gray."

"Jonah?" I felt my heart pounding.

"Yes?"

"It's, uh, Jeffrine. Hill. From the—"

"IRS, I remember." He sounded as friendly as ever, as if no time had passed. "How have you been? Where are you calling from?"

"Work," I told him. I leaned back in my chair and reveled in the sound of his voice.

"No, I mean, where are you working now?"

"The same place. I'm still at the Service."

"Really?"

"Why?" I asked.

"Because I called there. I asked for you."

I flew upright. "What? When?"

"Just the other day. I saw this documentary on horses and I thought of the whole hair-versus-fur issue and that got me to thinking of you. I didn't know your exact number or anything, but I called and, well, it was a little weird actually."

"Weird how? How weird?" I heard the panic rise in my voice.

"I was put through to a guy named Jeff Hill. Maybe they didn't hear me say Jeffrine."

"Jeff Hill?"

"You know him?"

"I think he's an archivist," I said, wincing at myself.

"Yeah, the archives. He said he didn't know any Jeffrine in your building."

"You talked to him?" My mind was racing. "Well, he's new," I said. "And I moved, I mean, my desk did. My cubicle."

"Does that mean you're not under the thumb of Ms. Gardner anymore?"

"Uh, yeah. I mean, I still help out over there."

"I shouldn't be too rough on her. I know she's having family issues."

"Family issues?"

"I understand her father isn't well," he said.

"You know that?" How would he know that?

"Don't get me wrong—I can sympathize. In fact, I wrote her this letter before my audit and told her about all this stuff with my dad. I wonder if she got that."

"I'm sure she did."

"Anyway, enough about the Gardners. Is everyone in the Hill family doing okay, Jeffrine? No run-ins with manatees?"

"We're surviving."

"It's funny, your name being so similar to that guy in the archives. I thought maybe you were related or something. He's not your husband, is he?"

"No!" It came out more forcefully that I'd intended. "I'm not— I mean—"

"You okay over there?" It was Cliff, calling through the wall.

"I'm fine, Cliff," I called back.

"So Jeff and Jeffrine, that's just a coincidence, then," Jonah said.

"Exactly. A coincidence. He's not my—we're not related or anything."

"I'll be right there," Jonah said.

"Here? In Oakland?" I ran my fingers through my hair.

Jonah laughed. "I'm sorry. I was talking to my editor," he said. "I've got to jump into a meeting now. Were you calling for any reason in particular? More looper issues?"

"No, those went away. My mother is eternally grateful."

"Excellent. It's always helpful to have someone's mother in my camp."

"Believe me, she's in your camp. I think she lives there."

"I'm not getting audited again, am I? Is that why you're calling?"

"Not that I know of."

"Because my accountant is supposed to be taking care of all the paperwork," he said. "I asked whether she met you at the interview, but she said that it was just her and Sasha Gardner."

"Just the two of them, yes."

"I kind of wish you'd been in the room. I get the impression you know my file at least as well as Ms. Gardner does."

"Probably about the same."

"They're buzzing me again. I should get to this meeting," he said. "So you're not calling with any particular request or news? Not that you have to."

"I just—" I paused. I didn't know what to say. Suddenly, it felt as if this were finally and definitely goodbye. "I just wanted to make sure you got through the audit okay."

"That's so kind of you. You're a good egg, Jeffrine. I feel like you get me," he said. "That's weird, huh?"

I didn't want to get off the phone. "Is it?"

"I'm coming!" he yelled to someone in his office. "I'm sorry. They're waiting for me."

"Sure. No, of course. Okay. Well, goodbye."

I hung up the phone and turned to the wall so that no one who passed would see my eyes well up. I sat there for a few moments, at first willing myself not to cry and, finding that ineffective, willing myself to stop. I would miss him. I already missed him.

"Oh, baby," I heard Jeff say.

I spun around and he was there. He walked around to my side of the desk and lifted me out of the chair into an embrace. He smoothed back my hair and shushed into it.

"It's your father, isn't it? I know. I know."

I nodded because it seemed the easiest thing to do. Maybe not the best, but the easiest.

"Just let it out," he said. "Go ahead and wipe your nose on this sweater. I've been meaning to throw it out anyway."

Chapter Twenty-Five

MY FATHER'S ILLNESS EXPRESSED ITSELF IN THE STRANGEST ways. The radiation therapy had slowed the march of lesions across his brain, but hadn't stopped them. And so in addition to the phantom smells he would announce—roses once, coffee, rotten eggs—he suffered continued headaches, a narrowing of his visual field, and sometimes rapid mood cycles and shifts in energy.

He had begun to lose weight again, which worried Dr. Fisher, who wanted to keep my father strong for the chemotherapy still ahead. But my father's sense of taste kept waning and, with it, his appetite.

But even as he lost physical stature, his personality continued to exert itself. "Now what?" my father said after dinner one night, maybe two weeks later.

"What are you in the mood for?" my mother asked.

"We haven't played Hearts in a while."

Blake groaned.

"What?" my father said. "You don't want to play a game with your old man?"

"I'll play," Marcus said.

"I'll play, too," I said.

"I'll get the cards," Blake said, sighing as he rose from the table.

"Lola? Will you join us?" Marcus asked.

"That's all right. Hearts is best with four. And I've got some reading I want to do," she said.

We cleared off the kitchen table, and Blake returned with a deck in hand.

"I always forget how to play," Marcus said.

"It's easy," my father said, grabbing the cards from Blake.

"I was going to shuffle," Blake said.

"I'll show you the right way to shuffle."

"I shuffle wrong?"

"I read that Hearts evolved from a game called Reversé that was played in Spain in the 1700s," I said.

"Fascinating," Marcus said, as if he knew that I was trying to create a distraction.

"That's a useless bit of fluff to keep track of," my father said. "Is that what I paid the University of California system to teach you?"

I felt my jaw begin to clench. "I didn't learn it in college. It's post-graduate fluff."

"Marcus can cut the deck," my father said.

"I'm still not sure how to play," Marcus said.

I turned to him. "The goal is either to get all thirteen hearts, plus the queen of spades—"

"Dirty Dora," Blake said.

"Or Black Maria or the Black Lady," I noted.

"We'll play an open hand until Marcus gets it," my father said. "He'll pick it up."

"Or we can do that," I said.

"We're starting," my father announced and dealt out the cards.

I was ordering the hand I'd been dealt when my father suddenly pushed back from the table. "Is everything okay?" I asked.

"I'll be right back," he said. "Keep going."

"I don't know what I'm supposed to be doing," Marcus said.

My father left the room, which gave Blake and me a chance to explain the rules in more detail.

"Supposedly, the queen of spades originally represented Athena, the Greek goddess of wisdom. But she gets no respect in this game," I said.

"Maybe because wisdom can be both powerful and dangerous," Marcus offered.

"Do you think that's why?" Blake asked.

"Ask your sister. She's the smart one."

"Where's Dad?" I asked. By then, he'd been gone nearly ten minutes.

Marcus stood and hurried from the room. "Jacob?" we heard him calling.

Blake looked at me.

"What?" I asked.

"Nothing."

"What?" I asked again.

"Do you ever wish it would just end?" he asked.

"Yes and no," I admitted. "It's hard, isn't it?"

"It totally sucks," he said. "And then I hate myself when I wish it would end." He looked miserable.

I nodded. "Yeah."

Marcus came back in a few minutes later. "He's asleep."

"Asleep?" I asked. "He was just here."

"I guess he was tired."

"Huh," Blake said. "Typical."

"I don't suppose anyone still wants to play," I asked. "No? Okay then."

As September eased into October, I began to take on new audits once again, first returning to my previous workload, then surpassing it. Fred Collins wondered aloud where my energy had come from, but I didn't tell him my secret. That I was sticking to the numbers. That I had stopped trying to imagine the various shades of life going on behind the sales receipts and income expense and itemized deductions.

Tagged taxpayers shuffled into my cubicle, as unhappy as ever.

"Some years are worse than other years," I'd tell them. "If you're going to gamble, you've got to be prepared to lose," I'd say. But mostly, I stuck to the form in front of me, skimming down it like a checklist, allowing or disallowing as I saw fit.

Susan had begun to ask me for advice again. "Nice catch on that return," she said one day. I took it as a white flag when she sent me a page from a return she couldn't make sense of. "I couldn't see what was wrong in there."

"All I did was compare income against mortgage interest. That's a fancy house to live in on forty-eight hundred a year," I told her.

"Well, anyway, thanks again," she said. Neither of us mentioned Jonah Gray. And even Ricardo stopped asking me about him.

When my workdays finished, I often spent evenings with Jeff. We tended to hang out in Fremont, in his apartment, though my house was closer. He was apologetic about it, but said that he slept better when he'd been the one to wash his sheets. I didn't mind. His apartment was spotless, and he did have a fascinating collection of insects, all carefully mounted. His favorites were flies.

Martina and I had stopped going to the Escape Room. I felt self-conscious in there, wondering whether she'd been right, whether I'd sought it out as a way of avoiding anyone with actual potential. It was just as well—Jeff didn't like the idea of me hanging out at a dirty bar with a single friend, though I wasn't sure whether my fidelity or the germs worried him more. Besides, my father's deteriorating condition provided a reason to meet in Piedmont and lounge around the pool as the sun dropped low. My mother approved of Martina's company and Marcus frequently pulled up a chair to join us.

One particularly warm evening, after he'd emerged without a shirt on, I pointed at his arms. "So which one was first?"

He smiled. "How long have you wanted to ask about the ink?"

"I've been thinking about getting one," I said.

"Yeah, right," Martina laughed.

"You and Blake," Marcus said, shaking his head. "Next it'll be Kurt."

"Now *that* I doubt," I said.

Marcus stood and began to unbutton his jeans.

"Am I going to be sorry I asked? Keep it clean. We're related, you know." I noticed that Martina didn't look away.

"Relax," he said. He stopped at the third button and only pushed his jeans low enough to reveal a tiny bit of text, neatly printed along his hip line. Rise Above, it read. "This one's the first."

"How old were you?"

"Sixteen," he said.

"Don't tell Blake," I asked him. "My mother would have a heart attack if he came home with one of those."

"Blake'll do what he wants," Marcus said. "But don't worry. Right now he's more focused on marching band. And Beth."

"Beth? Who's Beth? I thought it was Nancy."

"It was."

"Why 'Rise above'?" Martina asked.

"It's the name of a song I really liked. And a reminder. You know, not to let hurdles stop me. To rise above them, even when it's hard. The best stuff is usually hard."

"Is it?" Martina asked, meeting his gaze.

Only then did I realize that there might be something going on between them.

"I'm not sure I want you dating my half brother," I told her a few nights later.

"You don't think I'm good enough for him?"

"That's not it."

"Is it because he smokes? Is it the motorcycle?"

"Those things just make him more your type."

"I realize I'm a few years older than he is."

"I guess I just worry about him getting distracted. With Dad getting worse."

"Marcus is a professional, you know. And I care about your father, too. Neither one of us would let that happen. What is this about? Are you feeling bad because you're not dating anyone?"

"What are you talking about? I'm dating Jeff."

"Oh, right. Of course. So are *you* distracted?"

"No, but I'm not doing the work Marcus does." I realized that I was mostly worried that Marcus would suddenly have somewhere else to go. He'd been at my parents' house nearly every night and day since moving from Sacramento. None of my father's other children had put in so much time. In the month and a half since Marcus had moved in, Kurt had visited only a handful of times. Lori brought the boys every other weekend or so, and he had tagged along once or twice. But more often, he called to plead an excess of grading, a faculty meeting, a new class to prepare for or some academic crisis. I knew that he frequently checked in by phone, but in-person visits remained rare.

Blake's presence, too, had grown sporadic, and when we did cross paths, he never wanted to talk about anything but marching band. One evening, he showed me how his right arm, in which he carried the mace, was now noticeably larger than his left.

"That never happened with the trumpet," he said.

"I guess that's cool," I agreed.

"Blake," my mother called. "Come say good-night to your father."

I watched Blake deflate. "I thought he was already asleep," Blake muttered, before leaving the room.

I felt awful for Blake. He had been so excited about the drum-major position, but the achievement couldn't compete with meta-static cerebral lymphoma. Then again, it shouldn't have had to.

When my mother called, a week or so later, to remind me about Blake's performance that weekend, I promised to go. The marching band was debuting a new Dvorak piece during the halftime show. What's more, Blake was being given the chance to conduct it.

I invited Jeff to come along, but he'd been planning to clean his bathroom that night, and I knew he liked to keep to his schedule.

Then I called Kurt.

"You have to come," I told him. "Dad was really out of it today, and Mom doesn't want to leave him at home."

"I told you, I can't. I'm grading."

"What about Lori and the boys? Wouldn't it be fun for them? It's Uncle Blake. He's their favorite."

Kurt sighed. "Listen, even if I could make it, which I can't, I wouldn't go out of my way to bring my sons to watch their uncle Blake spin a baton. I don't see why he didn't go out for football. He's tall enough."

"It's called a mace," I reminded him.

"I know what it's called. And he wears that hat and marches all around. It's totally dweeby."

"I don't see what your problem is with it. It's not like he's skipping school and doing drugs."

"Given his recent influences, that's a relief to hear."

"Being chosen drum major is an honor. It means he's got talent."

"Spoken like the queen of the dweebs."

"Hey—"

He elevated his voice into a more feminine register, mimicking me. "Did you know that the California redwood is both the tallest and the heaviest living thing?"

"I can't talk to you about this. You're being an ass," I said, hanging up.

So I would go by myself. I'd been to a number of Blake's performances the year before. I knew how they worked. Not a football fan—particularly not of high-school football—I tended to sneak in around halftime and leave soon after. That was my plan for the night of Blake's conductorial debut, too. I didn't expect I was going to know anyone there.

I was walking by the bleachers when a piece of popcorn hit me in the face. I ignored it, but another one followed. I looked around, suspicious of every adolescent smile I saw. Then I spotted Marcus waving. I picked my way through a gaggle of rowdy fans to his place on the bleachers.

"Nice aim," I said.

"You liked that?" He offered me some of his popcorn.

"I see you asked for extra butter," I said, wiping my cheek. "I thought it might have been one of Jonah Gray's gardening thugs, taking a hit out on me. What are you doing here?"

"Blake is conducting," he said. "Sit."

"Where's Martina?"

"Some sort of jerky expo. Hey, do you have a problem with me seeing her? I realize it might be weird for you."

"It's only a little weird."

"She's not the kind of girl that usually goes for me," he said. "You told her about me, didn't you?"

"Some," I said.

"I mean, you told her about me being in jail."

I froze. What had she told him I'd said? "I might have mentioned something," I admitted.

"You mean she might not know?" he asked. Only then did he seem rattled. "I figured she knew and liked me anyway. Shit—what if she doesn't know?"

"You like her, huh?"

"She's real different. She makes such an effort."

"I think you'll be okay. She also gives people the benefit of the doubt," I said. I looked around at the crowd. "Have you been here the whole time?"

He nodded. "It's kind of fun to watch the teenage jungle from a safe distance. I've been trying to figure out which of these kids is most like I was. Of course, the kid most like me probably isn't at the football game. He's breaking into cars while everyone's watching the game."

"Really?" I asked. I began to stand and turn toward the parking lot.

"Sit down. You'll be fine. Hey, there's Blake!"

Chapter Twenty-Six

"DAD," I SAID. "YOU AWAKE?"

He bobbed his head a little, but didn't look away from the television. I knew he'd heard me.

"I'm going to the store. Do you need anything?"

It seemed to take a great effort for him to pull his eyes from the set. "The store? What kind of store?"

"The supermarket," I said.

"No."

"No, you don't need anything?"

"Not from the supermarket."

"Does that mean you need something from another store? I'm already going to be out. I could stop somewhere else."

He considered this for a moment before shaking his head. "Never mind. You're not a very good driver."

"What? You're thinking of Kurt. I've never gotten into a car accident. Not once."

"You're too cautious."

"So you don't want anything from the supermarket or any other store?"

"Nothing," he said. He turned back to the television.

When I returned from the market, my mother and I began to unpack the groceries. I had just pulled out two bags of Halloween candy when my father wandered in. Marcus followed at a close distance, watching carefully as Dad started to dig through the grocery bags.

"What are you looking for, dear?" my mother asked.

"Beans," he said.

"Sasha, did you get beans?" my mother asked.

"No," I said. "I didn't know—they weren't on the list. He didn't ask."

My mother sighed. "Do you mean baked beans, dear? That kind you like?"

My father nodded. My mother began to look for her purse. "I'll run out and get you some."

"I can do it," I said. "Dad, if you'd told me, I would have gotten them."

"No, sweetie, you stay here," my mother said. "I'll go. You have a nice visit with your father."

As if that was going to happen. The fact was that there were no nice visits with my father. Every visit, every stopover, every meal together was another flavor of unsatisfying. One evening, he'd be asleep. The next day, he'd be high on pain medication. Three times in a row, when I drove over expressly to prepare my father dinner, he'd refused to eat.

"The lesions are getting worse," Marcus said. "That affects everything. He's the same with me."

But I didn't believe Marcus. As far as I could see, my father managed to remain appreciative of Marcus's presence while he could barely stomach my own. And I knew that it was worse for Blake.

"Blake!" my father was always yelling. As he grew weaker, his voice seemed to take on a shape of its own, a hawkish, hollow echo that made me cringe.

"What?" Blake would yell back.

"Turn down that music!" or "Get in here!" or "What are you doing now?"

At which point Blake would pull off his headphones, on which he was probably listening to classical fugues and marches, and stomp to the master bedroom to explain that the lawn mower two doors down, or my mother's whistling teakettle, were not his doing.

After one such incident, I followed my little brother when he stormed back toward his bedroom.

"I hate him," Blake said, flopping onto his bed.

"You don't hate him."

"It's like he's trying to take me with him. He's up in my face about cutting my hair. You know that he's been after me to wear a tie to school? And not just for picture day." Blake's complaint became unintelligible at that point.

"Again?" I asked. "I couldn't hear you."

"I said that he says I mumble."

"Well, sometimes," I agreed.

"That's not the point!" Blake yelled.

A moment later, Marcus poked his head in. "Dude, can you lower it a little?" he asked. "Your mom is trying to sleep."

"Sorry," Blake said.

"I know it sucks," Marcus said. "It's not his fault, though. I'm not saying it's yours. No way it's yours. But your dad doesn't know he's being a dick."

Blake nodded. "I know," he said. "I'll try harder."

I thought of Jonah Gray, as I had on and off in the months after his audit. I wondered whether his father was ever so difficult. I could only imagine the old man on the lawn, the one who had offered lemonade to strangers. From my own father, it was lemons, just lemons.

But my father and Blake still had their sweet tooth in common. Both ripped into the candy I bought, finishing it off the morning of Halloween. My mother only realized it at the last minute and called in a panic to ask whether I could bring something to hand out to trick-or-treaters. I like to think that Martina's individually wrapped samples of beef jerky were viewed as a refreshing change of pace by the neighborhood kids, but I'll never know.

And then it was November.

Early in the month, my mother spent an entire weekend winterizing her garden. One chilly day, I wandered onto the patio and watched as she cut things back, mulched and covered her more tropical plants.

"I thought you usually replanted everything in the spring," I said.

"Usually."

"Not this year?"

"This year, I thought I'd try to keep things alive," she said.

I nodded. We were all trying to do that.

She'd given away her broccoli a couple of months before. "I began too late," she said. "If only I'd seen Gray's Garden earlier."

"Gray's Garden?" I repeated. "Have you been going to that site?"

"Oh, it's wonderful, dear. I'm so glad you introduced me to it. I went back and read a lot of the old discussion topics. They had some funny things to say about you, didn't they?"

"If by funny you mean nasty."

"Those people don't know you. They were just trying to protect Jonah. He had an awful time with that ex-wife of his. And poor Ethan," she said.

"You know about all that?"

"It came up a few times recently. Did you know that Jonah lives in the same town as Kurt?"

"Of course."

"You've got that nice space behind your house, Sasha," my mother said. "You should make something of that. You could get some great ideas from him."

"Maybe I don't need great ideas," I said.

She frowned, as though she hadn't understood.

"From him, I mean. Jeff has some good ideas, too, you know. Maybe not about gardening but about…" I thought hard. "Food preparation. And cleanliness. And insects."

"I've been thinking of signing up for some courses at the city college," my mother said, ignoring me. "They have a master gardener program. Maybe I'll become a professional."

"Ian Maselin is always talking about what a green thumb you've got. He'd probably get Ellen to hire you."

"Well, Ian, of course," she said. Whatever that meant.

"My mom's thinking about going back to school," I told Jeff as we lounged in his bedroom later that night.

"Good for her. I'm a big believer in lifelong education. And you said that she needs the money."

I told him that she was thinking of gardening.

"Gardening?" Jeff asked, his brow all wrinkled.

"Yeah, why?"

"All those worms."

I nodded.

"What about something that pays more? Didn't you say your mother was good with numbers? She could always do the books for a nursery or florist."

"But just because she's good at it doesn't mean she has to be a..." I petered off. I realized why I felt defensive and whom I was answering for. It wasn't my mother.

"Be a what?"

"A numbers person. You know, have a quantitative job. Especially if it's the plants she likes and not the numbers."

"Life's a lot easier when you do what you're good at," Jeff said.

I wasn't sure that was true. It wasn't easy if you'd stopped enjoying what you happened to be good at, if you were just going through the motions.

"So, have you thought any more about Fresno?" Jeff asked.

"Fresno. Right. You know, I think I ought to stay here. My dad and all."

Jeff had invited me to Fresno for Thanksgiving. I wasn't begging off because I didn't want to meet his family. My father had graduated from radiation to chemotherapy by then, and he'd been weaker than usual in recent weeks. On the plus side, the chemotherapy seemed to have sapped much of his churlishness along with his energy.

"Don't stay on my account," my father had told me when I'd mentioned Jeff's invitation.

"I'm not," I'd said. "I want to be here for Thanksgiving. Especially now that Kurt's coming." That was a lie, and he probably knew it. Much as people talk about honesty at the end of life, and coming clean about your regrets and forgiveness, a lot of lying goes on, too. Even when he was at his surliest, the rest of us tried to wear happy faces in front of my father. We didn't want to stress him more than necessary. Happy faces and good news and funny stories—as if our lives were made of spun sugar.

My father had begun to do it, too. He'd emerge from a round of chemo green to the gills and give a thumbs-up sign, as if he wouldn't have minded another shot of the stuff.

Marcus was the only one who consistently held my father to a more truthful standard. "You look like shit. You're trying to tell me that you're ready to go bowling?" he'd ask.

In response, my father would let out the sort of moan that made me miss his lies.

Jeff was understanding about Thanksgiving, especially after I explained that Kurt would be down with Lori and the boys, and that Blake would be there and Uncle Ed, too. Marcus was the only one who wouldn't be around. He had made arrangements to see his half sister in Florida. His *other* half sister, I should say.

"Man, I wish I was going to Florida," Blake said.

"Maybe next year," Marcus told him.

"You're going to have so much fun. You can hang out on the beach, check out the girls."

"Hello—you know that he's dating Martina," I said.

"So?"

"You're going to have fun, too," I reminded Blake. "Eddie and Jackie are going to be here. And Kurt and Lori."

"What if something happens with Dad?" Blake asked.

"Uncle Ed will be here," I reminded him.

"I wish Sara was going to be around," he said.

"Sara?" I asked. "I thought it was Beth."

Blake rolled his eyes.

"It's hard to keep up," Marcus said.

Kurt's contingent arrived on Thursday afternoon, just in time for the big meal. With such a sizable group around the table in the dining room, it almost felt like Thanksgivings in years past. Except that my mother looked exhausted and my father was too weak to cut the turkey.

"I can cut it," Blake offered, standing up.

"Have you carved a turkey before? It's a big job," my mother said.

"I'll do it," Kurt said. He stood, too.

"I asked first," Blake said.

"You could take turns," my mother suggested.

Blake sat down, disgusted. "Turns? Why do you have to treat me like I'm five?" he asked. "Forget it. Kurt can cut the turkey. Maybe I should go sit at the kiddie table, too."

"Uncle Blake's coming to sit with us!" Jackie yelled.

"I was kidding," Blake snapped.

"Now that we're all together, I wanted to read something," my mother said. She unfolded a sheet of paper.

"Is this that Ann Landers column you read every year?" Ed asked.

"This is new. I doubt you've heard it before," my mother said. "It's not exactly about Thanksgiving. But it reminded me of this past year."

"What's it about?" Kurt asked, carving into the bird. He was making a mess.

"Repotting," my mother said.

"Repotting?" Kurt asked.

"Moving a plant from a pot it has outgrown into a larger one. Transplanting."

"Sounds like organ donation," Kurt said.

"Where is it from?" I asked.

My mother just smiled at me, as if I knew better. She cleared her throat. "Repotting a plant gives it space to grow. Repotting ourselves means taking leave of our everyday environments and walking into unfamiliar territory—of the heart, of the mind and of the spirit. It isn't easy. The older we get, the more likely we are to have remained in the same place for some time. We stay because it's secure. We know the boundaries and, inside of them, we feel safe. Our roots cling to the walls we have long known. But remaining inside can keep us from thriving. Indeed, without new experiences or ideas, we slowly grow more and more tightly bound, eventually turning into less vibrant versions of who we might have been.

"Repotting means accepting that the way is forward, not back. It means realizing that we won't again fit into our old shells. But that's not failure. That's living."

My mother refolded the paper and sat down, patting my father's hand.

"Lemme see that, would you?" Uncle Ed asked her.

"I don't get it," Eddie said.

"Not exactly a Thanksgiving theme," Kurt said.

"Well, we're all Gardners here," my mother said. "Except you, Ed. I thought something from the garden would be fitting."

"I liked it," I said. Then again, I had a feeling that I knew who had written it.

"You would," Kurt said.

"Just hurry up and finish destroying the bird," I snapped.

"There's the Gardner Thanksgiving spirit," my father muttered.

After dinner, the phone rang. "It's for you," Blake said, handing it to me. "Again."

His intonation told me who it was. Jeff preferred multiple short calls to long catch-ups. He had checked in the night before, as we were baking pies. He'd called again on Thursday morning, and now on Thursday evening, as a few of us lounged around the kitchen, digesting.

"Hi Jeff," I said.

"How are things, baby?"

"About the same as before," I said.

"Well, I won't keep you. I just wanted to hear your voice."

"Okay," I said. "Say hi to Fresno for me."

Blake, Kurt and Uncle Ed were staring at me when I hung up.

"What?" I asked. "He's efficient."

"He calls too much," Blake said.

"This isn't that guy you were auditing a while back?" Uncle Ed asked.

"No, she works with this one," Blake told him. "His name is Jeff and he's serious and he doesn't like tattoos."

"There's more to him than just those things," I said.

"What happened to the one you were auditing?" Ed asked. "Didn't Kurt say you had a thing for him?"

"Jonah Gray," Kurt said. "Yeah, Sasha. What happened to him?"

"How should I know? You're the one who lives out there."

"Isn't that the same guy who wrote the repotting piece Lola read?" Ed asked.

"He wrote that?" Kurt asked. "I should have known."

"I thought it was nice," I said.

"Whatever. Don't listen to me," Kurt sniped.

"Best advice I've heard all day," I said.

My mother wandered into the kitchen, yawning. "Your father's resting. It took a while to get the pillows adjusted." My father's proprioception—his sense of where his body was—had begun to falter. It took some time to arrange his pillows in such a way that he wouldn't feel dizzy. Marcus had mastered it, but Marcus was in Florida.

"I wish you'd consider getting that hospital bed," Ed said.

"I thought that meant moving him into the den," Kurt said.

Ed nodded. "It would."

"These meds he's on now. It's been havoc on my sleep schedule," my mother said.

"Those hospital beds are awful," Kurt said.

"They're not pretty, but they're functional," Ed said. "Especially in this sort of situation."

"He can't sleep in the den," Kurt said, as if the conversation were over.

"Why is it your decision?" I asked.

"I talk to him. I check in. I probably call more often than you visit."

"I live here," Blake chimed in.

"Anyway, Marcus was saying—" I began.

"And if Marcus says it, it's golden?" Kurt asked.

"Not necessarily. But he's Dad's nurse. And we agreed that—"

"*We* didn't agree to anything. *You* agreed. All of you decided to open the door to some guy we know nothing about and now he's in charge and you're passing every decision to him," Kurt said. "I'm surprised you could even decide what to eat with precious Marcus gone."

"I like Marcus," Blake said.

"Don't do this, Kurt." It was my mother. "Your father's illness has been hard on all of us. You know I've had my misgivings about Marcus. I've talked to you about them. But his being here…" She glanced at Ed before continuing. "I'm grateful to him for coming here. It's hard to admit, but he has made this whole awful experience more bearable."

I wondered whether she would ever tell Marcus that, but it didn't matter just then. I left the kitchen and went to check on my father, who was watching television in the bedroom.

"You awake?" I asked. I kept reminding myself not to give up on my father. Jonah hadn't. Marcus hadn't. Maybe nothing would come of it, but I would keep trying all the same, because it meant that I wasn't sitting and waiting.

"Come on in, kitten," he said, patting the side of the bed.

I paused. He hadn't called me *kitten* for about fifteen years.

"Did you get enough to eat? I could fix you a plate of leftovers," I offered.

"Oh, I'm not too hungry," he said.

"Were you able to eat anything at dinner?"

He shrugged. "I've eaten a lot of Thanksgiving dinners in my time. I know what stuffing tastes like."

"That's the spirit."

"My hearing isn't gone," he said.

I glanced back toward the kitchen. "Kurt's just worried."

"I'm sorry for all of this. I know I haven't been the easiest guy to have doddering around the house."

"You're not doddering."

"You know what I mean."

"I know that it hasn't been easy for you, either."

"Actually, it's a lot easier on me. I get a little bored, but I'm not in much pain. That's the one thing modern medicine can do."

"Marcus promised to do his best."

"Marcus mentioned how accepting you've been," my father said. "Of him being here. In the house. It means a lot to me. He *is* family."

"I just looked at the economics," I said. "That's what I do. That's who I am."

"No, kitten," he said. "You're much more than that. You're the finest daughter a father could hope to have. I'm so proud of all that you do," he said. "You tell Kurt I want to talk to him, okay? Your mother deserves a good night's rest in her own bed."

A few days later, a hospital bed was delivered and wheeled into the den. My father spent his remaining nights there.

Chapter Twenty-Seven

IN THE FIRST WEEK OF DECEMBER, MARTINA'S COMPANY held its holiday party. Though early in the season, it coincided with the official launch of the new beef and turkey jerky line, and the marketing department wanted to pack the event with enthusiasts. Martina invited me, Marcus and Jeff to attend with her.

"Think of it as a double date," she said.

"With the added benefit of dried beef," I pointed out.

"And turkey."

"Jeff and Marcus didn't exactly bond when they met before."

"Jeff was probably nervous, meeting your parents, trying to make a good impression. This will just be us."

"And everyone from your work."

Jeff and I got ready at his apartment beforehand. When it was time to go, I grabbed my keys and walked toward the door.

"What are you doing?" he asked me.

"You always drive," I said. "I can drive."

"Of course you can drive."

"I mean, tonight. Why don't we take my car?"

"Oh," Jeff said. "Okay."

I realized I couldn't remember driving my car when Jeff was in it. Riding, sure. But not driving. "Have you ever seen me drive?" I asked.

"Sure, I have."

"When?"

"I know I have," Jeff said.

"It's settled then. We'll take my car," I said. I thought I saw him hesitate. "Are you coming?"

The restaurant where the holiday party was being held was only a mile from Jeff's apartment. We climbed into my car.

"You're a fine driver," Jeff said as we started out.

"I appreciate the support."

"There's a stop sign up there," he said, pointing.

"I see it."

"I thought maybe that you didn't. You weren't slowing down."

"I was slowing down."

"Sorry."

I pulled to a stop and looked both ways. I waited a bit longer than necessary, as if to prove that I wasn't reckless. Long enough that the car behind me honked.

"It's not you I worry about," Jeff said. "It's all those other drivers."

"Uh-huh."

"I would be wrecked if anything happened to you."

"That's a nice thing to say," I said, accelerating again. In my peripheral vision, I could see him clench. "What?" I asked.

"Nothing. So Susan said that the restaurant where they're hosting this party has great Italian food. Very clean."

"Did she?"

"Watch out for that—"

"Car," I said. "I see it. I was watching it." I found a space in the restaurant's parking lot. I turned off the ignition and looked at Jeff.

"You're so beautiful," he said. He leaned in and kissed me softly.

"You can drive on the way home, if you want," I said. He grinned. What did it matter in the larger scheme of things? I wondered. Here was a guy who wanted to be with me, who worried about me, who noticed things. And it was only a mile.

We found Martina and Marcus at a table in the corner. Marcus was as dressed up as I'd ever seen him. He looked uncomfortable and kept fussing with his tie.

"What's wrong?" I asked.

"I look like a drone," he said.

"You look handsome," Martina said.

"I can tell you don't wear a tie too often," Jeff said.

Marcus just looked at Jeff for a moment, as if trying to figure out how to respond. Then he shook his head.

"You'll get used to it," Jeff said.

"I don't really want to," Marcus said.

"You two don't look alike," Jeff said, looking from me to Marcus.

Marcus and I stared at each other.

"I think they do," Martina said. "Sort of."

"I look more like Sasha than I look like Blake," Marcus said. Blake didn't seem to have inherited any of my father's features.

"I look a lot like my mother," Jeff said.

"I take it she's tall and thin?" I asked.

"You'll meet her soon enough," Jeff said.

"Is she coming up?" Martina asked.

"No. I want Sasha to come to Fresno for Christmas," Jeff said.

"You do?" That was news to me.

"Of course."

"I'll have to see," I said.

"Don't you want to meet my family? I've met your family."

"My family lives nearby."

"But it's Christmas. I told them so much about you over Thanks-giving. Everyone's excited to meet you."

"It's going to be my father's last Christmas," I said.

"You don't know that for sure," Jeff said.

"I kind of do," I said.

"She kind of does," Marcus agreed.

My father was on a break from the chemotherapy at that point. The interim was meant to allow him to regain a bit of strength. In the past week, though, he didn't seem to have regained anything. Not his appetite. Not his sensory loss. Not the memories and words that overnight seemed to have begun to dissolve.

"Look, it's the Beef Queen!" Martina said. "She was my idea."

A young woman in a sash and tiara was moving through the party, shaking hands. She bore an uncanny resemblance to Linda Potter, so much that I wondered whether the Beef Queen was another one of the Potter girls. I found myself wondering what Jonah Gray was doing for the holidays. I hoped Ethan was still on the mend. I shook my head to clear it. Why was I still thinking about Jonah Gray? I was on a date, for goodness sake.

Martina jumped up to say hello to the Beef Queen. Marcus smiled, watching her.

"Did you ever imagine you'd be here?" I asked him. "With me and Martina and someone called a Beef Queen?"

He shook his head. "It's funny—say no and you'll stay in the same place. Say yes and who knows where you'll end up."

"Who's ready for a drink?" Jeff asked. He extracted a thermos from a bag he'd brought in with him. I just looked at him. "What?" he asked.

That next Monday, Marcus and my father returned from a doctor's appointment with troubling news. My father's white-cell count had dropped precipitously. The chemotherapy and radiation treatments meant to slow the cancer had damaged his bone marrow, which in turn blunted his immune system. Either that, Dr. Fisher said, or it was simply the way the lymphoma was progressing.

It didn't matter why. The question was what we could do about it. As my father received transfusions in a hospital bed down the hall, my brothers, mother and I gathered in Dr. Fisher's office to talk about the vagaries of bone marrow.

"It's called an allogeneic transplant," Dr. Fisher said.

"Allo-what?" Blake asked.

"A transplant between two individuals," Uncle Ed explained.

"Between Dad and one of us?" I asked.

"If one of you is a match," Dr. Fisher said. "We prefer to ask siblings first, but since your father doesn't have any, that's not an option."

"I wish your aunt Flor were still alive," my mother said.

"We've checked the tissue database. We're still hoping to find an unrelated donor, but it's prudent to test offspring. Just in case."

"So it's just a blood test," I said.

"If there's a match, there would be more, but we can discuss that if and when the time comes," Ed said.

"That sounds easy enough," my mother said.

"Lola, we'd love to get you tested, too, and in the database. Since you're not a relative, though, the chance of you matching Jacob is quite slight," Dr. Fisher said.

"So me, Sasha, Kurt, and Marcus?" she said.

"And me," Blake said.

"Are you sure you don't want to sit this one out, dear? Your midterms are coming up. You're already dealing with so much."

"But it might help Dad," he said.

"You heard Dr. Fisher. The chances are slim," she said.

"For you," Blake said. "You're not related."

My mother nodded, but looked away. I felt for her. Her husband was dying, and now her children were being asked to open themselves up to the possibility of surgery. Of course she'd be hesitant to let her youngest raise his hand. But he did. We all raised our hands and rolled up our sleeves.

"What if," I said to my mother, after the blood test, as I prepared to leave Dad's hospital room and return to work. "What if I come by this weekend and we go get a Christmas tree?"

My mother looked at my father and sighed.

"What? It's coming up. Didn't you notice the cardboard snowmen up and down the oncology hallway? If you'd rather, I could get a tree and bring it by the house. But I know you always like to pick out the best—"

"I don't want to buy a big, cut Christmas tree," she interrupted. She looked out the window, down across the parking lot. "I don't like them anymore."

"You don't?"

My mother had always been an enthusiastic trimmer and demanding about the particular tree she brought home. It had to be tall, dark green, without any bald spots or misshapen areas. It had to have needles neither too long and limp nor too short and sharp.

"I could cover the cost if that's—"

"It's not the money," she said. "I don't want to deal with another..." She stopped and stared at my father, who had dozed off during his transfusions. She motioned for me to follow her into the hallway. Outside of his room, she spoke more quietly. "I'm sorry, Sasha. I just don't want anything else in my house that I'm going to have to watch die."

"No tree," I said. I looked back toward my father's room. I felt as if I should be in there.

"I'd like to start a new tradition," my mother said.

"I thought a defining aspect of tradition was repetition over time," I said. Starting a "new tradition" rang to me as false as when people deemed something "first annual." First annual fall sale. First annual Easter brunch. How do you even know you'll be around in a year's time? How does anybody?

She looked at me, unamused.

"Sorry. What new tradition do you want to start?" I asked, which was the question she had wanted to hear.

"I want to buy a little, live tree, and after Christmas, we can plant it outside. In California, we have the luxury of living in an ecological zone that allows for that."

That didn't sound like my mother, but I had no energy to argue.

"So should I get a potted tree?" I asked. "I could do it this weekend."

"That would be lovely."

Back in my office, I realized that I had no idea what sort of tree to buy. If this were going to be the first year of a new Gardner family tradition, I wanted to get it right. What if I chose a tree that we lovingly planted, then spent the rest of the year watching as it withered? I needed a more auspicious beginning.

Why had I even offered? Sure, I'd been picking up some interesting horticultural tidbits in recent months, but few people knew less about actual gardening than me. I didn't even know where to look. And then it struck me. Of course I knew where to look.

Jonah had redesigned his site in the time since I'd last been there, and he had posted some beautiful pictures. One I recognized as having been taken in the backyard of his house, looking out over the cornfield. One was clearly Ethan. None showed Jonah himself, although one revealed a pair of work boots and another, his shadow. I examined that one closely, trying to discern a detail I could use.

I noticed that he'd recently posted a piece on Christmas trees. I wondered if he had recommended specific kinds.

I was at one of those Christmas-tree farms recently. A fell-your-own sort of place. It's something I've always done without thinking much about it. And this year, with my father unwell, I had set out to fell a most magnificent one. The owner of the place walked me into his field, until we found ourselves beside a gorgeous, fourteen-foot white fir. It was perfectly green and conical, the sort of tree that saplings want to be when they grow up.

The owner said, "You don't even need to decorate it. A tree like that speaks for itself."

And I started to wonder what a tree like that would say, if

it could actually speak. It seemed to me that "Don't kill me," might be the first thing out of its, uh, trunk. I knew that I couldn't cut it down. But this man had a business to run, and he'd probably sell it to the next person looking for the best tree on the lot.

So I paid a little extra, for the work of getting it out of the ground safely, and as of last week, my father and I have a new tree in our yard, across from where the great oak used to be. Maybe it will be our tradition, if you can call something a tradition that hasn't been repeated yet. We'll get a living tree, and we'll plant it in the yard. In California, we have the luxury of living in an ecological zone that allows for that sort of thing.

So that was the source of my mother's inspiration. Unfortunately, Jonah hadn't included suggestions for types of trees, and I preferred the idea of a nursery, rather than digging in the dirt of a Christmas-tree farm. But I knew he'd have a suggestion, and besides, it had been a while.

Dear Jonah, I wrote. *My mother read your piece on Christmas trees, and she's sold on the idea. Unfortunately, I have no idea which species of tree is most likely to thrive in the Bay area. Any suggestions? Jeffrine.*

By the time I was packing up for the day, he had written back.

Jeffrine, It's always a pleasure to hear from you. I was going to write, but I wasn't sure of your address, and I worried that the archivist might end up with my note. If your mother wants a tree that'll be around for years to come, she might try a silver tip or Scotch pine, or even blue spruce. Or go for a white fir like the one I got. You'll surely be able to find one of those varieties in your local nursery. Just be sure to keep the root ball moist (your mother will know what I mean). How are you, by the way? Jonah

I'm fine, I began writing back. *I've been—*

"Are you ready?"

I looked up to see Jeff.

"Almost," I said. "I'm just finishing something."

"What are you finishing?"

"A note," I said.

"I can see that. I meant, a note to whom?"

"It's nothing," I said. "I'll write it later." I shut my computer down.

"I didn't mean to stop you," he said, but I wasn't sure whether or not to believe him. "So?" he asked.

"So what?"

"Have you made a decision?"

"Decision?"

"About Fresno. For Christmas."

I rubbed my arm where the needle had gone in earlier that afternoon. "We'll be getting the results of the blood tests the day after tomorrow. Can it wait until then?"

"Of course it can, baby," he said. "Are we still on for dinner?"

"Dinner?"

"We were having dinner tonight and tomorrow because Friday you have that holiday party."

"That's right. The Maselins' party. You're so good at remembering."

"That's what they pay me for," he said. "So are you ready?"

I looked back at my computer and nodded.

* * *

Two days later, on Friday afternoon, the test results were in. Blake was still in school, Kurt was teaching in Stockton, and Marcus remained home with my father. But I had promised my mother that I'd meet her at the hospital, so we could hear about our options first-hand. We had agreed to meet in Dr. Fisher's office at two, but the room was empty when I arrived.

"Can I help you?" I turned around to see Dr. Fisher's assistant.

"I'm here for some blood-test results."

The young man looked at me warily. "Gardner, right?" he asked.

"Yes. For Jacob Gardner. The bone-marrow match."

"The doctor just presented them to your mother and uncle."

"He already did?" I looked at my watch. It was not quite two o'clock. "Where are they?"

"Out, I guess."

"Am I a match, do you know?"

"No. No matches. Not any of you."

"I guess it was a long shot."

"It was something," he said.

Leaving the office, I spotted Uncle Ed standing with my mother at the end of the hallway. He was in nearly the same place he'd been when I first saw Marcus, back before I knew that he was Marcus and my half brother. Back when the news of Dad's recurrence was still new and deniable.

Ed and my mother looked as though they were discussing something, but then Ed raised his hands and, even from a distance, I could tell that he was angry. He looked as if he could barely control himself. My mother shook her head, then shook it again, at which point Ed turned from her and came charging up the hallway.

"Uncle Ed," I said.

"Later," he snapped, barreling past me.

I hurried to my mother who sat now on a bench outside the laboratory door. "Mom?" I said. I could see that she was in tears. "What's wrong? What happened?"

"Oh, Sasha," my mother said. She reached for my hand. I sat beside her and put an arm around her. She seemed so small, so much slighter than I remembered. "I made a mistake, and Ed is angry with me."

"Is everything okay?" I asked.

She shrugged.

"What is it? Does it have to do with Dad?"

She sighed. "I suppose it does."

I waited a moment. "Will you tell me?"

"I don't know if you'll remember any of this," she began, "but back when you were in high school…oh, you must have been fifteen at the time. It was tax season and your father barely left his study, not even to come out and eat with us. Do you remember when he'd get like that? It was a bad year, and we were struggling a bit. Bills and things. I decided to spend some time in Tahoe."

"For spring skiing," I remembered. "I wanted to go but you didn't want to take me out of school for that long."

"That's right. That was the time. I should have taken you."

"It's fine. I don't harbor any resentment."

"Oh, Sasha. Dear, dear Sasha."

"What Mom? You're scaring me."

"I went to the condo for about a week, I think."

"Okay," I said.

"I left Piedmont angry. I shouldn't have, but I did. And during that week, I was not faithful to your father."

"What?"

"Now before you judge me—"

"I'm not judging. I'm just surprised."

"I was never unfaithful before or since," she said. "I've been a good wife. And your father was no saint. That much is obvious."

"So you had a fling. With whom?"

She took a deep breath. "You know Ian Maselin," she said.

I froze. Had she really said that name, of all names? Ian Maselin? Ian Maselin the slime? Ian Maselin the snake? Wasn't she better than that?

"Really?" I managed to say. "Mr. Maselin?"

"I ran into him at the ski lodge. I didn't realize he'd be in Tahoe."

"Ian Maselin?" I repeated. "But he's so...so obvious."

"He paid attention to me. He listened to me. He looked at me."

"He looked at you? Is that all it took? The man's looked at me a thousand times and I've never—" I didn't finish. I didn't want to say anything I'd have to envision. It was all wrong. Ian Maselin?

"I'm not proud of it, but it happened and then it was over."

"So it was just that one time? This wasn't something that went on for years and years or anything, was it?" I tried to think of all the times they'd socialized with each other. I checked my memories for signs of something larger.

My mother shook her head. "Oh no. I came back and things with your father improved, and then I found out that I was pregnant..."

I don't know if she said anything more just then. That's when it fell into place. That's what Ed was livid about. Not that she'd had an affair. Not that she'd fallen for someone other than my father. It wasn't about a moral lapse. It was about biology.

"Blake's not..." I couldn't say it.

"I never knew for sure. He's never needed blood tests. He's always been so healthy. Maybe I suspected it. Well, of course, I suspected it. But now with these tests…"

"No wonder he and Marcus don't look more alike. I'm always trying to find some resemblance, but I never do."

"I don't think you're ever going to."

"So, now what?"

"I don't know. Ed found out and he's angry."

"You don't have a plan? Are you going to tell Blake? Are you going to tell Dad?"

"No," she said. "What good would telling your father do? That's one thing Ed and I agree on. As for Blake, maybe after your father…" She petered off. "Sasha, I feel terrible," she said.

"You should," I said, thinking of Marcus. I heard my cell phone begin to ring, and I scrambled to pull it from my purse in time. "Hello?"

"Sasha, it's Jeff. Are you okay?"

"Enough. Why?"

"I swung by your office and you're not there. No one knew where you were. Where are you?"

"At the hospital."

"Oh my god, are you okay?"

"I just said I was. It's family stuff. It's not a good time. Can I call you later?"

"Call me later," he said.

Maybe I wasn't as angry as Uncle Ed, but I was plenty mad. I had to get some space from my mother, but I didn't want to go back to work. Instead, I found myself driving aimlessly around Oakland and then Piedmont. I passed Hunter's. I passed the Escape Room. I passed Blake's high school. He was in there, I thought, somewhere, oblivious. Finally, I pulled into a plant nursery not far from my parents' house. I was angry and confused, yes. But I still needed a Christmas tree.

I was browsing the evergreen section when I felt a timid tap on my shoulder. I turned around to see Ellen Maselin.

"Sasha, right? I didn't expect to see you here. Of all people," she said.

"I need to get a tree," I said. I looked at her, wondering whether she knew, whether she had any inkling, after all those years.

"Are you doing the living tree, too?" she asked.

"My mother wanted to start a new tradition."

"Someone's become quite a faithful reader," Ellen said. "It took me a while to convince Ian. You know how he likes to have the biggest tree on the street. You're coming tonight, aren't you?"

"Tonight?"

"Our holiday party. I wish your father could attend. Please tell him that we're thinking of him."

"Your holiday party," I repeated.

"And feel free to bring that young man who's been helping your father."

"Marcus? He's my half brother."

"I didn't realize you were related," Ellen said.

"There's a lot of that going on," I said.

Ellen cocked her head like a small bird trying to ascertain whether the crouched cat in the bushes was a statue or not. My cell phone rang again, so I didn't have to elaborate.

"Hello?"

It was Jeff. "I thought you were going to call me," he said.

* * *

I chose a little tree that the clerk informed me was a noble fir. It looked somewhat less than noble, standing two feet high at the most, but if my mother didn't approve, she could buy one herself.

It was almost dark when I finally pulled into the driveway of my parents' house. I carried the tree inside and found my mother at the kitchen table having dinner with Blake and Marcus.

"What's that?" Blake asked.

"It's our Christmas tree." I set it on the kitchen floor.

"Sasha, it's lovely," my mother said. "It's just perfect."

"*That's* our Christmas tree?" Blake asked.

"Ask her about it," I said, motioning to our mother.

"I was getting worried about you," she said.

I ignored her.

"Mom said that none of us matched Dad," Blake said. "Oh well."

"Oh well is right," I said. I couldn't meet my mother's eyes.

"Are you hungry?" she asked.

I shook my head.

"Is there going to be food at this party?" Marcus asked.

"I'm sure there will be," my mother said.

"You really want to go?" I asked him. "I was thinking that maybe I'd skip it."

"Oh, come on. Go with me. Just for a little bit," Marcus asked. "I've been planning on it. No offense, Lola, but I could use a night out."

"By all means," my mother said to him. "I'm happy to stay with Jacob tonight. You two should go. It's always a lively event."

"Fine. Let me wash my hands and we can walk down there," I told Marcus.

"No one cares whether I want to go?" Blake asked.

For a brief moment, I met my mother's eyes. Then I looked away. "Do you want to go to the Maselins' holiday party?" I asked Blake.

"No way," he said. "They're weird."

Marcus and I walked down the dark street.

"You seem a little off tonight," he said.

"Do I?"

"I hope you didn't get your hopes up about the bone-marrow match. It's a real long shot."

"That's not it."

"Everything okay with Jeff?"

"That's not it either."

"Fair enough," he said, backing off.

"Seems like you and my mother are getting along better," I said.

He laughed. "I caught her, out on the patio, smoking one of my cigarettes. It's been better since then."

"Strange bedfellows," I said.

"I'm not—there's nothing like that—"

"Oh, I know. I just meant, stressful times can throw people together."

"Kurt still takes exception to me."

"My older brother takes exception to any number of things. This is it," I said.

"Big house."

Inside, I recognized a few neighbors and introduced Marcus when I could, but it was true, I was a little off.

Ellen Maselin met us as I was getting a beer from the bartender. "Sasha, you made it. Is Lola coming?"

"I don't think so," I said. "She's home with Dad."

"Of course. And you're Marcus. I didn't realize you were family. Here I was thinking you were the help. It's nice to finally meet you. I'm sure you're a wonderful help to Jacob."

"I'm trying to be," he said.

"Have you seen Ian yet?" Ellen said, casting around for her husband.

"I'm sure we'll run into him," I said, leading Marcus away. I figured Ian was probably in the kitchen, trying to grope the wait-staff.

"She seems nice," Marcus said.

"She's fine."

"What do you have against the Maselins?" he asked. "Is it the house? It's a little gaudy."

I shook my head. "That's Ian, over there."

"The one who looks like an older Blake?"

I froze. Did Marcus know already? I looked back at Ian. Indeed, I could see a resemblance. I forced a laugh. "That's the one."

"Well, if it isn't the ever-radiant Sasha Gardner!" Ian had spotted us. "And who is this? You're not the same young man I met before."

"This is Marcus."

"Sasha, I didn't realize you were such a girl-about-town," Ian said to me, winking.

"I'm not."

He ignored my dour answer. "I expect to see you around the piano, later. I'm sorry your tone-deaf father couldn't join us tonight."

"Jacob's tone-deaf?" Marcus asked. "I didn't realize that."

"It's a shame, but the man can't carry a tune to save his life," Ian said. "Ever since I've known him."

"I'm tone-deaf, too," Marcus said.

"Then you're excused, as well," Ian said. "Hey, did you see the tree Ellen got us this year? Isn't it hilarious?" He pointed to a diminutive Christmas tree in a pot in the corner of the room. It stood about three feet tall.

"It's taller than ours," Marcus said.

"At least it's taller than someone's," Ian said. "I'd better mingle. Nice to meet you, Mark."

We sat on a couch, eating canapés and watching people socialize. I powered through my second beer, than began another.

"Thirsty tonight?" Marcus asked. "Good thing I'm the designated walker."

"I guess."

"Let me ask you something. Have you noticed that your mother's first instinct is to keep Blake away from your father's illness? The blood test is only the most recent thing."

"He's her baby," I said.

"Sure, but he's not *a* baby."

"Well, he got his way. He was tested. For all the good that did."

"What do you mean?" Marcus asked.

Though my mother had made it clear that she didn't want to tell either my father or Blake about the day's revelation, I felt as though I had to tell someone. And I'd had three beers, which made it easier. So I told Marcus.

"Him?" Marcus asked, pointing to Mr. Maselin, who by then was belting out tunes at the piano.

"Him," I said.

"So that's where he gets the musical ability."

"And maybe his way with the ladies. Please don't tell anyone yet.

I shouldn't have said anything. It'll all get worked out, but it can wait, can't it?"

He nodded.

"You must be so pissed at her," I said.

"Yeah," Marcus said, but he didn't sound like his heart was in it.

"The way she treated you. She's been acting like she's got this moral superiority. She's got no superiority."

"Yeah," he said again.

"Is that all you're going to say?"

"What do you want me to say? What am I supposed to do about it now? Sure, I'm pissed off. You think I don't get the hypocrisy? But now what? I'm not going to take it out on Blake."

"Of course not. He didn't do anything to cause this."

"Yeah, well, neither did I," Marcus said.

We sat in silence for a moment.

"We're a mess of a family, aren't we? You're probably sorry you decided to spend time with us," I said.

"Not at all."

I smiled at him for answering so quickly. "What do you think I should do?" I asked.

"Why are you asking me?"

"Because I trust your opinion. And because you're family."

Marcus smiled. He reached out and grabbed hold of my hand. "You're one of the good ones, Sasha Gardner."

I almost started to cry. "Oh, God, do you really think so?"

Chapter Twenty-Eight

"WHAT'S WRONG WITH YOU?" MY BROTHER BARKED AS soon as I picked up my office phone.

"Hello, Kurt," I said.

"Mom said you're not talking to her."

"Did she say why she thought that was?"

"No. Why?"

"I don't want to talk about it."

"She's going through a difficult time right now. Whatever it is, you should cut her a little slack."

"Typical you. Did you guilt-trip Lori into cutting you some slack, too? Was the anniversary party just your way of blowing off a little steam? No big deal?" I asked.

He paused for a moment before exploding. "That's none of your damn business. That's between me and my wife."

"How the hell did you get out of that anyway? The sick-father excuse?" I asked. "Or was it the new-job excuse? Or the 'I'm miserable in Stockton' excuse?"

"You wouldn't understand. You've never been married," my brother snapped.

"I've made promises I haven't broken."

I hated everything about my mother's actions—from the ease with which she had fallen for Ian Maselin's greasy charms to the hypocrisy of her previous treatment of Marcus. But was it the infidelity itself or its imagined effect on Blake that bothered me the most? My mother had had a point: my father was no saint. Then again, neither was she. Nor was Kurt. Was it just a matter of time before it was my turn?

I took refuge that evening in a trip to the mall with Martina. She was trying to find the perfect Christmas gift for Marcus.

"Everyone in my family has been unfaithful," I said to her. "My mother, my father, my brother."

"Blake hasn't," she pointed out. We were wandering the mall in search of a Christmas gift she could buy for Marcus.

"He's gone through four girlfriends this year already. It's not infidelity, but he's sure starting off on an acquisitive track. Not unlike his genetic father."

"You haven't," Martina said.

"Maybe it's just a matter of time. Maybe it's my gypsy blood. What if I get the undeniable urge to wander?"

"I don't see it," she said. "You know what makes you happy. I figure the next time you start dating someone, it's going to stick."

"I'm dating Jeff," I reminded her. "He's someone."

"Shit, you're right," she said. "Why can't I ever remember that?"

"You think I'm free from the Gardner curse?"

"I'm not saying you don't have issues," Martina said. "But yeah, I think you might be." She was sorting through a rack of athletic gear.

"You think Marcus would like it if I bought us matching track suits?" she asked.

I stared at her. "Are you serious? You think he's the one? That's great!"

Martina shook her head. "Marcus and I in his-and-her outfits? Oh, Sasha, I was kidding."

I agreed to go to Fresno. I was still worried about leaving my father, but even without a donor, his white blood-cell count had improved, and Dr. Fisher felt that he was stabilizing. So three days before Christmas found Jeff and me just off the highway, halfway between Oakland and Fresno.

Jeff had informed me that whenever he had to relieve himself while on the road, he would try to find a Denny's. "Their bathrooms are perceptibly cleaner," he said. And so, spotting a sign for a link in that particular chain, he had pulled off the highway and into a parking lot.

"I'll be right out," Jeff said, locking the car. He gave me a kiss and headed inside.

I spun on my toe on the curb. I looked out at the passing highway, wondering whether we'd make it to Fresno before dinnertime. I looked at the rows of newspaper vending machines that serviced the freeway traffic. The *Wall Street Journal*. The *San Francisco Examiner*. The *Stockton Star*.

I took a step closer. The *Stockton Star*? We had to be at the outer reaches of their readership. I crouched down to read the front-page articles—one on a town council meeting and another on immigrant health care. I found myself digging through my change purse for a quarter, but I didn't find any. I knew that Jeff carried a roll for tolls, but the car was locked and he'd kept hold of his keys. I hurried into the restaurant and walked up to the first waitress I saw.

"I need change," I said.

"They say that recognizing a need is the first step toward making it happen," she told me.

"No. *Change.* For a dollar." I held out a bill.

"Oh. That kind. The easy kind. Well, I just got on," she apologized. "I've only got…let's see. I've got two quarters and a dime."

"I'll take it. You can keep the rest. That's a forty percent profit in under a minute," I said.

She looked at me as if I were nuts, but she took my dollar and handed over the coins. I hurried back outside and bought a copy of the *Star.*

I scanned the bylines on the front page but none of them interested me. I was opening the paper wide when Jeff came back outside.

"What are you reading?" he asked.

I spun around. I had forgotten, for a moment, where I was. I had forgotten where he was, where we both were, and even that we were there together, on our way to Fresno to meet his family.

"The *Stockton Star,*" I admitted. He was going to find out anyway.

"Why didn't you get the *Journal?* It's a much better paper."

I faltered. "I tried but the machine was broken." As I said it, I thought of my family and the infidelity that seemed a more entrenched tradition than any living Christmas tree. Was this how it began? You got away with one lie, and the ones after that came more easily.

Jeff looked unimpressed. "We should get going," he said. "Are you going to bring that with you?"

"Well, yeah. I just bought it," I said.

As he pulled out of the parking lot, I looked back, only then considering what the waitress had said to me. Had I actually said "I need change" aloud? What did that mean?

Soon enough, we were pulling up to the Hill residence in Fresno. A tall, thin woman came out to greet us.

"There's Mother," Jeff said.

"So this is Fresno! I've never been," I told his mother, as we pulled our luggage from Jeff's car. "It's lovely."

"We prefer to call it Fres-yes," she replied.

"Are you serious?" I asked.

"What do you think?" I could see that Jeff had inherited her eyes.

In fact, Jeff was a lot like the rest of the Hills: tall, thin, fastidious. They were opinionated, but they took turns letting each other speak. They didn't smile much. They remembered details.

"How long has the Hill family been here in town?" I asked at dinner, unable to make myself call it Fres-yes.

"Four generations," Mrs. Hill said proudly. Jeff's sisters nodded, as if it were a story repeated many times before. "Herbert's grandfather moved here near around 1900," she said. "My grandmother moved here in 1910, so we're relative newcomers. Jeff is the only Hill to have left, and we're working on getting him back here as soon as we can." His sisters nodded again.

"It's only a three-hour ride to the Bay area," I pointed out.

"The way his mother sees it, that's three hours too many," Herbert Hill said.

Everyone nodded, even Jeff. I wondered what the Hills would have made of Jonah Gray's piece on repotting. I wondered what Jonah Gray would have made of the Hills.

"Jeff mentioned that your father hasn't been feeling well," one of Jeff's sisters said.

"He's got cancer," I said.

"That's a shame," Mrs. Hill said. "I hope it's not too serious."

I turned to Jeff, wondering what he had told them. "It's very serious. Actually, it's terminal," I said.

"Your mother must be beside herself."

"She seems to be handling it all pretty well."

"That's probably just an act," Jeff's mother said. "I'm sure it's worse when she's alone."

"Maybe," I said. I hadn't spoken to my mother before I left. I knew she was grieving. I believed she was sorry. But I was still angry at her.

Later that night, Jeff emerged from the guest bathroom to find me leafing through the *Stockton Star.*

"I didn't see you bring that in," he said.

"It's something to read."

"I could get you a copy of the *Fresno Bee.* I'm sure it's a better paper."

"My brother lives in Stockton. I like to know what's going on out there."

"Does that guy you were auditing still write for them?" Leave it to Jeff to remember.

I hedged. "I haven't come across any of his articles yet." I didn't say that I was still hoping to.

"Well, I'm beat," Jeff said, crawling into bed. "It's so nice to be here with you, in our home. How long do you think you'll keep reading?" He was wearing his come-hither smile and caressed my arm.

I pretended not to notice. "For a little bit," I said. "Will that keep you awake?"

"No. It's fine." He closed his eyes and turned over.

I just sat there. For a moment, I didn't read. I didn't look at Jeff. I didn't look at anything.

The bed was comfortable and the guest room was neither too warm nor too cold. The man beside me, I knew that his body would fit nicely along the curves of my own, were I to turn and press up against him.

Is this what I've chosen? I wondered. I looked over at Jeff, curled onto his side. He was a fine man. He wanted to include me in his life. Why was I fighting it? I told myself that I was tired from the drive, and I folded the newspaper. I was about to drop it to the floor when an article caught my eye. I leaned closer to the light.

New Strain of Strawberry Blight Worries Farmers by Jonah Gray.

I brushed my finger over his name. I was glad to see that he was covering agriculture now.

I had never written him back after he'd offered Christmas-tree suggestions. I had intended to, even thought about what I wanted to say. That I'd been thinking of him through the fall. That he had served as an example for me. That I understood why his readers had been so fiercely protective. But instead my workdays had filled with audits and holiday gatherings, and soon a week had passed and then another.

Maybe Martina had been right. Maybe I preferred detachment to diving in and making a change. Maybe Marcus was right. Saying no— or not saying anything—meant staying in the same place.

All the same, I didn't have any actual gardening questions, and I didn't want to make one up just to talk to him. My Jeffrine persona was enough of a lie, even though everything I'd said through her was true. What was I supposed to say now? That though we'd never met,

I felt some weird pull to him? That I understood how hard it must have been to give up his life in Tiburon, and that I was drawn to him even more for having done it?

I shook my head. I should listen to the advice I doled out to my auditees. If you're going to gamble, you've got to be prepared to lose. Calling or writing to Jonah Gray at that juncture was a gamble, and I was already in the process of losing someone I held dear.

It was late. I stared at the article a while before dropping the paper to the floor of Jeff's bedroom. I could still see his name when I turned out the light.

Two days later, around noon on Christmas Day, we were raking leaves in the Hill's backyard when Jeff's mother called from the kitchen.

"Sasha," she yelled. "Phone call."

I hurried inside.

It was Marcus. "I was really hoping I wouldn't have to call," he said.

"Something's wrong,"

"Things took a turn for the worse."

"Should I come back?" I asked.

"That's your decision," he said. "I can't tell you what to do."

"What would you do?"

He paused. "I would come back."

I went outside to tell Jeff. "I'm sorry," I said. "I thought he had stabilized."

"Do you think Marcus might have been exaggerating?" Jeff asked. "Your family probably just misses having you at Christmas. Mine would feel the same. They'd make up any excuse to get me back here."

"Marcus is a nurse. He knows the difference between bad and worse. Besides, he wouldn't do that."

"I think maybe he doesn't approve of me and doesn't like the fact that you're here in Fresno."

"He's my brother—" I began.

"Half brother," Jeff said.

"Why do you always point that out?"

"Because it's not the same as full."

"Do you have any half brothers or sisters?" I asked.

"No, but—"

"That you know of."

"Hey!"

"So you don't know," I went on. "I don't hear you doubting Blake." I had told him about the blood test in the car on the way to Fresno.

"That's different."

"I'm going to call about bus schedules," I said and went back inside.

I was back in Oakland that afternoon. The man in the bus seat beside me looked out the window as we pulled into the station.

"Watch it when you get off the bus," he said. "Lots of unsavory types hang out at these stations, just preying on single women, like yourself."

"I'll be okay. My brother is picking me up."

"That's good. Family will watch out for you." The man had spotted Marcus, pacing, just inside the station doors. "Jesus, get a load of that guy. Bus stations are always full of creeps, aren't they?"

"That's my brother," I said.

The man harrumphed. "I guess you know best."

"Merry Christmas," Marcus said when I met him inside the station. "You made it."

"More or less."

"How was Fresno?"

"How's Dad?"

"Not so good," Marcus said.

The hospice nurse, who had begun her visits the week before, called it "active dying." I hadn't realized that there was such a thing, or that the body could begin to power down a full two weeks before a person stops breathing. All the systems slow. The heart rate drops, the blood pressure drops. The hands cannot keep warmth.

By the time I returned to the house on Christmas evening, my father had already eaten for the last time. We didn't know that yet, but the hospice nurse said it was normal for his appetite to have cut out completely.

"Dying doesn't work up an appetite," she said. "It's the normal process of things."

"He's got to eat something, doesn't he?" I asked.

"Or what?" she asked and looked at me. "Child, he's dying right now," she said more gently.

"No, I mean…" I struggled to find words that made sense, but I came up empty. Was it really happening? Wasn't there anything left to do?

Christmas evening was quiet. We had agreed to skip the gift exchange, though Lori had brought presents for the boys, who seemed unaware, in their excitement, that they were the only ones unwrapping anything.

My mother had retired early, and Kurt and Blake played video games on the computer in my father's study. While my father slept in the den, I dug into a plate of Christmas leftovers. Lori and Marcus sat there, watching me, too spent to say much.

"Dying doesn't make you hungry, but sitting around waiting apparently does," Marcus said.

"It was a long bus ride," I pointed out.

Marcus got up to check on my father, leaving me with Lori.

"You've got nice nail beds," she said. "You ought to try polish sometime."

"It's not really my thing," I told her.

"I know you know," she said.

"Know what?"

"I was very angry at Kurt. I still am."

"Oh, that," I said.

"People are always saying what they would put up with and what they wouldn't, but you never know, until…"

"I believe you," I said.

"And it's not just me I've got to think of. I mean, your mother stayed."

"She did," I agreed.

"We're trying to work things out," she said. "He's not perfect."

"Maybe you haven't noticed, but you didn't exactly marry into a flawless family," I said.

"I'll be glad when this year is over," she said.

"I always tell people I audit that some years are worse than others. It's kind of true, isn't it?"

A slow and patient tide was pulling my father out to sea. You can't fight a tide—maybe you can for an hour or two, but not for months. It's larger than one person's will. And this was a tide that the rest of us could neither fathom nor follow. In the days before we lost him, I didn't feel any great calm; I felt helpless. I couldn't do anything that mattered, and what I managed to do, I did poorly. I left the coffeemaker on all day. I burned soup. I locked my keys in my car.

When we spoke at all, he and I, it was of little things. The weather outside, the temperature of my food, the show on television. I held his hand and watched him as he slept. Then I'd leave and Blake would take my place, and after him, my mother, and so on, so that someone was always there.

You hear those stories about people sensing that they're about to die and summoning loved ones to their bedsides to say goodbye. It didn't happen like that for us. There was no more denying what was coming. I could see it in the continued presence of the hospice nurse. I could see it in the length of time my father slept each day, in the number of pills he took each night, and in the morphine drip that was brought in when he could no longer swallow. There would be no reprieve, no last-minute surprises. Death had camped out in our den and waited beside the bed. It was a smell just beyond reach. It filled in the lull when people had nothing more to say.

My father died around eight in the evening, three days shy of New Year's Eve. Eddie and Jackie were asleep, but the rest of us were around his bed when he slipped away. And with that, it was over. The disease that we'd all been focusing on, fighting, talking about, railing against for months, it had won. I wish I could say that I'd said all that I wanted to. I wish I could say that I even knew what I wanted to say. But you live with what you're dealt, and my father died without any cathartic shift in our relationship. It hadn't been easy, but he knew that I loved him, I guess. And by the same token, I knew that he loved me. There are worse ways to go.

If that seems anticlimactic, that's cancer for you. It kills as thoroughly as a heart attack or gunshot, but with an insidious subtractive quality. Little by little, it eats away, sapping strength, then appetite, then memory, then locomotion, a hundred smaller farewells before the last one.

But even I was surprised by how quietly it all wrapped up. Death carries such huge expectations. I thought my father's final breath would grind everything to a halt, that a great, yawning loss would follow it, a chasm I would disappear into. Instead, the next day began much as the day before had, with dawn breaking and the birds out trilling. One's own loss doesn't slow the course of the sun across the sky.

The worst of it happened in smaller, unexpected moments during the weeks and months that followed—seeing a can of my father's favorite beans on the pantry shelf, hearing his voice on the outgoing answering machine message, getting a bill for the renewal of his CPA license. Those little things cut more quickly and more deeply than his last breath. Those little things were what took my own breath away.

I knew she'd been prepared by the hospice nurse, but I was still surprised by how well my mother handled things in the days afterward. She worked with Lori on floral arrangements. She worked with Ed to get notices to the local papers and my father's alumni newsletter, back in Virginia. She chose the music and readings for my father's service. She set Eddie and Jackie to making cookies, so that well-wishers might have something to eat if they stopped by.

What you'll find, if you ever suffer the misfortune of losing a relative during the height of the holiday season, is that you're forced to wait out the festivities. It's a strange limbo to inhabit. Everyone else is celebrating, rattling around with champagne bottles, exchanging gifts, enjoying their vacation time. And you're just riding it out, waiting until January second, when you can give people the specific time and date of the funeral service.

My father's service was scheduled for the end of the first week of January. It would be small—first at a local church and then at a cemetery. Maybe it was macabre, but I kept thinking how convenient it was that we lived in California, in an ecological zone that allowed for planting in the dead of winter, whether of live Christmas trees or coffins.

Two days before the funeral, I was driving along the freeway when I was startled by a strong vibration from below. I thought it was a blowout, then maybe that I'd thrown a rod. The car was jerking around so violently, it was all I could do to slow down and head for the shoulder. Up ahead, other drivers swerved and moved off the road as well.

And then, just as suddenly, the vibration stopped. I pulled onto the shoulder and turned off the ignition, my heart beating fast. Another car had pulled over just ahead of me. The driver jumped out and yelled something.

I rolled down my window. "Excuse me?"

"Sure felt that one," he said. "You okay?"

At that moment, the earth burped again. The man grabbed hold of his car, then gave me a nervous wave before he ducked back inside.

I turned on my radio. "Not sure yet what the magnitude was, but in this office, things were sure sliding around. Let's get someone on the phone. Hello, you're on the air. Tell me where you're calling from."

"Hello?" a woman said. "We just had an earthquake."

"We're aware of that. Where are you calling from?" the radio announcer asked.

"San Leandro," she said.

"And you felt it down there?"

"It went on for a long time," she said.

My cell phone rang. It was Jeff.

"Are you okay?" he asked.

"I'm fine. A little shaken. You?"

"I'm fine."

We hadn't spoken much since his return from Fresno. I think he felt guilty for doubting the extent of my father's illness or was embarrassed that, for someone so detail-oriented, he had misread so much about the situation. But I had been focused on events at home and had to admit that I'd barely noticed his absence.

"Where are you?" he asked.

"On the freeway," I said.

"Will I get to see you before I go?"

For a moment, I thought he meant that he was moving to Fresno. "Go?"

"You remember, the archivist conference. We talked about this before. It's always in early January."

"I guess I thought you might not go this year."

"You did? Why? I go every year."

"My dad's funeral," I reminded him.

He paused.

I looked out into the highway. Cars were moving but cautiously, as if they didn't trust the earth anymore.

"I gave it serious consideration," Jeff said. "And if you said that you wanted me to stay, you know I'd stay. But you haven't said that."

"No, you're right," I said. "You should go."

"Can I see you before?" he asked.

"Sure. But I'm going to stop by my parents' house first. To make sure everything survived. The quake, I mean."

I listened to the radio as I made my way toward Piedmont. Now they were saying 5.8, but a radio caller said it felt way stronger than that. Emergency personnel were reminding people of numbers to call if they smelled gas.

"Hello?" I called out, as I walked inside my parents' house. A tremor rolled past just then, and I could hear car alarms along the street sounding. But inside the house, no one answered. "Mom? Blake?"

I poked my head into the kitchen. A few of the cabinet doors had bounced open, and cans of food had been jettisoned onto the counter. Nothing looked broken.

I passed through the den. My father's hospital bed was neatly made and pushed to the side of the room. A few framed family portraits had been knocked to the floor.

"Marcus?" I called. I didn't expect him to answer. He had gone up to Sacramento for a few days, the first time he'd had to himself in a long while.

The sliding door to the patio was open, so I stepped outside. My mother's garden was a shamble of toppled plants and potting soil. The Christmas tree I'd bought was tilted against the house, its trunk bent. As I leaned over to set it straight, I noticed my mother. She was kneeling at the far side of the pool.

"Mom?" I called. "Are you okay?"

She held up a hand, as if to say that she had heard me, but she didn't turn around. I walked over to her.

"I guess you felt the earthquake here, too," I said, looking around at the mess.

She still didn't answer. She was looking down at a plant she held. Its ceramic pot had shattered, and she was trying to pick shards of pottery out of the roots.

"The stem is broken. It won't survive," she said.

Then she sobbed, a low, guttural moan that came from deep inside her chest. "How am I going to do this by myself?"

I dropped to my knees beside her. "The garden?" I asked.

"All of it. You try to take care of them. You do your best and then something like this. How do you plan for something like this? What am I supposed to do?"

It hit me that she had, indeed, been trying to protect us this whole time, to protect Blake and Kurt and me, her children, from the pain of loss. Maybe it came across as manipulation, but there was a method there. "It's okay, Mom," I said. "It'll be okay. We'll get through it." I met her eyes, and for the first time since that day at the hospital, I held her gaze. "What do you need me to do?" I asked.

"Oh, sweetie. I know you don't like to get your hands dirty."

"I can get my hands dirty," I said. "It'll wash off."

She wiped her eyes and managed a smile. She took a deep breath. "I have some other pots in the garage," she said.

Six of her plants were damaged beyond repair. Seven others had suffered cracked or shattered pots. We found spare containers for all but the largest, a small tree, and that one my mother and I secured with a torn piece of burlap, like a field dressing.

"You know what Jonah Gray would say about this, don't you?" I asked wiping my hands on my shirt.

"What do you think he'd say?"

"Sometimes we do the repotting, and sometimes repotting is forced upon us."

She smiled.

When we were done, my hands and knees were filthy and my nails were embedded with potting soil. To my surprise, I found that I kind of liked the looks of it.

Chapter Twenty-Nine

AT FIRST, I THOUGHT THAT MY MOTHER WAS SIMPLY replacing what she'd lost in the earthquake. Or else that she was expressing her grief via acquisition. On the day of my father's funeral, all sorts of plants began to show up at the house. Four times that day, five times the day after, three times the day after that—and that was only what I counted in the hours I was around. Each time the doorbell rang, another delivery van waited with another plant. Not cut flowers, but living things full of roots and dirt and leaves.

"Look at those bleeding hearts," I heard her cluck. "Oh, and a tillandsia. I adore those."

"Who are all these from?" I asked. I'd checked a few cards, but I didn't recognize the names.

"Friends. Colleagues."

"What colleagues?" I asked.

"I can't have colleagues? Oh, and look at this. Do you know what this is?"

I shook my head.

"You're asking Sasha?" Blake asked. He was doing his homework at the kitchen table.

"I'm learning," I told him.

"It's a miniature yew," my mother said. "How thoughtful."

Even I could see that the little tree was lovely, both young and alive and somehow wise at the same time.

"Mrs. Maselin dropped something off, too," Blake said. "I put it out on the patio."

My mother ran her hands through Blake's hair and smiled down at him. She had decided to wait to tell him about Ian Maselin, and I had decided to trust her decision. Maybe once the school year was over, she said, depending on how he was doing. He was no longer a child, but facts doled out judiciously seemed a kinder thing than the whole truth just then.

"What did Mrs. Maselin bring over?" I asked.

Blake just shrugged. "It had leaves."

I glanced at the card attached to a cachepot of daffodils. "So how do you know Gordon?"

"Gordon is the tulip guy."

"Who's Gordon the tulip guy?"

"Well, I've never met him face-to-face. But I understand that he works over at DePlains Nursery, where you got our Christmas tree. And he's a frequent contributor on Gray's Garden."

"Gordon? I bet he's one of the people who called me when Jonah Gray first posted my name. If it's the same Gordon, he wasn't very nice."

"I'm sure he didn't mean anything by it. He was just concerned."

"I'm pretty sure he did mean something by it. Why is he sending daffodils? How did he know about Dad?"

"He must have read my post."

"Your what?"

"About your father's passing."

"You posted that on—"

"Gray's Garden," she finished for me. "Yes."

I saw Blake giggling.

"It's not funny," I snapped.

"This is a major trauma in my life, Sasha. I wanted my friends to know—"

"Those people aren't your friends. You've never even met them."

"I can't like someone I've never met? I can't develop an appreciation for someone from afar?" She stared at me. "Do you think that has never happened? Perhaps you can even come up with an example from your own life."

"That's different," I said.

"Just look how supportive they've been. You know I love Martina, but if I get another box of beef jerky—"

"Yeah, well, we'll all be glad when she's onto another account," I said.

"Why don't you take one of these plants back to your house?" my mother suggested. "I've got more here than I can deal with."

"I don't know," I said.

"Or put one in your office. Fred told me that you don't have a shred of greenery in there."

"Fred who?"

"Fred Collins. Your boss? He came to your father's funeral?"

"Oh, Fred. Sure." My boss and my father had met years before, when Fred was just a junior compliance clerk for the Service. They hadn't kept in close touch, but he had come by to pay his respects all the same. I was wondering when he expected me to return to work. It had been a while.

My mother grabbed the yew tree. "Take this one," she said. "As a reminder of the world beyond the IRS."

"What if I forget to water it?"

"Don't."

Jeff called me the following night, just back from his conference. It was four days after my father's funeral, and I appreciated his offer to drop by my house. I couldn't remember the last time he'd been there.

"So what's new in the archivist world?" I asked, trying to sound like a supportive girlfriend.

"A lot of new software. Some interesting approaches to cataloging. Why?"

"What do you mean, why? You've been gone a week."

"You don't have to pretend that you're interested."

"Why would you assume I'm not interested? You know how I like to learn new stuff."

"Your posture says that you're bored."

We watched television in silence for a while, until I realized that I wasn't following the story. I yawned. "I'm so tired," I said.

"You've been tired a lot recently," Jeff said.

"I know. It's been a difficult few months. I'm tired of being tired."

"I hoped to make your life easier," he said. "I tried to."

"It's not you, Jeff," I said. "It would have been difficult no matter what."

"I guess."

"You guess? Do you want to see my father's death certificate?"

"Don't get sarcastic," he said. "Maybe if I'd been someone else, it wouldn't have been so hard for you. Whatever. I'm going to be the bad guy either way."

"What are you talking about?"

He stared at me with his serious eyes. "This isn't working for me."

I felt my cheeks start to burn. "What isn't working?" I asked.

"You and I. I did some thinking when I was down in Fresno, and later at the conference."

"You mean Fres-yes?"

"See, that's just it. You don't get me. Besides, my family doesn't think you're right for me. They didn't see a real connection between us."

"I don't get you? Wait a minute—you're breaking up with me?"

He shrugged, but it was a shrug in the affirmative. A definite affirmative. "I wanted to wait until after your father died."

"Give yourself some credit," I said. "You even waited until after the funeral. That must have taken discipline."

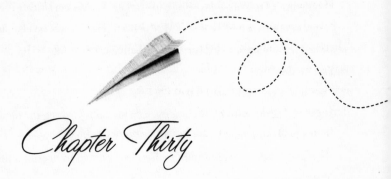

Chapter Thirty

IN MARCH, I OPENED MY DOOR, DRESSED TO GO JOGGING, and nearly plowed into Gene. He was standing there, catalogs in hand, leaning toward the mail slot.

"Sasha!" he said.

"Gene! It's been a while." In the previous few months, my mail had come as regularly as ever, but it seemed that I was always gone when Gene made his rounds. Of course, I'd been gone a lot.

"How are you doing?" He asked with a delicacy that I knew referred to my father's passing. "I'm so sorry I missed the funeral. I was away for the holidays."

"I thought you were obligated to deliver through rain, sleet and even snow," I said.

"I am, but not through two weeks' paid vacation. That's the loophole. How's your mom holding up?"

"She's okay. Well, she will be. She started working over at DePlains Nursery, in Piedmont," I told him. "If you're ever near there, you should stop by. I'm sure she'd love to see you."

"That sounds like a new beginning," Gene said.

He really was remarkable, I thought. For the first time, I felt lucky to have dated him, lucky that he'd been in my life, for however long. There was nothing ugly about Gene. Nothing controlling. Maybe he wasn't as observant as I'd have liked—but he was humane and he was kind. I hadn't appreciated it at the time, but I found myself wondering whether I could again.

"It's something," I said. "It's her first job in ages."

"And you? Still at the Service?"

"Year seven, can you believe that?" I asked.

"They should give the person who hired you a medal," Gene said.

"I don't know about that."

"Oh, I do. They really lucked out."

"What about you, Gene?" I asked. I was finding it a pleasure just looking at him again.

"Same old, same old," he said. "The mail keeps on coming. Speaking of which." He looked at his bag and motioned down the street.

"Of course," I said. "You're on the clock."

"But it was nice to see you," he said.

"You, too," I told him.

He turned to go.

"Hey, are you doing anything this weekend?" I asked.

"This weekend?" he asked.

"Yeah. I was thinking maybe we could have dinner. Catch up."

"Catch up," he repeated. "That would be fun, but, well, I'm seeing someone now," he said.

"Oh." I deflated a little.

"Remember, ages back maybe, I mentioned that guy at work's sister?"

"I think so."

"That's working out real nice. Actually, we're living together."

"Wow," I said. "That was quick."

"I know, right? And it was my idea, if you can believe it. But it feels right. I was going to tell you, but with your father and all, I didn't know how to bring it up."

"I'm happy for you, Gene. Really, that's great."

We stared at each other for a moment.

"Well, I don't want to keep you," I said. I closed the door and sat on my couch, dressed to go running, but headed nowhere. Gene had found someone. Martina had found Marcus (and vice versa). Blake had no trouble finding dates. But why was I always on the outskirts?

I looked at my bookshelves, full of dusted, alphabetized accounting books. I looked at my kitchen, spotless, everything in order, everything in its place. Was there simply no extra space in my life? I wandered through my house, eventually landing in front of my computer. There, I did what I often did—logged on to Gray's Garden and read what Jonah Gray had written that day. I liked to imagine that we were keeping up, although I realized that he knew nothing about me.

Every so often, I'd stumble across one of my mother's postings. In the past week, on behalf of one of her customers, she had asked why a certain plant was failing to thrive. Did he think it needed more sun? More bone meal? A more acidic soil? Or was it something else? Was there something intrinsically wrong with the plant, something invisible to the naked eye that weakened it from within?

That day, he had answered her question about a gardenia bush that was yellowing unexpectedly. He had asked how old the plant was and about its history, before expounding.

You see, plants can be exquisitely sensitive to their environment, just like people. Sometimes, their failure or success is a comment on care and nourishment. But it's also true that some plants are weaker than others, and others simply won't last long. Maybe they resented transplanting. Maybe they were bruised in the process. Try to find out what happened to bring these plants to this moment in their lives. It's a fact of life that at some point, options start to diminish. Sometimes it's better just to let go.

I sat there at my computer, thinking of my father and of Ethan Gray and of the lost oak tree up at 530 Horsehair Road. Then I thought of myself. If I was sure about one thing, it was that I didn't want to look up after twenty years with the Service, the same books on my shelves, the same numbers in my head, and all my options gone.

At the lamb end of March, my mother organized dinner at the Banner Hill house, to mark that we'd all survived the first full season without my dad around. Uncle Ed was at a professional symposium, and Blake's marching band was down in Anaheim that week, performing along the streets of Disneyland. But the rest of us came. Kurt, Lori and the boys, Marcus and Martina, me and my mother.

"Actually, Stockton's beautiful in the spring," I heard Kurt telling Marcus. "It took me a while to give it a chance, but now I'm convinced. We'd like to put down roots there."

"I'm still recovering from my move to Oakland," Marcus said. Martina squeezed his shoulder.

"Speaking of moving, guess who's headed back to Fresno?" I asked.

"Jeff is going to leave the file room?" Marcus asked.

"Ricardo told me that he and Susan are headed there by the end of April," I said.

"I never thought he was good enough for you," my mother said, shaking her head.

"I know you didn't."

"Either did your father and either did Blake."

"How is Blake?" Lori asked. "The boys have been asking about him."

"Better and better," my mother said. "His last report card wasn't great, but he's been getting his homework done this quarter. Marcus has been helping me stay on him about academics. It's been hard to get him to focus on anything but this band trip."

"Except maybe prom," Marcus said. "And Elaine."

"Oh, right. Elaine." My mother smiled.

"Elaine?" Kurt asked. "I thought it was Sara."

"Sara was December," I said. "Way back."

Lori stood and walked to the sliding glass doors. She looked out across the pool, still closed for the winter. "The tree looks really great, Lola," she said.

My mother had ripped up some of the concrete patio to reveal the earth beneath, and we had planted our Christmastime noble fir in that spot, in honor of my father.

"It reminds me of that thing you read at Thanksgiving, about plants," Lori said. "Like all it needed was a new place."

I walked over and stood beside her. There was something satisfying about seeing the little tree I had picked out growing nobler every day. Maybe it would make a fine Gardner family tradition. Better than infidelity, in any case.

Chapter Thirty-One

IT TOOK A COUPLE OF MONTHS TO WORK UP MY NERVE, but that May, I gave notice. Senior auditor was the highest rank I would reach at the IRS, and that was just fine. In the months since my father's death, I had tried to dive back into auditing with the same energy as before, but I couldn't do it. I didn't want to keep people at a safe distance. I wanted to be out in the world. I wanted to get my hands dirty, even if I wasn't sure just how.

Just because I was good at auditing didn't mean that I was meant to audit. At sixty, my mother had started down a new career path. Who was to say that I couldn't? I was a different person than I'd been the year before. I belonged in a larger pot. Sure I'd never met Jonah Gray. Maybe I'd never meet him. But I'd learned a thing or two from the guy, and I was better for it.

Wherever I ended up, I'd keep the yew tree nearby. It had made itself very comfortable in my cubicle. I had already repotted it once, bringing in a bag of soil and a new container and managing to make a mess of the sink in the kitchenette. So much for forgetting to water it; it reminded me of my father too much. I wanted it to thrive.

At Fred Collins's request, I agreed to stay until June. The new cycle of audits had begun by then, and I was able to help my replacement get comfortable with the chaos. And so a month after I'd given my notice, I was finally and absolutely cleaning out my double-wide cubicle. My books were already at home with my calculator, ledger pads, mug of pens and picture of Kurt and his boys. The cubicle I'd spent so much of my working life in was now empty, save the government-issue furniture I'd happily leave behind and the yew tree, which would leave the building when I did.

I didn't have much to do but wait until the day ended. I said my goodbyes to people, hung out in the kitchenette and filled out my final pieces of paperwork for a sad-eyed Ricardo. At four o'clock, Fred caught me in the hallway.

"Do you have a moment?" he asked.

"You've got me for another hour. What do you need?"

"I agreed to oversee a call-in audit. Would you mind sitting in on it?"

"You need a witness?" I asked. Sometimes, auditors brought in witnesses, usually when they were worried an auditee might become violent during the interview.

"It couldn't hurt," Fred said. "If you're not doing anything else."

"A call-in, huh? What's the story?"

There were three ways individuals could find themselves audited by the IRS. There were random compliance audits. There were audits generated when certain numbers veered too far from the mean. And there were audits prompted by a call to the IRS fraud hotline.

I'd always wondered about the motives behind the hotline calls. Some were surely the work of honest citizens who felt a civic obligation to report money laundering or evasive schemes. But some no doubt stemmed from spurned exes, retaliatory colleagues or jealous relatives. There was a screening process to all of them, but whoever had reported Fred Collins's auditee must have made a believable accusation or just said the right things to get an investigation started.

I followed Fred into his office. At his table sat a handsome, dark-haired man I didn't recognize. He looked about my age, and he was reading one of Fred's tax manuals. At first, I wondered if he was a new employee. Just my luck that Fred would manage to hire an attractive auditor only after I left.

As soon as the man noticed us, he put the tax manual back on Fred's shelf. "I'm sorry," he said. "I was killing time, but I got sucked in. I didn't realize there were so many options for innocent spouse relief. That's awfully understanding of you guys." He smiled then, and his green eyes lit up. I liked him immediately, but it was clear that he was no auditor. Still, he seemed familiar. I wondered if I had met him before.

"I wanted to bring in someone more familiar with your file," Fred said. "We might get you out of here more quickly that way."

"Who else are you bringing in?" I asked my soon-to-be ex-boss. I wondered what Green Eyes had done to require the attentions of three of us. He didn't appear particularly evasive. Instead he seemed welcoming and easygoing, down to his work boots and jeans with dirt at the knees. Suddenly, he stood and looked at me. He began smiling broadly.

"You're the one who knows my file? Are you Jeffrine Hill?"

I froze. Only one person could have asked that question, and with that voice. No wonder he seemed familiar.

"Who's Jeffrine Hill?" Fred asked. "This is Sasha Gardner. She oversaw your audit last year."

"*You're* Sasha Gardner?"

"You're Jonah Gray?" I asked. But it had to be. Now I placed the voice, at once interested and amused. So this is what he looked like. Exactly as I'd hoped he would. Exactly as I'd imagined him. But how? And me, with no time at all to prepare. "What are you doing here?" I managed to ask.

"I'm being audited," he said. He smiled, as if it didn't bother him in the least. "Again."

I looked from Jonah to Fred Collins. "*He's* the call-in?"

"I guess someone turned him in," Fred said.

"But we didn't find any fraud last year. Not willful."

Who would have reported him? I wondered. Who would have been mad enough, or self-righteous enough, to do that? Could it have been his ex-wife, all the way from Argentina? A rival gardener? A disgruntled *Stockton Star* reader? Everyone liked Jonah Gray. He was one of the good ones.

"So I guess Jeffrine doesn't work here anymore," Jonah said. "I tried calling, but I was told that she moved to Fresno. You don't happen to have her phone number, do you?"

"Who is Jeffrine Hill?" Fred asked again.

"Ms. Gardner's assistant. Last year at least," Jonah said.

"You had an assistant?" Fred asked.

"Fred, could we have a moment, please? I'd like to go over a few things with Mr. Gray, uh, regarding his file from last year."

"Be my guest," Fred said, and he left us alone in his office.

"So you're Sasha Gardner," Jonah said. "Wow, you're not at all what I was expecting. Hey listen, I'm really sorry all those people harassed you like that."

"Oh, that. It's fine. Really."

"I wrote to you. I don't know if you got—"

"I did. I meant to thank you for that. I should have."

"Well, you're welcome. Listen, can I ask if Jeffrine—"

"No wait!" It came out as more of a bark than I intended. "I can't talk about her. I've got a few things I feel I should tell you." I took a deep breath. Unprepared or not, I knew I didn't have much time. "I went by your house once, and I talked to your father."

"You met my dad? In Stockton? When?"

"Last August. I was up there to see my brother and I took a bike ride. It's a long story, but I took a bunch of random turns and then a couple not so random ones and I ended up at your house. I'm sorry about the oak tree, by the way. That must have been tough."

Jonah nodded. "My grandfather planted that tree when my dad was born. Kind of hard to see it go."

"I realize that my actions were inappropriate and if you want to submit a formal complaint, I can give you the forms to do that."

Jonah waved me off. "My dad thought you were one of the Potter girls," he said. "He must have talked about you for a week. Were you with a kid or something?"

"My five-year-old nephew."

"Wow. Gutsy play," Jonah said. "Dad told me to invite you back, but none of the Potters knew what I was talking about. I thought he must have imagined you."

"You wish," I said.

"I don't," Jonah said, smiling.

I didn't know what else to say. I knew that I should tell him that I was Jeffrine, but I couldn't. It seemed okay to shoulder my share of the blame, but I didn't want to erase whatever positive memories he might have of her—or me. Whichever.

"How are things at the *Stockton Star?*" I asked.

"My job? It's fine. They keep me busy."

"Think you'll ever go back to Tiburon?"

"I guess that would depend on why," he said.

I was trying hard to keep my professional demeanor intact. I just wanted to smile at him and smile again. After all this time, I was talking to Jonah Gray, face-to-face.

"Are you keeping this?" I looked up to see Fred, standing in the doorway of his office, my yew tree in his hands. "Or were you going to leave it for your replacement?"

"I'm keeping it," I said.

"Because I'd take it," he said. "If you didn't want it."

"It's not a giveaway, Fred."

Fred shrugged and disappeared again with the little tree.

"Nice yew," Jonah said. Only I heard "Nice you," which I took to be some sort of endearment.

"You seem awfully nice yourself," I said. "Though I didn't expect to meet you this way. I would have liked a little more warning, you know, to prepare."

"I said I like your yew tree."

"Oh. Right. The tree." I was embarrassed. "Did you know that years ago, the yew was known as the tax tree?" I asked, trying to distract him.

"I did indeed," he said.

"My mom ended up with a lot of plants back in January. I figured I'd try to turn over a new leaf, so to speak."

"Well, it's thriving. This is the exact home I would have wanted for it."

"How do you mean?"

"I grew that tree."

"*You* grew it? My tree?"

"For the first two years."

"How do you know?"

"Because I sent it to Lola when your father died."

I froze. "You know my mother? And that she's my mother?" It was not what I'd expected to hear.

Jonah smiled. "She mentioned Virginia in one of her posts on my Web site, and we got to corresponding. I'm originally from Roanoke, but I think you must already know that."

I nodded.

"And once I realized that she was my auditor's mother...I'll give her credit—the things she said about you, she made me realize I probably judged you a little quickly. You know, based on your job. That's kind of why I didn't send Linda Potter in today."

"You just made it. This is my last day."

"Really? I guess I can thank Fred Collins for getting me onto your schedule then."

"There was a Jeff Hill." Speaking of Fred, he was back again, now holding a staff directory. "But no Jeffrine. I feel like I would have remembered that name. Sasha, didn't you date Jeff Hill for a while?"

"Aren't we supposed to be focusing on Mr. Gray's audit?" I asked.

"Call me Jonah," Jonah said. "I'm not in a hurry. I took the whole day off."

Fred stuck a return in front of me. "I just need you to vet this. Since you covered it last year."

There was a knock on Fred's door. It was Cliff, the auditor from the far side of my cubicle.

He waved. "Hey, Sasha, thanks again for that info on loopers. That spray is working great. Fred, can I see you for a minute?" Cliff asked. Fred excused himself yet again.

When I turned back to Jonah, he wore a strange look.

"What?" I asked.

"I'm such an idiot."

"No," I started to say. "You're not an idiot. You're nothing close."

"You probably thought that was pretty funny," he said. "Me asking about Jeffrine like that. Pretty hilarious."

"No," I said again.

He frowned. "Do you do that with all your audits? Make up a fake persona to try to get to the person? Try to get them to open up and unveil their secrets or something?"

"No. I've never—not before you."

"I feel so special." He sounded sarcastic.

"You were," I agreed. "You are."

"Why did you pretend to be her? Why would you do that?"

I felt my cheeks burning. This is what I was unprepared for. I'd just have to dive in. "Because you wouldn't have talked to me otherwise. Not the way you did. You wouldn't have opened up like that. And once you opened up—"

"You figured you could stick it to me?"

"No. I just wanted to keep you open. You talked to me like you were actually interested in the same stupid things I was interested in."

"You said you liked manatees. What was I supposed to do?"

"See?" I asked.

But Jonah was still frowning. Finally, he looked up. "I don't know what to tell you. I feel like I don't know what to believe. I feel like a dupe."

"I'm sorry," I said.

"I think I'd rather finish this—all this—" he said, motioning around Fred's office, "—without you here."

I nodded. "That's fair." I stood up. "When Fred gets back, you can finish up with him."

I started to leave Fred's office.

"So what are you going to do now?" Jonah asked. "Head to Fresno?"

I turned around to look at him, for what I knew would be the last time. "Fres-no-way," I said. "I don't know. I just want to be out in the world."

I thought maybe I saw him smile a little, but I didn't have anything else to say. I turned and left.

Then I called my mother.

"I can't believe you didn't tell me that you've been writing to Jonah Gray," I said to her.

"On and off. You knew that."

"I knew you were going to his site. That's different from writing to him directly."

"I think he's handsome."

"You've met him?"

"At the nursery. But that was months ago. I hope this second audit wasn't too uncomfortable. For him, I mean."

"He seemed to take it in stride," I said. Then I froze. "When did he tell you he was being audited again?"

"He didn't," she said.

It hit me. "You didn't, did you?"

"What?"

"Are you the one who turned him in?"

"I didn't realize you'd mind," she began.

"Why would you put him through that? How did you even know what to say?"

"I had a good feeling about Jonah. Ever since you first mentioned him. So when I saw Fred Collins at your father's service…"

"Fred was in on this, too? You guys have no boundaries at all, do you? What ever happened to not trying to set me up with every random man you come across? Didn't you claim to have learned some sort of lesson about that?"

"Did Fred ever tell you how he met his wife?" she asked. "It's the sweetest thing. He was auditing her. When I heard that, I thought, well why not?"

"Excuse me, but can I have a say over my own life? You're still betting with Ricardo, aren't you? That's not fair."

"To whom, dear?"

"To either of us. It's not right. It should just happen. And not because you or Fred prodded the poor guy."

"All I did was get him an easy little audit. I didn't make him go in person. How'd it go?"

"Well, he's gone again. For good this time."

"Oh, sweetie," she said.

"He found out that when Jeffrine was calling him and writing to him and asking him for gardening help about loopers, that it was actually me. He trusted me when I was Jeffrine. He doesn't trust me as Sasha."

"You told him your name was Jeffrine? But that's so unflattering."

"There was a context. I really don't want to get into it."

I wanted to get out of the building. I was afraid that Fred was going to stop by my cubicle, his face expectant, and I'd have to explain how Jonah Gray was gone completely this time, even after his well-intentioned assistance. I took my yew tree down to the reception area and stayed there until the clock struck five. With that, I was gone. Gone from the building, gone from the IRS, gone from my life as an auditor.

Once home, I walked up to my porch and pulled the mail from my mailbox. As soon as I turned toward the door, the phone inside started to ring. I pulled open my purse and dug frantically for my keys, bending my mail and shoving my coat under my arm.

"Shit," I muttered as I upended my purse on the porch, grabbed my keys and managed to force them into the lock. I flung the door open and lunged for the phone. Why do I do this? I wondered as I went through the motions. It would be a telemarketer, or a survey, or the newspaper selling subscriptions, or my mother apologizing for meddling in my life yet again.

"Hello," I gasped.

"Why Jeffrine, you're not in Fresno after all." It was that voice. His voice. The voice that wrapped around you like a warm day.

"I really am sorry," I said.

"Actually, I'm flattered," he said. "I thought I was the one who wanted to talk to you. I didn't realize it was also the other way around."

"I knew you'd be mad and think I was a crazy person."

"You disappeared," he said. "I didn't know how to find you. Do you know how many Hills there are in Fresno?"

"But I'm not in Fresno," I said. "I'm still here."

"Thank God. You sound like you're out of breath," he said. "I hope you didn't rush on my account."

I smiled. I looked at my keys, still in the door. My purse upended on the porch. My mail in a bent pile. "It was worth it," I said, and I sat on the floor to talk to Jonah Gray.